**WILL KIRK, McCOY, AND THEIR FRIENDS BE REIN-STATED BY STARFLEET COMMAND?**

**WILL SAAVIK BECOME A PERMANENT MEMBER OF THE STAR TREK FAMILY?**

**IN *WRATH OF KHAN*, WHY WERE KLINGON SHIPS PRESENT IN THE NEUTRAL ZONE?**

These are just some of the questions explored in this latest collection from *Trek* magazine. You'll find out why the Klingon commander, Kruge, met his end; discover some of the possible futures that await Kirk, Spock, and the rest of their crew; and be able to compare your likes and dislikes, and your knowledge of Star Trek, with both fellow fans and casual viewers.

# THE BEST OF TREK® #8

𝒪

## More Science Fiction from SIGNET

# THE BEST OF TREK ®#8

## FROM THE MAGAZINE FOR STAR TREK FANS

### EDITED BY WALTER IRWIN AND G. B. LOVE

A SIGNET BOOK

NEW AMERICAN LIBRARY

Copyright © 1985 by TREK®
Copyright © 1985 by Walter Irwin and G. B. Love

All rights reserved

TREK® is a registered trademark of G. B. Love and Walter Irwin

Cover art by Paul Alexander

SIGNET TRADEMARK REG. U.S. PAT. OFF. AND FOREIGN COUNTRIES
REGISTERED TRADEMARK—MARCA REGISTRADA
HECHO EN CHICAGO, U.S.A.

SIGNET, SIGNET CLASSIC, MENTOR, PLUME, MERIDIAN AND NAL BOOKS
are published by New American Library,
1633 Broadway, New York, New York 10019

First Printing, March, 1985

1  2  3  4  5  6  7  8  9

PRINTED IN THE UNITED STATES OF AMERICA

## ACKNOWLEDGMENTS

As always, thanks are due to the many, many readers, contributors, and fans who have helped make our magazine and books successful. Special thanks go to our editor at NAL, Sheila Gilbert; Jim Houston; Leslie Thompson; Marc Schooley; Chris Myers; and, especially, to all of the writers in this volume. To all of the above, and to our faithful readers, this volume is dedicated. Thanks.

# CONTENTS

# INTRODUCTION

Thank you for purchasing this eighth collection of articles and features from our magazine, *Trek*. We know that you will enjoy it just as much as you did the previous seven. And we feel you regular readers will be pleased to know that there will be at least two more collections to come—and, it is to be hoped, many more after that!

As always, we selected the articles and features included in this volume with an eye toward diversity. As is postulated in the Vulcan philosophy of IDIC (Infinite Diversity in Infinite Combinations), each type of article, just like each type of person, is equally important and valuable. Most important, however, we chose articles which we think you'll find informative, fun to read, and maybe just a tad educational.

The release of *Star Trek III: The Search for Spock* this past June reaffirmed our belief that Star Trek, Star Trek fandom, and the ideals embodied by both will continue to thrive and grow. The movie broke even in its first nine days of release, and promises to be one of the biggest moneymakers of the year. At the bottom line, this means that there will be more Star Trek movies. As a matter of fact, as this is written, Paramount has announced definite plans for *Star Trek IV!*

If you enjoy the articles and features included in this volume and would like to see more, we invite you to turn to the ad elsewhere in this book for information on how you can order individual issues of *Trek*. (And, please, if you have borrowed a copy of this collection from a library, copy the information in the ad, and leave it intact for others to use. Thanks!)

If you have been stirred to write an article yourself, please send it along to us! We would be more than happy to see it, as we are always on the lookout for new contributors with a fresh outlook on Star Trek and related subjects. (Please, please do not send us Star Trek stories! We do not and cannot publish Star Trek fiction!) If you feel a little timid about submitting your work, remember that *every* contributor featured in this issue sent us an article after reading a previous *Best of Trek*. They made it; you can too.

We want to hear from you in any case. Our lines of communication are always open. We welcome (and heed!) your suggestions, comments, and ideas; you readers are the bosses. Although we cannot give you the address of the Star Trek actors or forward mail to them, or help anyone get a professional Star Trek novel published, we *do* want your comments on *Trek* and Star Trek in general. It is only by the letters you send that we can know if we are doing a good job . . . or a bad job. Either way, let us know. Our address is:

Trek

1120 Omar

Houston, TX 77009

Thanks again, and we hope you'll enjoy *The Best of Trek #8*!

WALTER IRWIN

G.B. LOVE

# NIMOY'S THE SEARCH FOR SPOCK: UNREPENTANT

## by Kyle Holland

*Kyle Holland is gaining quite a reputation among our readers as something of a gadfly. His penetrating and, frankly, somewhat offbeat looks into Star Trek (particularly the films) have drawn a number of unflattering letters. As always with our most controversial writers, however, the letters of praise are equal in number. In the following article, Kyle takes a look at Star Trek III: The Search for Spock. As a matter of fact, he takes a look at BOTH Star Trek III AND The Search for Spock. Confused? Read on. . . .*

We all had clever ways of bringing Spock back to life plotted out in our heads. The Genesis Planet, with its promise of life from lifelessness, had to be the key to the whole thing. The territorial dispute between the Federation and the Klingons over the new ground was inevitable. The only details that needed to be worked out were the exact circumstances of Kirk's return to Genesis and the precise moment of Spock's reappearance. Here, many strategies were possible. Only one was truly unthinkable: that Spock would never return to material existence.

In retrospect, it is interesting that no one seriously entertained that particular possibility. Absolutely every person I knew who saw the film, whether enthusiastic about Star Trek or not, was certain that Spock would return. Some, of course, were of the opinion that on aesthetic or philosophical grounds it would be best to let our hero rest in peace. But this was different from the assurance that he would, nevertheless, be brought back to life. The signals, of course, were glaring, with the spooky "Remember" exchange with McCoy and the repeated descriptions of the nature of the Genesis experiment. Two questions were raised by this certainty: One, why was everybody so sure, and, two, why did the suspense remain, as everyone trundled off to the cinemas to join *The Search for Spock*?

After all, the powers behind *Wrath of Khan* had clearly not committed themselves to the continued existence of Spock. The Spock that appeared in the second film, I have argued earlier ("Indiana Skywalker Meets the Son of Star Trek," *Best of Trek #7),* was only a caricature, meant for the broad masses of space-movie goers who, in the opinion of the producers, only knew that "Mr. Spock" was a loyal sidekick with no surface emotions and big pointed ears. His death would be a payoff scene, and would contribute to the trite character-building process to which the entire film was subjecting Kirk. If the survivors are so sure, at the end of the film, that they will see Spock again—well, Luke Skywalker saw Obi Wan Kenobi plenty of times, too, after he was dead. The confusion of the producers regarding their intentions for Spock at the end of *Wrath of Khan* was evident; somehow, it was clearer to the viewer that Spock would again be walking among us.

That being so, reviewers of *The Search for Spock* have still refrained from actually revealing whether or not Spock lives, and those who went to see the film during its debut weekend admitted to a bit of uncertainty regarding the outcome of the story. The big mystery, of course, wasn't whether or not Spock would return to life, but how it would be done. There would be that moment, a moment of drama and irony, when the viewer would see that they had done it after all. They had really brought back to life the creature that commercial powers in television and films had been trying, at various times and in various ways, to kill off for two decades.

But there was no Big Moment. What a strange way to make a film. What an incredible blunder, what amateurishness, what failure to exploit one of the easiest dramatic marks in current popular culture.

Or was it?

Let's look at this two ways: first, *The Search for Spock* as a cinematic production; then, *Star Trek III* as the further adventures of the good guys.

## I. *The Search for Spock*

Most of the questions relating to the creation of the film begin and end with Leonard Nimoy. He was a party to the original decision to kill off Spock; he could single-handedly have prevented Spock's return, no matter what pressures mounted for his resurrection. For many years, the notion that Nimoy is Spock's enemy has been common. But Nimoy has always been open about the complexity of his feelings for the character. It is his creation, it contains a lot of himself, but like all successes, Spock has threatened in the past to obstruct his creator's artistic adventurousness. In retrospect, it can be seen that Nimoy and Spock have indeed worked out a relatively peaceful and mutually beneficial coexistence; Nimoy is the first to admit that he has been much luckier than some of his fellow Star Trek actors in this regard. So, their domestic problems worked out, Nimoy seems to have been perfectly willing to aid in Spock's recovery.

That Spock would live again was in fact proposed early on, and many people have seen copies of Harve Bennett's original outline for the third Star Trek film. Some features of this proto-story are particularly intriguing in light of the finished film. The Genesis locales were set, and the Klingons were closing in for the conquest. The destruction of the *Enterprise*—at first glance, an outrageous idea—was fully mapped out there, nearly identically to the film version. Sarek had much the role he had in the film (a brilliant stroke, on many counts), and Lieutenant Saavik was still aboard the *Enterprise*. But there were many changes made from this old outline, and among them was the deletion of the Big Moment. Spock—a deranged Spock, to be sure—was originally supposed to be discovered on the Genesis Planet by the *Enterprise* crew.

By changing that element in the story, the entire dramatic

chemistry of the film was altered. Instead, an odd conceit was substituted: Spock and the planet were now one process, both growing from infancy to old age in a series of violently eruptive episodes, both headed for oblivion unless Kirk and friends could save Spock and restore his soul. A good science fiction idea, but very problematic filmmaking. To work out this theme, the audience must see the infant Spock on the young Genesis Planet, and they must see him early in the film. Spock is revealed not in a theatrical burst, but in a series of slow, teasing glimpses, inching toward the familiar presence they are expecting.

Technically, this cast the burden of suspense onto the story's subplots. David's death was, in part, necessitated by the new responsibility of supporting characters to provide dramatic muscle for the plot. The dementedly violent Klingon commander, played to pathological perfection by Christopher Lloyd, was another tension-generator, and the pyrotechnical self-destruction of the Genesis Planet filled in some of the potentially slack moments. On its surface, the film is so action-happy that the tempo is actually frenetic. In real time, *The Search for Spock* is a little on the short side for a feature film, but its nervous editing has allowed an overflow of action and reaction into the show. The overall effect forces the viewer to feel that *The Search for Spock* is more than a little defensive about the fact that it has given away its major dramatic device, and hopes to compensate with an overload of plot and action. The film could have benefited from a little pacing.

Most science fiction films pace with high-tech displays. It's easy to see why Nimoy did not choose to linger over the technical ambience of *The Search for Spock*. This movie is distinctly low-tech—intriguingly, self-consciously, unapologetically indifferent to the glossy technical backgrounds that were so prominent in *Wrath of Khan*. The *Enterprise*, once the pride of the fleet, is now a battle-scarred hulk—and we are told straight out that it will not be repaired. We don't get to drool over the engine room or the torpedo run. Spock's quarters we see only as an unlighted, abandoned chamber. The ship has actually been detechnologized; Kirk had to push a button on the turbolift to get to his deck, a contrast to the insipid talking elevator of the *Excelsior* that speaks volumes (even without Mr. Scott's help) on the relationship of technology in *The Search for Spock* to that in *Wrath of Khan*. The bridge will certainly not bear close scrutiny, and the same can be said for the animated special effects. With the exception of Kirk, who gets a tasteful tunic, the clothing our heroes don once they leave their official attire behind is strictly from a twenty-third-century K-Mart; unless you're an admiral, it seems, you don't get rich working for Starfleet.

So Nimoy presents himself as uninterested in cheap dramatic thrills or expensive technical thrills. What *is* he interested in?

If *The Search for Spock* reveals anything, it is that Nimoy is interested in acting, first of all; he is also interested in actors, and he is also interested in—we can see this indisputably— Star Trek. All three distinguish him from the director of *Wrath of Khan*, and all three account for the eccentric quality of *The Search for Spock*. And Nimoy has, for good or for ill, indicated in this film that he is more interested in all these things than he is in following current commercial formulas.

Unconsciously—but unavoidably—these values have led Nimoy to more or less explicitly repudiate the values of *Wrath of Khan*. Kirk's peaceful, philosophical acceptance of Spock's death at the end of *Wrath of Khan*—an acceptance totally out of character for the stubborn, hopeful Kirk known to Star Trek fans, no matter how old he gets or how many times he reads *A Tale of Two Cities*—is essentially erased in the first moments of *The Search for Spock*. In the same voice we heard Kirk announcing last time that "all is well" he is now saying, "I am troubled. . . ." That's more like it. And that's the beginning of a journey back toward a series of directorial and thematic elements that are classic Star Trek, as it was brewed for its small-screen existence so many years ago.

Nimoy's actors created characters that are now part of American folklore, and he lets those characters out of the straitjackets they were put into during their duel with Khan. The original cast was a milestone in serial television; instead of the tall, blond, broad-shouldered heroes who had done all the good deeds up to that time, Roddenberry largely won his struggle to bring to the screen an unexpected variety of shapes, colors, and facial features. The result was one of the most interesting collections of faces to be seen in any acting ensemble, and those faces alone would serve any director well. Fortunately, behind those faces are solid acting talents, and by getting Spock off the screen for a while, what has always been feared is proved: If the true potential of each of these characters was fully developed, they would each be ruling some quadrant of the galaxy and that would be the end of the show.

William Shatner's performances in the three Star Trek films prove two things about him that, on the strength of something like *T.J. Hooker* alone, would never be appreciated. One, he is a skillful and very creative actor. Two, he is a terrifically good-looking fellow. Viewers of his Saturday-night cop show, who are accustomed to seeing the hypertensive Hooker waddling gamely after street scum and barking his contempt for them into their faces as he drags them off to the lockup, are likely to miss both of these qualities. Kirk, in his original television incarnation, had no easy tags—as did Spock—for the actor to latch on to; Shatner crafted the character out of very subtle gestures, voice tones, and attitudes, and after a lull of nearly ten years he was able to conjure this personality up again. Kirk learns and changes, but remains Kirk. Unlike many television series actors, Shatner was not just playing himself week after week. Like his fellow Star Trek actors, he shaped a character so palpable that it could be recalled, revivified, relived after long absences. This is a remarkable feat of sustained creativity, and an unusual task for an actor. Of course, it is one thing to admire an actor's talent; I am assured by various females that Shatner's looks are equally admired, and that he only gets better-looking as he gets older. The young Shatner's face was perhaps too much on the pretty side, a very interesting contrast to the gritty spirit that was supposed to dwell behind it. And I do not see anything particularly attractive about T.J. Hooker. But for Kirk, Shatner works a kind of magic, becoming a compact, finely tuned dramatic instrument confidently playing the entire range from light humor to crushing sorrow. Kirk is now the major repository of Shatner's serious intentions. And, I think, the vehicle has served him well. Nimoy has let Shatner give back Kirk's soul, as well as Spock's.

*The Search for Spock*, unlike its two predecessor films, does not attempt to showcase new and supposedly exciting characters. Instead, it gives center stage to the actors who have served it well over the years, who created Star Trek, have unrealized ambitions for their characters, and have unexhausted support among the audience. Its statement is polite but firm: "That's right, we're not thirty-five years old anymore. What about it?" (Get in the closet.) An interesting face is an interesting face, and character only deepens with experience. Nimoy's camera played those faces the way the old camera did on the TV show, and as in the old days, benefited profoundly by doing so. Kelley's soulful mug is more expressive than ever; Takei has not lost a bit of his dash. Nichols seems, incredibly, more beautiful than she appeared in the previous films. Koenig is at last allowed to present Chekov as a mature, responsible man (no screaming, a bold innovation); and Doohan—are there really words to describe the inventor of Montgomery Scott, who can blow away whole atmospheres of cinematic pretension with a remark in an elevator? Surely, Nimoy's major task as director was sometimes just to stand back and watch. Instead of ambitious new characters, Bennett and Nimoy wisely engaged the remarkable Mark Lenard to revive Sarek, a truly charismatic figure who underscores the limpness of the youthful nobodies the second film tried to make stick.

*The Search for Spock*'s commitment to the human essence of Star Trek is evident, and is to be expected in light of Nimoy's outspoken concern with acting. What was a little less expected was his playful attention to the trivia of Star Trek. I had the distinct sensation, at times, that Nimoy and Bennett had pulled up in front of the theater with a dump truck and covered the sidewalk with every odd and end from the seventy-eight stories: We got your nerve pinch; we got your *pon farr*; we got your Vulcan gongs; we got your self-destruct sequence; we got your mind meld; we got your Tribbles; we got your two-consciousnesses-in-one-body; we got your female computer voice; we got your star bar (in style, a *Star Wars* rip-off, but in concept a tip of the hat to "The Trouble with Tribbles"). Even the flimsy soundstages and plastic armor harkened back to the soulfully chintzy props of the televised episodes; the only thing that was missing was blue eye shadow on everybody, which would be a daring affectation in our punk present. The rain of cultish detail sometimes tied small knots in the story, and ran a serious risk of turning off nonenthusiasts. Still, the message was clear. For Nimoy, the film was not just a star play that he happened to be directing; it was a tradition, in which he is a proud and willing participant. He was taking a chance. Would the audience feel the same?

It will be a year before the commercial success of *The Search for Spock* can be fully assessed. But I admire Nimoy for his boldness, for taking a fantasy world that many have derided as a "cult" and presenting it, unreconstructed and unrepentant, for popular consumption. He may have guessed that the "cult" knowledge is, in fact, common knowledge, and that Star Trek lore is so ubiquitous that there is little reason to hold back or delete its true character. If he made such a guess, he may have been correct. The Star Trek cult myth probably will be exploded by this film; toddlers and grandmothers are going to recognize the trivia here, because it's something we know, just as we know how many strikes it takes to eliminate the batter in baseball. When I saw the film the first time, in a large commercial theater packed to the corners, the audience laughed loudly, together, at McCoy's unsuccessful nerve pinch. A friend next to me could not understand why everyone was so amused. My friend was from China.

Like *Star Trek: The Motion Picture*, *The Search for Spock* is a complex film that reveals new nuances with each viewing. The ultimate significances of the film lie in its responses to the attempts of *Wrath of Khan* to mainstream the characters and over-technologize the Star Trek universe. Just as the sleek, smug *Excelsior* proved no match for the battered, outmoded *Enterprise*, no flashy directional strategies can replace the human energies that created Star Trek and placed it in the American cultural heart. And never again, one hopes, will the Star Trek producers feel a need to deny the little traditions that have trailed this remarkable creation.

As for Nimoy himself, one cannot help but suspect that he found the motif of Spock's rebirth and growth on the Genesis Planet—despite its destructiveness for the film's dramatic coherence—so attractive because it spoke on two levels. For Spock, the resurrection was in accord with a grand old theme in folklore and religion; and after the nullification of Spock's character as well as his life in *Wrath of Khan*, it was a necessary catharsis. For Nimoy, it was an immersion in the continuing adventure with which he and his fellows have struggled, not always happily, for almost a generation. It was a literal search for Spock. It seems he has truly been found in the mawkish last scene. That particular look after McCoy's nonverbal revelation, that irony and indignation in the one raised brow, has not been done for fifteen years. Spock has been hiding in McCoy's skull for a time, but he may have been hiding in Nimoy's, too.

## II. *Star Trek III*

The events of this story return Star Trek to its central concern— the "adventure," the search for meaningful existence—and prune away many of the distracting or compromising themes introduced in the earlier films, particularly in *Wrath of Khan*. At the same time, it takes two dramatic symbolic steps forward: The *Enterprise* is destroyed, and Kirk kicks an enemy off a cliff. Both are self-consciously contradictory of the former rules of the Star Trek universe, yet both are authentic, and challenging.

At the end of the Khan story, we are left with our characters in a very tenuous position. Kirk has been, in essence, bourgeoised. A sometime soldier, a sometime adventurer, the remarkable friend of remarkable friends, he is not encircled by new structures of relationship. Spock is dead. The love of his life (whom we have never heard of), Carol Marcus, has resurfaced, and with her a previously unknown son, David. The ship is heading back toward Earth, Kirk resigned to his friend's death and feeling "young," the future of himself and his remaining friends an open question.

Presumably it is a long way back to Earth, for by the time Kirk arrives his tone has changed. He is now disturbed, feeling that, in fact, he has lost "the best part" of himself. And McCoy is actually deranged, possessed by an inexplicable but, in time, fully identifiable presence. In accord with a previously unknown but completely acceptable Vulcan practice, Spock, when close to death, deposited his soul into the closest companion—not Kirk, who was separated from Spock at the time of the Vulcan's death, but McCoy. With Sarek's help, Kirk discovers the truth, and the search for Spock is on.

In a verbal introduction, Kirk dispelled the middle-aged placidity that had closed out *Wrath of Khan*. He is restless, dispirited, and the *Enterprise* reflects his mood; as it pulls into space dock, the extent of its damage is a wonder to the onlooking crowd. McCoy is also not the gamely philosophical man on the bridge muttering platitudes the way he had been as the group left Genesis. He is hurt, spiritually wounded in a way that he cannot quite understand. They are a tired crew, and upon returning to Earth are, in effect, rejected. Starfleet is putting them all (except Scott, who for reasons of plot must go directly to the *Excelsior*) on leave. And the *Enterprise* is headed for the junk heap. They are being turned out.

On the Genesis Planet, David Marcus and Lieutenant Saavik are doing scientific survey work to determine the progress of the Genesis experiment. They discover a life form, to no one's great surprise. It is the child Spock, regenerated like the microbes that had surrounded his coffin. But before their finding can be reported, the *Grissom*, which brought them there, is destroyed by a Klingon cruiser equipped with a cloaking device. With the *Grissom* was destroyed its buoyant Captain Esteban, one of the more promising characters to be introduced into Star Trek. Alas, this is an antiestablishment story, and as an official servant, Esteban is expendable.

For reasons that are never made perfectly clear, in the film official permission for Kirk to return to Genesis is denied. But now, convinced that Spock's soul and McCoy's sanity are at stake, Kirk resolves to go anyway. His friends join him, with Uhura handling the details of their actual acquisition of the *Enterprise* and Scott sabotaging the *Excelsior*, the new flagship of the fleet, which can be expected to block their departure. The *Enterprise* is now their own; they have stolen it from officialdom and, in doing so, irreparably severed their ties to "the establishment." "She is a beautiful lady, and we love her," Kirk told the Alice android in "I, Mudd." Now their fate is wedded to the ship's for better or for worse. As they trusted her to, the *Enterprise* takes them to their destination, but the ailing ship loses her first encounter with the deadly Klingon cruiser and is essentially stranded in space.

As Spock grows, the confrontation with the Klingons comes to a violent resolution. But in the meantime, Spock's body (his "marbles" are all with McCoy) appears to experience *pon farr*, and is "aided" by Lieutenant Saavik. This is, perhaps, a very crude use to which to put this unsuccessful character. She has been played by two mediocre actresses (who do not much resemble each other), and now that we have Spock back, she is as interesting as an imitation light bulb. If you consider the rate at which Spock was growing and if you accept Saavik's blithely mouthed law that Vulcan males "must" experience *pon farr* every seven years, you can appreciate that her services here must have been considerable. Saavik's future after *The Search for Spock* is not bright. It would probably be a waste of plot to kill her; she should be allowed, like Carol Marcus, to just fade away.

But David, Kirk's son, comes to a stunningly dramatic end. The young scientist confesses to Saavik that he used "protomatter" in the Genesis Device. (The use of protomatter, Saavik informs the air, has been disavowed by all ethical scientists. David used it to solve "certain problems." These problems, we fear, are more in the structure of *The Search for Spock* than in the structure of the universe.) Soon afterward David, Saavik, and Spock's physical self are captured by the Klingons, and in a brutal and very tense scene, David is murdered. A clever boost to the film's dramatic level, and a necessary demise for another character with no future. In the aftermath, Kirk, despite his pain, is back on course.

The admiral now appears to have no choice but to surrender his ship, and in a fulfillment of one of the earliest sketches of he story, he lures the Klingon raiders aboard the

*Enterprise*, which is set to self-destruct, and beams down to the planet with his own crew. As they stand on a precipice over a molten plain, the great ship explodes, its famous serial numbers disintegrating in the blast, and the remains soar down into the atmosphere. The magnitude of the loss is later acknowledged by Sarek. "Your ship, your son . . ."

On the surface of the planet, Kirk confronts the Klingon commander, Kruge, and after a short debate, during which Kirk's sentient friends are transported to the Klingon ship, Kirk and the Klingon have a fistfight over whether or not Spock's unconscious body will also be transported up. It's a close fight for Kirk (no, Spock does not jump up and rescue him), and it ends with Kruge, the man who ordered David murdered, hanging by his hands from a cliff as the planet melts down around them. Kirk, our familiar Kirk, offers his hand, and when the Klingon attempts to drag him over the cliff by grasping his ankle instead, Kirk exclaims, "I have had enough of you!" and kicks the villain squarely in the forehead, dropping him to his doom.

Interesting. I saw an offer for a commercial poster of Kirk offering his hand to the doomed Kruge; I wonder whether there will be an attempt to sell one of him bashing in the alien's forehead with his boot. Many of the seventy-eight televised stories ended with Kirk's using his refusal to kill as a demonstration of human worth. Of course, nobody killed his son in the old days, or caused him to destroy his ship. Still, he presented this as an absolute; he wanted to kill, but he did not. Here, his first impulse was not to kill, and in exasperation he finally did kill. It was a killing everyone enjoyed, and carried off with an irony that played off the old Star Trek theme of mercy. We agree with Kirk that this particular one, just this one, really doesn't deserve to live, and we are relieved and amused to see Kirk get mad as hell and not take it anymore. Good sense. Now what?

Using the Klingon cruiser, the group takes Spock's body back to Vulcan, where they are met by Uhura, and the film winds down with a not very thrilling ritual and a hackneyed recognition scene. Intriguingly, the story ends with the group all on Vulcan, with assurance that the adventure continues. For the first time, we wonder if they can really go home again. Starfleet can drop charges resulting from the theft of the *Enterprise*; but do our friends really have a future with the Fleet? Would the Federation ever give them a starship again? More important, would they want one? With their Klingon vessel they can cruise the galaxy, doing . . . you fill in the blanks. Will they settle on Vulcan, if only temporarily? And as for Spock—now that he has come back from the dead, would he not find some of his scientific duties mundane?

It is a curious feature of science fiction that it is easier to bring a person back to life than a spacecraft back into existence. There is no need to speculate whether or not the *Enterprise* will come back from the dead. In the original outline there was some suggestion that the ship might be rebuilt; in the film as it stands, no such idea is offered. The *Enterprise* has been a Star Trek character, as surely as the men and women who pilot her, and, like Spock (and like David), she died for her friends, counting down the seconds to her self-destruction. But unlike Spock, she seems not to have had an eternal soul. She has cradled the crew, and now they are truly free. They are liberated not only from the *Enterprise*, but also from Starfleet. In fact, with *The Search for Spock* these vigorous characters have declared themselves free of many of the authorities that had bound them.

It was a sorry sight when old *Enterprise* went down, but Star Trek is left with its vital organs intact, and unlimited possibilities stretching ahead. A very different situation from that with which we were left by the previous film. Then, the problem was how to get back to where we had been. Now, the question is which way to go from here. Spock had to come back, because Star Trek is part of our culture, and Spock is part of Star Trek. He came back as he did because Nimoy refused to play games with the audience or with the Star Trek legacy. From now on, at least one thing should be clear: Star Trek can go right on being Star Trek, and this time they will keep on watching.

# BENEATH THE SURFACE: THE SURREALISTIC STAR TREK

## by James H. Devon

*James Devon, a newcomer to* Trek, *surprised us with this submission; seldom have we seen a first-time effort so well thought out and skillfully written as is this article. James took a look at Star Trek from a new angle—surrealism—and found that the series manages to stand up even under that offbeat and demanding discipline's scrutiny. We're awfully proud of this article, for it supports our contention that if you look hard enough, you can always find something new in Star Trek. And after you finish reading James's article, we think you'll want to go back and watch some of the episodes again, from a new and slightly different viewpoint.*

There's a stranger within the man. He looks out cautiously, secretively, curiously . . . impatient with the intellect and trained personality which rules him. He's angry, yet respectful of those strict limitations which are the sign of civilized man, and looking out, he wonders about a way to speak, longs to express his own undefinable presence.

The subconscious is the alien in every man or woman; the truest, deepest part which desires so strongly to speak of matters for which his conscious being has no precise words. That subconscious can be wild, untrained, amoral, inventive, undefined, and, in its own way, extremely beautiful. It has been called many things and *is* many things: the subconscious, the id, the sex drive, the creative unconscious. It's the powerful raw material of personality, and as such is a fit topic for science fiction.

It has always played a large part in the work of the genre's best authors, but it is difficult to put a label on just what these writers are referring to. Their material deals with something beyond the consciously evident, beyond the practical and recognizable, and consequently splits the audience into two halves: Those who simply shrug and turn away, complaining that there's "no plot, it makes no sense;" and those who read or watch, entranced, mystified, as they receive a message which is not transferred so much through the trained intellect as it is by a sort of logical/emotional creative subconscious. To this second audience, the work becomes something *more*, something very personal. It is no longer something which can be cleanly converted into words of definition.

Undoubtedly, the finest accomplishment of science fiction is the explicit portrayal of that mysterious part of man known as the subconscious. Science fiction, at its best, is the art of revelation of the creative subconscious. Using dialogue, story, and special effects, it expresses symbolically the workings of the subconscious mind. It is surrealism.

And this is the point at which Star Trek fans and general science fiction fans often take up arms against one another. Those who consider themselves sophisticated, well-rounded science fiction fans might point to Star Trek, their lips curled in disgust, and say "Space opera." And the avid Star Trek fan, always ready to defend his old friends, Kirk, Spock, and McCoy, will, just as rudely, point to some fine piece of surrealistic science fiction and mutter, "It doesn't even tell a story." He would then go on about how Star Trek is, after all, a series which tells stories about people and "the human adventure," about things of the human heart.

So, like the two Lazaruses of "The Alternative Factor," our polarized fans will battle eternally, each defending his own little corner of his own little self-defined world. And all for nothing, because they're not only missing the point of it all, they're missing much, much more.

Like the legendary prophet without honor in his own land, Gene Roddenberry has come under a great deal of criticism for his work and for some of the things he "said" through that work. Yet that very work, Star Trek, helped to make science fiction a popular medium, bringing it and its surrealistic themes out of the dusty back corners of the library and into the living rooms of not just the United States, but the entire free world. And if his episodes lacked the finely tuned sophistication of the best science fiction, they did tell lively science and futuristic stories with all the love and subtle grandeur of a Heinlein. You just can't *sell* the tough surrealism of a Clark to a meat-and-potatoes audience.

But Roddenberry did his best to retain science fiction's surrealism in Star Trek. Again and again we find episodes containing themes which deal with some aspect of the subconscious mind: "Man Trap," "The Enemy Within," "The Menagerie," "Shore Leave," "The Return of the Archons," "This Side of Paradise," "Amok Time," "Mirror, Mirror," "Charlie X," and "Catspaw," to name just a few. These are stories which can and *should* be viewed on many levels, levels which would often prove complex and self-revealing in nature. These episodes speak of the mysteries and power of the human mind, sometimes glorying in that mind's ability to reach beyond the mundane, oftentimes in awe of the mind's dualistic power to create and destroy. Often, this subconscious or surrealistic motif deals with the most powerful, driving force in and of the human mind—sexuality.

Even the good ship *Enterprise* is generally thought to have been designed in a fashion which would bring to mind symbols of male and female sexuality: The ship's round, feminine hull, and her accompanying oblong, phallic warp engine nacelles are representative enough of the shapes which stir the sexual subconscious ever so slightly. Done laughing? Now consider the psychosexual themes of such episodes as "Amok Time," "Metamorphosis," "Elaan of Troyius," and "The Empath." These episodes deal more with human sensuality than with sex, and range from the agonizing, logic-ripping sex drive of the Vulcan *pon farr* in "Amok Time" to the gentle, very feminine and healing tenderness of Gem in "The Empath." We're not talking about sex here any more than we're talking about sex when describing the shape of the *Enterprise* . . . we *are* talking about that aspect of sensuality which exists in a given episode and which might be speaking directly to our subconscious. Its only relation to sex is as a catalyst that touches or even awakens the deepest, most powerful areas of the human subconscious. Such episodes *use* sensuality to draw our attention to the story and its message—nothing more. A story like "Amok Time" cuts through the barriers of sexual/emotional taboos by presenting us with a being who is not human and whose sex drive need not be embarrassing to us for that reason. It's damned interesting, but not threatening. So considered, "Amok Time" is probably Star Trek's single most sexually powerful episode, and yet its passionate story is "safe," not an overt threat to a non-Vulcan audience.

It would be narrow-minded to claim that surrealism or the surrealistic mood of science fiction deals with only the sexual subconscious. In "The Empath," an episode which is more theater than television, something entirely new is added to Star Trek. Yes, the show certainly has undercurrents of sex and sadism. There is the stripped, tortured Kirk, the brutalized but not defeated McCoy, the lovely, innocent Gem. But the story itself does not have a sadomasochistic theme. Quite the opposite, it is a story of simple humanitarianism and human devotion, bringing the friendship of the Three closest it ever comes to spirituality. It reveals something of the good and evil, the negative and the positive of the human subconscious, calling to mind the depths of man's cruelty, and, more important, the powerful force of his compassion. In this sense, of all the Star Trek *television* episodes, "The Empath" is the most progressive and daring statement about the personal destiny of man. But it relates its message quietly, not so much by word or deed, but by the craftsmanship of the artists involved.

Whenever you are dealing with "good" science fiction, especially in the surrealistic sense, you are also dealing with the theme of the destiny of man. Roddenberry, most of his actors, and at least some of the directors and producers knew that. But only so much can be done on television, so it was not until Star Trek took to the big screen that the Big Story happened.

And when it did, Star Trek fandom split right down the middle.

The Movie. It is to the discredit of the science fiction motif of Star Trek that many fans disinherited Paramount and Roddenberry at the film's release. *Star Trek: The Motion Picture* is one of the finest *science fiction* films ever made. The fact that a good number of fans resent the movie will not change that fact. But if many fans were turned off by the fact that it wasn't the soap opera or action-adventure that they had expected, others were awed by the scope of the film.

Yes, there were flaws. Poor editing, for one, rectified too late when the movie finally aired on network TV. A certain amount of nepotism: too many friends and relatives—and, most especially, too many fans—were involved in the film . . . some of whom turned on Roddenberry when a new producer and new "opportunities" came along. This hurt the necessary overall look and "feel" of professionalism in the film. Then there was some plain, ordinary bad acting. To make things worse, someone seemed to have forgotten that there *is* no single star in Star Trek—resulting in a show "over-Kirked" (as were most in the third season). Most unforgivably, William Shatner forgot that he was acting on the movie screen, not the TV screen, and so came across as overblown and uneasy.

But despite it all, *Star Trek: The Motion Picture* held to a powerful, hard-core science fiction theme: the evolution of mankind. The story uses a multiplicity of themes and subplots to work its way to a masterfully orchestrated, unifying climax. And Nimoy and Kelley, whose strong affection for their characters was evident, held the friendship together at its darkest hour.

But first and foremost, of course, is Kirk and his tragically wonderful headstrong determination, not only to face the alien V'Ger, but to once again command his beloved *Enterprise*. Thus the continuing all-important symbolism of the masculine sex drive is established at the outset. Kirk's courageous determination is, at times, almost blind, driven—and one might even say that on the subconscious level it matches the desire to reproduce, to rule, to *live*. Kirk *is* very much acting out of instinct here, and on a larger scale it is that primitive instinct of his that ultimately leads to the confrontation wtih V'Ger and the saving of planet Earth. So while some fans seem unfairly annoyed with Kirk's masculine sex drive—and perhaps even turned off by it—it's clear enough that this facet of man is extremely important to the part he is to play in the surrealistic Star Trek.

As if to mirror the masculine and sometimes virtually out-of-control passion of Admiral Kirk, we are introduced to Lieutenant Ilia, the Deltan navigator. She is beautiful; she is very, very feminine, evoking completely the idea of sensuality—but she is also very much in control of her sexual "self." She has to be, as she is Kirk's (and all other humans') sexual superior. Her calm sense of sexual identity and security gives her maturity and emotional well-being that contrasts perfectly with Kirk's almost childlike need to "prove himself" through command.

Persis Khambatta, as Ilia, is certainly one of the unsung heroines of *Star Trek: The Motion Picture*. She is to be commended for her insightful portrayal of the alien, achieving the delicate balance of eroticism and innocence so necessary to this being who is pivotal to both the overt and the symbolic storylines of the movie. Ilia is, after all, the mother of a new race in which the feminine is to be combined with the masculine, the emotional to be combined with the logical, flesh and blood with the living mechanical. Because of her great passion, she is the connecting line between Decker and V'Ger, ultimately to lead the human Decker (symbolic of the god/man/creator) and the alien V'Ger to *understand*. Even though the machine entity has *destroyed* her actual carbon-based body, it is not able to erase that superior aptitude for passion and love. Thus, she becomes both the enticer and the savior/mediator (memories of Gem?) and the mother—as well as the child—of a new life form.

In *Star Trek: The Motion Picture*, Kirk and Decker are, on a symbolic level, the same man. Or at least Decker *represents* the same kind of man as Kirk. He is ambitious, determined, strong, and sexually impulsive and has a great genuine love for people, human or otherwise. The admiration he holds for Mr. Spock matches Kirk's, although, of course, it is backed up by legend, not years of personal friendship. Figuratively, he steps in for Kirk at the end of the story, sacrificing his life despite Kirk's pleadings, because—through his very sexually oriented communication with Ilia—he feels it is his duty, his destiny, even his *right* to join with V'Ger. Decker, symbolic of the evolving human race, takes over where the more primitive form of mankind, represented in Kirk, cannot. It's almost as if the personality represented in Kirk takes over in the new, younger, and perhaps a bit more emotionally advanced figure of Decker to take that next step in human evolution.

It's been said before, but it cannot be said enough: Emotion/Imagination/Logic = Ilia/Decker/V'Ger = McCoy/Kirk/Spock. These combinations are really one combination, read on many different levels. To some, it is simply the Friendship. To the science fiction fan, it is the evolution of man to something greater. To the lucky person who allows himself to fit into both categories, it is a great deal more: It is the achievement of something that is very difficult to put into words. But if examples help, it might be apt to point out here that the thing that happens with/through the Friendship in *Star Trek: The Motion Picture* is the same sort of thing which goes on throughout the series. What occurs in the movie is, on the subconscious, symbolic level, the same thing which occurs in "The Empath:" the preservation and even advancement of a race through the qualities exemplified in the friendship of McCoy, Spock, and Kirk.

And the best part of it is, it doesn't matter *who* makes the sacrifice. In "The Empath," it is McCoy. In *Star Trek: The Motion Picture*, it is Decker. It seems, in Star Trek, that it is not the individual who makes the sacrifice who is alone responsible for what that sacrifice achieves. The value of his "gift" is measured ultimately in the way in which these personalities who are closest to him respond and contribute. In this way, the very surrealistic quality of the Friendship is made apparent. The great value to the viewer on a subconscious level is that McCoy/Kirk/Spock are, as Roddenberry himself has explained, representative of one man. The qualities they display as a team are the qualities which go into the making of any man. That, in itself, might be one explanation for the phenomenal charm the Friendship holds for fans. Like all such phenomena, it cannot be explained in simpler terms. So we might say here that we like McCoy and Kirk and

Spock because they show us our own potential. Never has there been a more positive, more compelling team of characters. And never before has a group of actors combined so cleverly to portray a theme which is essentially surrealistic in nature.

It is ironic that *Star Trek: The Motion Picture* fell short for many of us because of its failure to present the Friendship the way we were used to seeing it on the series. The reeditied TV version is much better than the original release print. This second edition of the film makes it obvious that in the first release, the characters of Spock and McCoy were shorted for the sake of Kirk. The only explanation for this is that those with editorial power had absolutely *no* instinct for the surrealistic nature of the Friendship and the importance of the balance contribution of the three leads. Someone obviously thought that Star Trek was, or is, Kirk's story. It is, as we all know, the story of all three . . . the Three. And it takes place on such a sublime, surrealistic level that to change or tamper with or ignore that fact leaves us with something that is not Star Trek at all. Paramount may someday be able to get away with putting new characters on the bridge of the *Enterprise*, but they will never be able to continue the magic of Star Trek without the same kind of combination which McCoy, Kirk, and Spock represent to the subconscious mind.

But while the Friendship is the ultimate key to the underlying mood and success of Star Trek, it is not all. In *Star Trek: The Motion Picture*, we have the achievement of something that goes even beyond discussing the personality of man. It is, after all, through the qualities of the Friendship that a *new being* emerges. Cosmically evolved from the rudiments of man's logic, V'Ger, the machine/entity, comes in search of its creator. V'Ger is an emotionless entity—at "heart" still only a machine, after all—and unmoved by those things which touch man. It knows neither beauty nor ugliness. It only follows its creator's command: to learn all that is learnable. But by the time it returns to Earth, it has, through its achievement of so much, reached a crisis point: It has come, through the process of its own evolution, to know that it is alone. Rather than a monster, it is, as Spock tells us, "a child," terrified in the night and on that brink of self-awareness and questioning we all reach during childhood. And, on an even deeper, symbolic level, we might say that it is not even really a child, but that still, powerful, pre-life "nothingness" which exists even before infancy. The prime, untouched, unmoved force of life.

The special-effects genius of Doug Trumbull takes over to give the audience the subliminal sexual/intellectual message of V'Ger; a surrealistically erotic joureny through the curling labyrinth of V'Ger's protective cloud membrane—the very womblike core of the machine entity. There, the Voyager probe waits with an eerie kind of patience, symbolic of the egg waiting for fertilization. Throughout the special-effects journey, in fact, the viewer is treated to a number of subliminally erotic scenes, from the first mystically swirling entry into the cloud, with its rich, hypnotic blend of blues, pinks, and grays, always soft and beckoning—to the mutedly devilish features which peer at us from the cerebral psychosexual "landscape" of V'Ger's surface. It is, none too subtly, a mind-enlivened imaginary journey to the sexual center of the subconscious of man. The *Enterprise*, commanded by the virile Admiral Kirk, penetrates the V'Ger "orifice" (take that allusion as you will; for as each individual member of the audience takes it, so it was meant to be received) and drives onward through the deep, ovarial recesses of V'Ger proper. In the erotic vastness of V'Ger, the *Enterprise* becomes tiny, fragile, seedlike, as the sperm would appear as it makes its long, mystical/biological journey to the ovum. And as if to reinforce this subliminal message in the minds of viewers, the scientific symbols for the male and female are portrayed clearly just outside the orifice . . . as if to say, "This way, folks! Proceed with caution!"

Could it be that V'Ger has unknowingly developed a sexual subconsciousness of its own, and that its cerebral/mechanical landscape is portraying it for us? We are, after all, now deep within V'Ger's most secret places. And if, as Spock tells us, V'Ger has achieved consciousness, would it follow that it would also have achieved its own unique form of a subconscious? And it is just as possible that some form of its creator's subconscious sexual symbolism would have found its way into the programming and building of the Voyager probe itself. The basic sex drive is, after all, sublimely evident in all we do, certainly in art, mechanics, or any such creative design. Man is first and foremost a sexual creature, so it stands to reason that he leaves that mark on all he touches. It is no different with the V'Ger probe, and no less likely that it would have picked up on those strange, compelling seemingly unnecessary points of design (with the curiosity of a child?) and, as it evolved, would have programmed and transcribed them in a logical, technical way. In short, V'Ger, as it matured, contrived a technical map of its own sexual subconscious. It was too innocent to know what else to do with the curious, seemingly impractical "knowledge" of sexual identity.

V'Ger's original command and purpose, to go into the unknown and bring something back for the benefit of man, can also be interpreted on a deeper level (if a more organically basic one). V'Ger was designed for the benefit and survival of the race which was its creator. As a mental probe of man, it was a mechanical extension of the sexual urge. And the human sex urge must be recognized (as portrayed in Kirk) as the primitive basis of man's need to discover the secrets of the universe, to venture into the dark unknown for the sake of extending mankind. It's a matter of growth and plain evolution. In Star Trek, it is instinct.

The sexual experience has often been equated with a kind of death. In the final V'Ger scene, we have the powerful, all-giving/all-receiving orgasmic union of Decker/Ilia/V'Ger. Is it a death or a rebirth? Kirk reports Decker and Ilia as "missing." McCoy gloats like a new father as he pronounces the "birth" of a new life form. One thing is for sure, the Friendship of Kirk/Spock/McCoy is very, very happy. The race of man has been saved, has evolved. It was perhaps the most satisfying and rewarding of all their missions together. They have a right to be proud.

If *Star Trek: The Motion Picture* has fallen out of grace with the fans, it is only a temporary thing, very likely due to the vast popularity of that charming shoot-'em-up *Wrath of Khan*. Unlike *Wrath of Khan*, the first movie is just too complex, too intense and sincere in ambition, with its intricately interwoven themes of positive/negative, virility/barrenness, emotion/logic, man/machine. From its celebration of

IDIC to its insistence that man can accomplish more through understanding than through fighting, it was just too completely "Star Trek." Too much mental work, not enough phaser fire. Paramount has since learned the hard lesson we fans taught it—thus, the death of Spock. Don't blame Paramount for giving the public what it wants.

Nevertheless, *Star Trek: The Motion Picture*, as a whole, is not a story about good versus evil. It is a story of the evolution of human values and worth. It is, perhaps, too powerful, too threatening a story for the average viewer. It is one of those science fiction stories which, like *2001: A Space Odyssey*, must sit on the back burner of American consciousness for a time before it is truly and honestly appreciated.

But Star Trek, from "The Cage" to *The Searth for Spock*, has always dealt at its deepest level with the inner growth of man. Of course, this growth is often portrayed in a phychosexual sense—it is the way of the art, the way of legitimate science fiction, the way of man. From what we have discovered about the underlying themes of some of the episodes (including the movies), from what we have seen of the Friendship—probably the cleverest combination ever to be achieved on film—and from what we know to be the basis of man's subconscious self, it's certainly fair to say that Star Trek does indeed speak with the charming, surrealistic tongue of true science fiction. And through the magic of its science fiction, special effects, and symbolism, the "alien" within each of us is allowed its brief, beautiful, and very revealing hour in the sun.

# SOME THOUGHTS

### by C. J. Nicastro

*C.J. is another first-time contributor, and we found his collection of short articles so enjoyable that we decided to break one of our rules and present them all at one time, so that you readers could enjoy them that much more. We think you'll especially enjoy C.J.'s profile of Transporter Chief Kyle, and, we'll be the first to admit it, it's about time!*

## "Spock Savage" or the Vulcan of Bronze

Both *Best of Trek #2* and *#4* have promising articles on the ancestors of the *Enterprise* crew. "A Theory of Relativity" states that perhaps Sherlock Holmes was a Vulcan. "The Star Trek Family Tree" states that not only Holmes but many other heroes of the past (Zorro, the Lone Ranger, etc.) were related, through the Wold-Newton Family of Philip Jose Farmer, to the Star Trek universe.

One article, "Kirk's Career," even states that Doc Savage is a member of *his* family. However, here I must disagree.

While Sherlock Holmes *seems* to be a good candidate to be a Vulcan, there is just too much evidence that he is *not*. If nothing else, Holmes did not have pointed ears. No surgeon of the time when Holmes was supposedly born—the 1850s—could have "fixed" alien ears to resemble human ones.

Doc Savage, however, is a very likely candidate for Vulcanhood.

Doc was supposedly born onboard a boat in the Caribbean. His mother supposedly drowned a few days later, leaving her adventurer husband to raise the child; he raised him to start a career of righting wrongs.

What really happened is this:

Mrs. Savage did, indeed, drown—while still pregnant. A few nights later, a small craft fell from the sky and struck the nearby shore. Clark Savage, Sr., went ashore and found the strange craft—a small experimental spaceship from Vulcan. The adults aboard were dead, but one small infant survived. Seeing that the craft was about to explode, Savage rescued the child and grabbed up a small, glowing box.

The box, a universal translator and recorder device, enabled Savage to learn of the ship's origin and peaceful mission to explore other planets.

Savage took the child to a friend, a surgeon who was perfecting the new art of plastic surgery. Swearing him to silence, he had him operate on the boy's ears so that they would appear human.

The career of Doc Savage is only too well known. World War I hero at just age sixteen. Graduate of Johns Hopkins at eighteen. A super-crimefighter whose career spanned two decades.

Always, Doc retained his Vulcan heritage. Rarely did he show emotion. Hardly ever did he smile. He studiously avoided women. He used logic in both his careers, as surgeon/scientist and crimefighter.

Many have speculated on the purpose of the Fortress of Solitude to which Doc would periodically retreat. The reason becomes evident when one considers that Doc was Vulcan, not human. He needed it as a place to mate, in the Vulcan manner, with the chosen woman of his life.

And who might that have been? Many women pursued Doc, but none ever caught him, so only one candidate seems very likely—his "cousin," the earthborn Patricia Savage. Farmer does often speculate that Doc and Pat had been having a secret sexual affair for years, since he treated Pat differently than he did other women—much as a Vulcan would his mate. In short, with respect and more kindness than he allowed himself to show to, say, any of the "normal" women who wanted him.

And Pat was anything *but* normal! She was often described as being almost Doc's female counterpart. It is obvious that she and Doc were "mated" at an early age by the Vulcan ritual described on the translator tapes Clark Savage rescued from the spacecraft. Savage's brother, Alex, knew of Doc's true origin, as, later, did Pat. The undercurrent of a "shared secret" that Doc's friends detected between him and Pat was indeed that—the secret of his origins and their love.

So, a Vulcan did, indeed, come to Earth. Doc "vanished" in 1949, shortly after his last recorded adventure against a decidedly alien force. It just may be that Doc (along with Pat, who also disappeared about that time) may have constructed, from directions on the tapes, a spacecraft which enabled him to travel to the stars. Perhaps, after many years of "exile," a Vulcan finally returned to his homeworld. . . .

## A Note on Spock

It is important to note that Spock also fits into the Wold-Newton list via his mother, Amanda Grayson. She is the great-great-etc.-granddaughter of Richard "Dick" Grayson, who, in the late 1930s, was adopted by millionaire Bruce Wayne. Wayne became police commissioner of Gotham City, and when he died in the late 1970s, Grayson inherited his role as a crimefighter—Batman! So, a tradition of righting wrongs—and a strong element of emotionalism—exists in Spock's heritage.

## Another Look at Women in the Federation

*The Best of Trek #2* contained an especially interesting article: Pamela Rose's "Women in the Federation." Being not only male, but a "male feminist," I think a man's look at women in the Federation is in order.

It was never explicitly stated anywhere in the Star Trek canon—on television or film—that women couldn't be starship captains. On the contrary, the fact that the Romulans had a female commander makes it all the more likely that there are indeed female captains. The twenty-third century is doubtless an extremely liberated age, an era of almost total equality; a place where if a woman is more qualified than a man for the job of starship captain, she'll get the job.

The example of Janice Lester doesn't hold water when one considers that she was mentally unbalanced. Starfleet wouldn't allow anyone, male or female, in a captain's chair unless that person was 100 percent mentally and physically up to it (witness the case of Ben Finney in "Courtmartial").

There are a few women we have met in Star Trek who qualify as captain material. Uhura is the most obvious choice; she is mentally and physically fit for the job and extremely well trained. (She is the most obvious choice among the fans as well, it seems—how about all those "Uhura for Captain!" buttons worn at cons?) But there are other women, human and alien, just as qualified.

T'Pring immediately comes to mind. Many male fans like T'Pring—for obvious reasons. Many female fans despise her—for reasons just as obvious. Her natural coldly logical viciousness aside, it is apparent she would make a fine captain. She is, above all else, a Vulcan. Even Spock complimented her on her logic. If T'Pring ever tires of Stonn (or vice versa), she should try Starfleet.

Daras of Ekos is another likely candidate. Her militaristic background and training under the Reich of Führer John Gill will make it nearly impossible for her to settle back into a "homemaker" role. If the Ekosian system of military rule is completely dismantled, it is likely she will look to Starfleet for an outlet.

And what of Yeoman Janice Rand? Despite the fact that she is seen in *Star Trek: The Motion Picture* as transporter chief, replacing the legendary Mr. Kyle, it has always seemed to me that Rand had the right stuff in her to earn a command. The few times we see her during the first season, she is often in danger and taking it in stride. In fact, in "Balance of Terror," she comes onto the bridge to be with Kirk in the event the ship should be destroyed. It not only speaks of her love for Kirk, but speaks volumes for her courage. She doesn't *have* to be there—she *wants* to be there.

It has been mentioned that there are no females in Security. Really? What about Yeoman Tamura in "A Taste of Armageddon?'' She's left with a phaser to guard a female prisoner. It's obvious she's a security person, since few other females with other duties would really be intimately acquainted with a phaser.

In the novel *Vulcan* by Kathleen Sky, Dr. Katalya Tremain is very efficient with a phaser when defending herself and Spock against hostile creatures. Despite her alleged bigotry against Vulcans, she protects a wounded Spock, even mindmelds with him to save his life. A promotion to captaincy in her future would be pretty much of a sure thing.

In their novels *The Price of the Phoenix* and *The Fate of the Phoenix*, authors Sondra Marshak and Myrna Culbreath expand on the character of the Romulan commander from "The Enterprise Incident," giving her both a name—Dion Charvon—and a detailed homeworld background on the planet— Romula. The setup on her home planet seems to be more a matriarchy than a patriarchy, and in some parts of *Fate of the Phoenix*, it seems more as if we're reading a John Norman novel than a Star Trek novel (with, of course, male-female roles reversed.)

Perhaps the best example of recent Star Trek fiction is Vonda McIntyre's *The Entropy Effect*. This excellent novel, which obviously takes place two years or so after *Star Trek: The Motion Picture*, is set (like the *Phoenix* tales) in an alternate Star Trek universe. (You can see this in many ways, the most obvious of which is the change in Mr. Sulu's first name from Walter to Hikaru.) Whereas the *Phoenix* novels are so adult in content as to shock, this novel moves along at a nice clip and offers us not one but two superior females.

Captain Hunter is near Kirk's age and commander of the Starship *Aerfen*. She is a female warrior in the mold of those of *Star Wars* and *Battlestar Galactica*, and if you're a Star Trek purist, she obviously has no place in Kirk's past. This tale does answer one question, however: In this timeline, women in the Federation *do* command Starfleet ships.

The other heroine is Lieutenant Commander Mandala Flynn, the *Enterprise*'s new security chief. A wild, tomboyish lady, she comes from the "border patrol" (which we never heard of in aired Star Trek) and juggles a tough-as-nails personality with a tender love for Sulu. One is especially reminded of the tough female officer played by Sigourney Weaver in *Alien*. If Vonda McIntyre writes any more Star Trek novels, it is hoped by this writer that Mandala Flynn is again prominently featured.

Fandom is obviously divided over the question of females in the Federation. There are probably many fans who have written their own tales of female captains and security chiefs, doctors and science officers. And who knows? In the growing Star Trek universe, we may yet see a starship with a crew where females are in the majority. After all, if there can be an entire starship of Vulcans . . .

## A Look at the Prime Directive

What is the most rigid rule a starship captain must uphold? What is the single most important thing he must always remember?

The Prime Directive.

Simply stated, it means noninterference in an alien culture. Federation crewmembers may beam down to a planet, mingle with the culture's natives (if prior study indicates that they are sufficiently humanoid so that the crew can do so without being detected), learn if the culture is ''up to'' Federation standards (i.e., if they hold the same, or nearly the same, values as the majority of Federation worlds, and if they are sufficiently advanced to avoid ''culture shock''), then report their findings back to the captain. He then forwards the findings and his opinions to Starfleet, and (probably months later) a decision is made. If the planet is to be offered membership, other crewmen and diplomats, specially trained in such duties, reveal their presence, explain about the Federation and its enemies, and proffer membership.

Fine. Understood.

So how come James T. Kirk consistently destroys computers, deposes leaders, helps arm natives, takes sides in battles, etc., and otherwise screws up lives and civilizations?

Seriously, Kirk is a good commander, but a bit emotional where ''human rights'' are concerned—or, rather, human rights according to the definition of James T. Kirk!

The most blatant violations of the Prime Directive by Kirk

appear in "The Apple," "A Taste of Armageddon," and "Patterns of Force."

In the first two of these episodes, two extremely similar setups are presented—computer-controlled worlds. In "The Apple," a computer gave an entire people almost everything they wanted, but Kirk believed they needed free will—the right to make a choice. *They* didn't want or need it—yet Kirk went ahead and destroyed the computer-god Vaal, and the people were left, like little children, to fend for themselves (until the Federation missionaries and such could arrive, of course).

In "Armageddon," a computer played out a bloodless war with the population of two planets. As morbid as all this seemed, the fact remained that it was *their* solution to the problem of war. It was their right to do so—nobody ever said that a person had to choose freedom. The very fact that a people *can* choose to turn over all their rights to a computer proves that they have made the choice, and it's their own business. Does Kirk heed this? Nope. He just walks in, wrecks the computers, and gives the planet full-scale, real *war*!

"Patterns of Force," a very controversial episode, is a very strong example of how Kirk uses his *own* opinions and judgments to throw the Prime Directive to the winds.

Sociologist John Gill has been on the planet Ekos for some years, and he has established a society paralleling that of Earth's Nazi Germany. As soon as Kirk beams down and sees this, he sets out to topple the system. Despite the very controversial remark from Spock—that the Nazis were "a near-perfect state—a small nation, beaten and broken a few years before, eventually came close to world domination!" —Spock does not approve or disapprove. He merely states the same idea that Gill tells Kirk when they find him drugged and near death—that, handled correctly, it could have worked. Unfortunately, unscrupulous men in his own party seized power and history repeated itself.

Kirk's reason for wanting the system destroyed is: "It was evil." A value judgement. Hardly an impartial observation.

Despite the fact that the prejudiced part of the system is destroyed in the end, it is unresolved whether the planet will remain as a Nazi state. From hints dropped in the show, the Ekosians had had Gill as Führer for a good many years, and only during the last few, when Melakon seized power, was the program of prejudice against the neighboring planet Zeon implemented. (Though it was not stated, Gill had to have been on the planet at least twelve years. Daras, in her early twenties, says she grew up respecting the Führer—Gill—and that her father was an original party member and an old friend of Gill's. Gill was also one of Kirk's instructors at the Academy, and since this episode takes place when Kirk is about thirty-seven, we can be sure he has not seen Gill in about fifteen years.)

One society that Kirk does *not* attempt to change is the Roman world of "Bread and Circuses." Perhaps that world is too violent, and Kirk is just glad to get his crew out of there before they can fall apart as another crew and captain did before them. It's not cowardice on Kirk's part—these people, like the Gorns, the Klingons, and the Romulans, are better off outside the Federation.

In the humorous "A Piece of the Action," Kirk insinuates that the gangster society of the Iotians is going to be helped "in spite of itself." Though he doesn't here actually interfere in the culture—it's left relatively unchanged when they leave with Iotia enlisted as a new Federation member—the hope that contact with the Federation will change the Iotians is uppermost in Kirk's mind.

Kirk's specialty is computers—short-circuit 'em, make 'em explode or implode, burn up their memory banks. Anything to free those "poor people." And then what? Many of those "poor people," despite Kirk's contentions and his "good intentions" (and over Spock's frequent admonitions—"But Captain, the Prime Directive clearly states . . ."), just don't know or care for any other way of life. But that doesn't matter to Kirk. In "The Apple," he actually orders Chekov and some security men to hold off, at phaser-point, the people who are trying to protect their computer-god, Vaal. It's almost as if Kirk wants to say, "This is for your own good; grow up and take your medicine."

And take it they do. Computers blow up. Ancient gods die. Systems crumble into dust.

And all for what?

In *The Price of the Phoenix* and *The Fate of the Phoenix*, the two excellent novels by Marshak and Culbreath, the villian, Omne, wants to have the Federation investigated and broken up for consistent violation of their own noninterference laws. And Kirk is the chief culprit. Though the "conferences" Omne convenes are only a cover for his real intent, to kidnap and clone Kirk, one cannot help but sympathize with the idea. Somebody *should* make Kirk read over that section on noninterference in the Starfleet manual again!

In the TV movie *Goliath Awaits*, the whole idea of noninterference was beautifully summed up in a quote from the captain of the sunken ship whose people didn't want to be rescued.

"What if a spaceship landed on Earth, and the inhabitants got out and told the people, 'We have come to rescue you'? The answer might be: 'To rescue us from what?' "

From what, indeed?

## Enterprise Crew Profile: Transporter Chief Kyle

Lieutenant Commander Winston Matthew Kyle was born in Sydney, Australia, thirty-seven years before the five-year mission of the *Enterprise* under Captain Kirk began. His parents were both in Starfleet: His father, Nayland Andrew Kyle, was a commander in Starfleet Intelligence, and his mother was on the Australian Embassy Staff.

From his earliest years, Kyle was groomed by his parents for Starfleet. His father wished him to enter either the Intelligence division, or if Winston decided he wanted deep-space life, to try for Security. Both choices appealed to the young man, but as he grew, he realized he possessed a wanderlust that would be satisfied only by space travel.

He listened to his father's tales of his ancestors, of their contributions not only to Starfleet and the Federation but, in the early, pre-spaceflight days, to the Crown and the Empire. Two such ancestors were both in intelligence work. One, Sir Denis Nayland Smith, was an inspector with Scotland Yard and later a member of various British intelligence departments. Another, later in the twentieth century, was

Major John Steed, of the British Secret Service and Special Branch.

Kyle listened with admiration and pride to these tales of his heritage. And although most of his ancestors seemed to have been involved in "spy" work, an equal number, men and women alike, were swashbuckling adventurers who struck out on their own, cutting their way across an early and savage world.

Kyle entered Starfleet Academy and did fairly well during his four years. At the end of his training, he was assigned as a security guard on the *USS Paul Revere*, an ironic twist of fate, in more ways than one, for the Britisher. Here he would meet a friend he would later work with on the *Enterprise*—Helmsman Walter Sulu. Like Kyle, Sulu had a love for Earth's past, and he and Kyle had long talks whenever they could. They seemed a Mutt and Jeff pair—the not-so-inscrutable Oriental and the giant, blond, stoic Australian. But Kyle's time on the *Paul Revere* was all too short; following a wound received in battle, he was left behind to recuperate at a starbase, and his friendship with Sulu would not be revived for many years. (During that time, Sulu would love and lose Lynn Mihara, and Kyle would forever feel slightly guilty that he was not there to comfort his friend as best he could after Lynn's tragic death.)

Kyle was reassigned to Security on the *Queen Victoria*, a predominantly British starship made up of residents from the Isles and Australia. Feeling more at home, he rose to the rank of assistant security chief. He also met another man with whom he would have a long friendship—Engineer Lee Kelso, one of the few Americans on the ship.

It was on this ship that Kyle was to have his first serious love affair. And, like his friend, Sulu, he would know the tragedy of loss.

T'Lina was a young Vulcan science officer assigned to the *Queen Victoria*. Since some British share with Vulcans a stoic, "proper" attitude, they can work in concert much more easily than, for example, Vulcans and Americans. For Kyle, in the process of becoming a seasoned space warrior, the cool logic and (for him) the extreme, almost painful beauty of T'Lina were something new to his experience.

Both became aware of a mutual attraction, but Kyle, true to his own British code of sparing a lady any embarrassment, remembered Vulcan custom and tried to avoid showing his feelings. For months, they remained "just friends," each afraid to make the first move which would carry the relationship further. (Kyle learned that T'Lina had some human blood. He was somewhat amazed, for there were very, very few half-Vulcans around, and he had heard of only one other in Starfleet—the science officer aboard Captain Pike's *Enterprise*.)

Even this knowledge still was not enough for Kyle to declare his feelings. Eventually, T'Lina made the first move, seeing it as the "logical" thing to do. Soon, she and Kyle were meeting whenever they had a free moment, and they even began discussing marriage. T'Lina had been pair-bonded to a Vulcan who had died on a deep-space mission, and so was free to choose her own mate.

Some time later, a party of explorers from the *Queen Victoria*, led by T'Lina, beamed down to a planet to search for dilithium crystal deposits. They were attacked by a band of renegade Klingons, and before Kyle and other security people could come to the rescue, all in the landing party had been slaughtered.

Swearing vengeance, Kyle devoted months of his R&R time to tracking and killing, on his own, the Klingons who had been responsible for the tragedy. When his vendetta was completed, he felt that T'Lina had been avenged—but that his own life was now hollow. Most of all, he wanted out of Security. He wanted out of death, destruction. He hadn't formed many friendships in Security; a friend could be dead a day later. Or you yourself could.

He asked for, and received, a transfer. He was assigned to the *Enterprise* as a transporter operator. In three years, he rose to transporter chief, and saw Captain Christopher Pike leave and Captain James T. Kirk take over.

Some months before Kirk arrived, Kyle had been glad to see his old friend Lee Kelso assigned to the *Enterprise* as assistant engineer. And, with Kirk's coming, another old friend arrived—Walter Sulu, who had served on the *Hua Ching* with Kirk.

After the harrowing events at the edge of the galaxy, Kyle knew that there were disadvantages to serving in any capacity in deep space. For Lee Kelso had died out there, and again, something died in Kyle.

Still, he stayed on. He got on well with the rest of the crew and was highly rated by the demanding Kirk and Spock. By the time of the end of the five-year mission, he had become something of an institution in the main transporter room. When Kirk and Spock decided to leave and Captain Decker took over, Kyle decided to sign on the *Enterprise* again.

Fate intervened, however, and Kyle was again injured while helping to install the new transporter equipment during the *Enterprise*'s refitting. He was sent Earthside to recuperate and Janice Rand was transferred back to her old ship and made transporter chief.

Kyle was now nearing middle age. His father had died and his mother persuaded him to apply for desk duty on a Starbase. He was given charge of the transporter facilities on Starbase 4.

Kyle remained at this position for over three years, and although the duties were enjoyable and he had many friends, he was not happy. So when Captain Kirk, again in command of the *Enterprise*, beamed down to ask Kyle to sign on as security chief, Kyle readily accepted.

Kyle served on the *Enterprise* until Kirk, again accepting desk duty, asked him to accompany Chekov to his new position as second officer on the *Reliant*, and serve as security chief. Kirk knew that Chekov liked and respected the stoic Britisher, and that his advice and experience would be invaluable to Chekov and Captain Terrell.

So Kyle was again on a new ship. It had been many years since the loss of T'Lina's love and Kelso's friendship. He had learned to live wtih loss. He was older and more experienced; and, on the smaller *Reliant*, he was needed more than ever. His love of adventure had not diminished, and, for Lieutenant Commander Winston Matthew Kyle, a whole new adventure was just beginning.

# STAR TREK III: THE SEARCH FOR SPOCK—REVIEW AND COMMENTARY

## by Walter Irwin and G.B. Love

*It's a pretty well-known fact that G.B. doesn't often turn his hand to writing. Usually we're lucky if we can get him to contribute one short article every other issue or so. So you can imagine Walter's surprise when G.B. insisted upon sharing the duty of reviewing* Star Trek III: The Search for Spock. *It seems G.B. so enjoyed the movie he couldn't stand not having a hand in* The Best of Trek's *"official" review of the film. Walter, of course, equally enjoyed the movie, and was not at all averse to having some help with the review. As always when two strong-minded (some, uncharitably, might say "stubborn") writers work together, you may see a little of their disparate opinions slip into the review itself.*

Spock is alive. Were any of us really surprised to find out that the search would not be in vain? Did anyone out there *really* think there was a chance that Spock would not return to us at least by the end of this film? We doubt it. If it is true, however, that virtually no one was surprised by the ending of this film, then why is it so successful? Why does it work so well?

*Star Trek III: The Search for Spock* works very well indeed. It is definitely a Star Trek story in the finest tradition, working on several levels at once, filled with excitement and suspense, leavened with humor and pathos, showcasing the

47

series regulars (if only for a brief moment each) and celebrating human emotion and will.

It works, mostly, because first-time director Leonard Nimoy had the courage and the insight not to shy away from the Star Trek legend. Instead of (as in Robert Wise's *Star Trek: The Motion Picture*) attempting to replace one mythic structure with a similar, but nonetheless different, one, Nimoy— somewhat daringly for an untested film director—decided to take the plunge and go all the way in the opposite direction. He immersed the film in Star Trek lore, and it works beautifully.

More than this, Nimoy went beyond the inclusion of simple trivia and made sure that the classic Star Trek story elements were not ignored or discarded. This movie, unlike *Star Trek II: The Wrath of Khan*, has a definite commitment to the original series' Theme of "friendship above all." To those of us who fondly remember Kirk ignoring orders to take an ailing Spock back to Vulcan or Spock keeping the ship too close to a dangerous interphase zone to rescue Kirk, *The Search for Spock* is like greeting an old friend.

The plotline of the film is almost classic Star Trek: Kirk discovers that Spock's "soul" is residing in McCoy's mind, and both McCoy's body and Spock's essence are in danger of being destroyed unless he can get to Genesis, pick up Spock's body, and take it and McCoy to Vulcan for an ancient "burial" ritual. In the name of friendship, Kirk disobeys Starfleet orders and steals the *Enterprise*. Meanwhile, Saavik and David Marcus have discovered a regenerated Spock on Genesis. Complicating everything is the arrival of a Klingon battlecruiser intent on learning the secrets of Genesis.

What more could anyone ask? Friendship. Sacrifice. Drama. Humor. Evil villains. Tribbles. . . .

*The Search for Spock* is a film which was obviously carefully crafted to embody all of the best features of a typical Star Trek episode in the form of big-screen movie entertainment. This was no attempt by filmmakers to bring something new or different to the Star Trek universe; instead it was almost a complete return to the style and content of the series. In a number of scenes which pay homage to various episodes, Leonard Nimoy lets us know that his love for and appreciation of Star Trek is no less than ours, and that he is just as happy as we are that there is yet another movie, a new Star Trek story to be told.

As a whole, the film works very well indeed. The story is an involving, well-crafted use of the characters and situations left over at the end of the previous film, *Star Trek II: The Wrath of Khan*. *The Search for Spock* is a direct sequel to *Wrath of Khan*—usually a situation which leads to a film remarkably like the predecessor and therefore remarkably dull—but instead of rehashing a proven successful formula, Nimoy and Bennett decided to do something more difficult and give us a continuation of the Khan story, but with a completely different style and feel. *The Search for Spock* is really nothing like *Wrath of Khan* in tone or substance, yet the two films could be watched back to back without any discomfiture or confusion.

It is therefore no surprise that many, many fans have expressed the opinion that *The Search for Spock* is a better Star Trek movie—and a better Star Trek episode—than *Wrath of Khan*. We feel that since the movies are so different, it's kind of a senseless thing to argue about. Like comparing apples and oranges, it's a waste of time to debate the merits of one kind of filmmaking over another. Of course, we agree that the story in *The Search for Spock* is a richer, more involved one, but it would be difficult to say that *Wrath of Khan* made any less use of the characters and the Star Trek milieu. Again, there's no sense comparing. . . . We, like most of you, will simply be grateful that we've been given two superior Star Trek films in a row.

Many fans (more than would be expected, surprisingly) feel disappointed by *The Search for Spock*. Many reasons are cited, the one most often mentioned being a lack of action and direction of the film. A lesser number feel that a glaring number of mistakes were made in the story proper; the killing of David, the destruction of the *Enterprise*, etc. Still fewer feel that it was a mistake to have brought Spock back at all, and the movie fails simply because it accomplished that feat.

However, the vast majority of fans, like us reviewers, found the movie enthralling. (This is also true of the average moviegoer, but as "civilians," they don't count, except to

make the movies financially successful so we can have more
of 'em.) As mentioned above, Leonard Nimoy and writer/
producer Harve Bennett went even further in the direction
they began in *Wrath of Khan* and have almost completely
returned to the spirit and style of the original series.

The story proper is a rather simple one. Kirk must get
Spock's body from the Genesis World and return it to Vulcan
so that Spock's *katra*, his essence, can be removed from
McCoy (whom it is driving slowly insane) and laid to final
rest. That is it, friends. Kirk doesn't go flying off to Genesis
expecting to find Spock hale and hearty; his is a mission of
mercy. He must save Spock's immortal soul, and he must
save McCoy from a living death. Which of these is more
important to him, which is the driving force behind his
actions, is moot. The point is that he acts out of friendship—in
one case friendship to a dead man—and friendship alone.

This is why *The Search for Spock* is so reminiscent of
many series episodes. Everything that Kirk does stems from
his passionate desire to be steadfast to his friends. Unlike the
series, however, the film is not constrained to weekly
continuity, and change is possible, almost inevitable. Thus,
Kirk must suffer the consequences of his actions (or inaction),
as well as gain the rewards. Rushing off in search for Spock
is all well and good, but in doing so, Kirk (directly or
indirectly) disobeyed orders from a superior officer, freed a
prisoner from jail, assaulted Starfleet personnel, gained access to a restricted area by unauthorized transporter use, stole a
starship, sabotaged another, entered a restricted area of space,
and, finally, destroyed a ship which, technically, was not
under his command. In addition to the fact that Kirk committed all these crimes, his son died as a direct cause of Kirk's
failure to finish off the Klingon ship when he had the chance
to. All of this because of friendship. Was it worth it?

Let's go back to something stated earlier. Even on repeated
viewings of *The Search for Spock*, many fans take it for
granted that Kirk, having once learned of the survival of
Spock's "spirit" within McCoy, made a mental jump and
decided that the *katra* could be reunited with Spock's body.
In effect, Spock could live again. This would nicely explain
why Kirk went slightly berserk.

However, Kirk had not the slightest suspicion that they would find anything more than Spock's body upon Genesis. His first concern was to take that body and McCoy to Vulcan, where Spock's *katra* could be removed, allowing the Vulcan eternal rest and easing McCoy's pain. The film does not make clear how or when Kirk learns of Saavik's discovery of Spock's tube on the surface of Genesis. Had he not known of it, wouldn't he have told Sarek the body was cremated by entry into the atmosphere? Then he and Sarek would have taken McCoy to Vulcan for the ritual transfer. This is a minor complaint, although it's one of those niggling little things which should have been taken care of. In any case, it is Spock's body Kirk is after, in order to save Spock's, McCoy's, and, undoubtedly, his own soul.

William Shatner, once again called upon to serve as the focal point of the film, turns in yet another excellent performance. It is especially fine when one considers that it would have been ridiculously easy for him to have fallen into the trap of simply playing Kirk as a "man obsessed"—much as he played Kirk in *Star Trek: The Motion Picture*. Such a Kirk is unpleasant for us to watch, and although such obsessive single-mindedness would be more acceptable and understandable when it concerns Spock, a harsh, demanding, unyielding Kirk is not the one we know, love, and want to see.

Wisely, Shatner (under Nimoy's direction) decided to deliver a somewhat low-key performance—so low-key, in fact, that a number of fans have complained about Kirk's seeming "disinterest." But it was the correct decision, for Kirk's undeniably reckless decision to steal the *Enterprise* and storm away to Genesis would be totally disturbing if it were not for the cool and controlled manner he displays throughout the operation. And it is not an emotionless Kirk; oh, no, it is an almost rueful, reflective Kirk who does these things. His are the emotions of a man doing the only thing that his conscience will allow him to do.

And we know Kirk does not like it. One of the major failings of the film is the lack of a scene wherein Kirk must fight an inner battle between his loyalty to Starfleet and his loyalty to his friends. For surely such a battle must have taken place. . . . We have seen the depth of Kirk's loyalty to Starfleet and his sense of duty too many times for us to believe that he could so lightly make a decision to betray that loyalty, for whatever reasons. Very few fans felt that Starfleet would have won out over Spock (although a few wish that it would have); your reviewers would have preferred that the script find some way to get Kirk, crew, and ship back to Genesis without such a betrayal.

Bennett and Nimoy, however, obviously felt that the most effective way to display Kirk's debt to Spock and McCoy was by having him serve that debt above all else. It does make for effective moviemaking—the theme of a man giving up all that he has, all that he is, for those he loves is classic in fiction.

What must be considered in this equation, however, is the eventual response of Spock. We may be sure that he will eventually regain all of his faculties (now that the processes of memory have begun again), and will be, in attitude and intellect, the Spock we all know and love. If so, then, logically, he should condemn Kirk's actions in *The Search for Spock*. Why? Well, it has been stated over and over again that Vulcans, having once declared their loyalty, would rather die than betray their oath. To do anything else would be illogical. Spock, although he has learned not to expect logical behavior from humans, and certainly would not presume to judge them by Vulcan moral standards, would probably expect better from James. T. Kirk. At the very least, he would be bitterly disappointed. It's doubtful that it would cause any permanent rift in their friendship—Spock knows that once the decision is made and the deed is done, the result is no longer important to Kirk—but what if similar circumstances should arise when Spock is at Kirk's side to advise him? We might then see the first serious disagreement and perhaps split between the friends.

Alongside Shatner are the same faces—not same old faces, because they are eternally fresh and new to us: DeForest Kelley, James Doohan, George Takei, Nichelle Nichols, and Walter Koenig. As always, they are all excellent. Nichelle Nichols and George Takei have perhaps the most memorable turns, but it is the spirit of camaraderie and unspoken, understated *friendship* which truly marks their performances. We have no trouble believing that these people actually do like to work, talk, play, and break people out of jail with each other.

Because of the circumstances which force Kirk to gather together his crew and steal the ship, the supporting actors are more important to the story this time around. In past films, just about any bunch of competent officers could have sat around and set courses and fired phasers and opened hailing frequencies, but it was and could only be the faithful bridge crew of the *Enterprise* who would follow Admiral Kirk upon what, if anyone else had attempted it, would be a fool's mission.

Even though Chekov and Sulu have moved on to other positions (we don't know the exact status of Uhura and McCoy; we must, without contrary evidence, assume they were part of the *Enterprise* training crew under Captain Spock), it is clear that all of these people still consider themselves members of the "*Enterprise* crew." "The finest crew in Starfleet," Kirk called them once, and it was true. We know that they were handpicked by him, nurtured by him, driven and pummeled and urged on by him until they became the very best that they could be, which was the very best that Starfleet had to offer. It was a time and an experience which they can never forget. In a way, it spoiled them. It is not impossible for us to imagine that they will never be truly happy anywhere else or doing anything else during their entire careers.

We get the distinct impression that the crew goes along with Kirk in this thing not for the sake of Spock, not for the sake of McCoy, but for the sake of their captain, Kirk. It is he they are loyal to, it is he they will follow unhesitatingly, unblinkingly into whatever danger or unknown. It is clear that they do not really understand what is happening to McCoy— they appreciate the fact that he is ill, of course, and know that it has something to do with Spock—but they cannot comprehend the inner torment which is driving Kirk. They can only trust, and follow.

This is not to say they are not sympathetic. It's even money that any one of them would give his life to bring Spock back, perhaps even to cure McCoy. But it is Kirk they really care about. It is his pain, his obligation with which they can more easily empathize and therefore they can more readily see how failure to resolve the dilemma will destroy him. Consciously or unconsciously, each of them realizes that it is Kirk who makes it all work. Without Kirk, there can be no "*Enterprise* crew"; without his leadership and his inspiration they would become no more than ordinary Starfleet grunts, faces in the crowd with unrealized potentials and unrealized dreams. Kirk is, and always will be, their captain.

We couldn't really bring ourselves to number Saavik among the regular crew members. And, apparently, neither could Nimoy or Bennett, for Saavik, while important to the plot and definitely not neglected when it comes to the amount of time onscreen, was not included in the "family" scenes and adventures of the series regulars.

This seemingly intentional failure to have Saavik fully integrated into the circle of Star Trek characters is one of the strangest things about *Star Trek III: The Search for Spock*. The character of Saavik was one of the most intriguing things about *Wrath of Khan*, and we were absolutely sure that she would become the first new regular cast member to be introduced since the second year of the series. It was taken as a matter of fact that she was intended to be, and would be, at least on this one mission, Spock's replacement. Now we cannot be so sure.

Why Saavik should be shunted aside in this fashion is a mystery. The character proved immediately and immensely popular with fans, and objections to the possibility that she would stick around even after Spock returned were virtually nonexistent. In fact, most fans looked forward to Saavik being the very first of the "new crew" which would eventually supplant the series regulars. But to have Saavik remain an effective and viable character, she has to be, literally "one of the gang." Astoundingly, this was not done in *The Search for Spock* until the last part of the picture.

To be sure, plenty of screen time was devoted to the adventures of Saavik and David and the ever-growing Spock, but they were adventures away from and—except for circumstances—remote from the *Enterprise* and her crew. For all we know, Saavik's assignment to the *Grissom* could have been permanent, and only circumstance aligned her with Kirk and his people once again. It would have been simple enough to design the plot so that Saavik would have at least have been established as being assigned to the *Enterprise* before going to the Genesis Planet, if for no other reason than to let us know that Kirk still considered her a friend and a member of his crew.

Not only was Saavik removed from the company of the regular crew throughout much of the film, her actions throughout much of the film were also not very consistent. Part of the blame for this can be assigned to Robin Curtis, for her interpretation of the role was obviously different from Kirstie Alley's, but much of the blame can also be assigned to the script and/or Leonard Nimoy's direction.

For example, Saavik seems to consider David's presence more of an annoyance than a pleasure, or even a help in her work. She continually snaps at him, looks at him askance, and, when he finally confesses his error of using protomatter to "cheat" in the development of the Genesis Device, she is decidedly unsympathetic. (The tone of this scene is, for some inexplicable reason, seemingly designed to lay all of the blame for the events of *Wrath of Khan* at David's feet; actually, even if Genesis had worked perfectly and his actions had been pristine pure, it wouldn't have affected what Khan, Kirk, or anyone else did one little bit.) Most importantly, when Saavik discovers Spock's empty torpedo tube, her reaction is almost nonexistent. This isn't Vulcan stoicism, it's decided noninterest. Even the fabulously cool Mr. Spock would have raised an eyebrow at such a startling sight.

Even more astounding is her reaction to finding the Vulcan child. It is obvious that this is Spock, yet Saavik displays no emotion at all—no surprise, no pleasure, no fear, nothing. Throughout the subsequent events, Saavik's absence of emotional reaction is maddening to the audience. She watches David die and her voice barely trembles. She initiates the adolescent Spock into *pon farr* and the look on her face is one of clinical detachment. She comes face to face with a restored Spock on Vulcan and she lowers her eyes—the only thing in the movie from Saavik we can call an honest emotional reaction, and it is good old Vulcan embarrassment. Haven't come very far in twenty years, have we?

The issue of Spock passing through *pon farr* (and the whole idea of having him be literally reborn) will be assuredly discussed at great length in other articles and letters. We'll say only this, then go on: We felt that it was a mistake to have Spock reborn as a child, and a compounding of that mistake to have him somehow mystically "tied" to the "aging" of the Genesis Planet. It would have been much more effective to have simply kept Spock offscreen until the climatic moments, the sight of him alive and well, but essentially mindless, perhaps providing Kirk with the final incentive he needed to defeat the Klingons. As we said, this view and those opposing it will no doubt be covered in depth elsewhere; but it is appropriate here to say a few words about Saavik's role in things.

Saavik, as portrayed in *Wrath of Khan*, was definitely a Romulan/Vulcan halfbreed. She displayed all of the best traits of each, and because she obviously desired to have Vulcan training and control while still keeping her Romulan capacity for emotion, she was potentially a more interesting and well-rounded character than Mr. Spock. In *The Search for Spock*, however, we see nothing of the Romulan influence. All of it is gone—the fire, the emotion, even the rounded eyebrows, which marked Saavik as a true genetic sport (and perhaps bespoke a long-ago human influence)—all gone in favor of a Junior League Vulcan.

Because Saavik is now a more or less official Vulcan, her cool and logical decision to engage in sexual congress with Spock becomes totally uninteresting. Saavik, while still following the dictates of logic, should have shown some sign that the situation was, at the very least, uncomfortable for her. Spock was not only her teacher and her friend, he was the closest thing to a father she had ever known, and that fact alone should have caused her to hesitate for a bit. (We must presuppose that incest, if not outlawed on Vulcan, is at least considered illogical.) Too, she was expecting David to return at any time, and although he wasn't the sharpest fellow that ever lived, he'd probably have figured out something was going on sooner or later, so Saavik should at least have been slightly embarrassed by his presence . . . not to mention the presence of the Klingons! If, as she so calmly stated, Spock would go through *pon farr* every time the equivalent of seven years of growth occurred, Saavik would have had to have joined with him again at least twice or three times while the Klingons were present. This surely would have caused her emotional pain, and we should have seen the results of that pain.

We saw nothing of the kind, however. The act took place tastefully offscreen, but for all the drama and (to the audience) emotional interest of it, it might as well have been shown up there in 70mm with Dolby sound. The whole affair smacked too much of script manipulation, of titillation, of a desire to make us care something about a character whom the entire rest of the script forced us to care nothing about. Most fans greeted this event with a resounding "So what?"—and that is exactly what it deserved from the treatment given it in the film.

Miss Robin Curtis may be a fine actress, but she failed to bring anything new or interesting to the character of Saavik in *The Search for Spock*. And although Curtis is undoubtedly a lovely woman (a TV commercial starring her appearing at the time of this writing confirms this), she makes a strangely unattractive and decidedly unappealing Saavik. Why Leonard Nimoy and Harve Bennett ever decided to fill the vacant Saavik role with Miss Curtis is a mystery. Obviously, they must have seen something in her which, somehow, totally failed to come across in the finished production.

As mentioned above, the Saavik character is now slanted more toward being Vulcan, and the makeup given Robin Curtis unfortunately reflects this. She's given very thin slanted eyebrows, a pair of overly pointed ears, and a too-thick application of yellowish facial tone. Then, inexplicably, she's allowed to keep her own hairstyle, which is just about as Southern California 1980s modish as it's possible to get. (One local female fan said, "God, poor woman! She must have cried when she saw herself onscreen!") The final result is a Saavik who almost perfectly matches David's preppish good looks, and together, they look like students on their way to a pep rally.

Poor David. It's strange (and must have seemed even stranger to Paramount executives, not to mention exasperating), but fans never really warmed up to him. Shortly after the release of *Wrath of Khan*, one fan commented, "Nobody's fallen in love with him yet," and that comment was even more true by the time 1984 rolled around. So, while many fans were surprised by his death in *The Search for Spock*, it's safe to say that very few of them were upset by it.

From the very beginning, David seemed to be one of those characters whose job was to hang around and bitch and screw up and generally make the leads look good. Instead of presenting us with a son for Jim Kirk that we could immediately like and admire, the producers gave us a snotty, whining snob with a superiority complex and an almost pathological fear and hatred of authority in general and Starfleet in particular. David was indeed his mother's son, for there was little or nothing of Jim Kirk in him.

Kirk, however, must have thought otherwise. Or maybe it was just the sheer shock of losing the son and heir he had never been allowed to know or even acknowledge. In either case, we're not allowed to know, for David's death had no bearing on the outcome of the film. Unlike Spock's sacrifice, which resulted in the escape of the *Enterprise* and the saving of many lives, David's death was an act of malicious violence, seemingly designed primarily to show us how rotten and evil the Klingons were and to give William Shatner a big grief scene.

The only reason this happened is that David became an expendable character. As a person, as a foil for stories, even as Kirk's son, David was a bland and rather unlikable dead end whose place could more than adequately be filled by any of the regular cast, or Saavik in a pinch. The fault of this does not lie with Merritt Butrick. He is a competent, if unexciting, actor, and whatever appeal the character had was thanks to him. Even the best of actors cannot work with a bad part, however, and Butrick simply couldn't overcome the failings of the character as written.

In *The Search for Spock*, David reveals to Saavik that he "overcame certain problems with Genesis" by using "protomatter" in the matrix of the Genesis Planet. Saavik replies that protomatter is disdained by all "ethical" scientists (without telling us why), then goes on to accuse David of following in his father's footsteps—changing the conditions of the test. This is, obviously, supposed to make us more sympathetic to David, while at the same time giving us a fond chuckle at the similarity between father and son.

However, it has no such effect. If we do not immediately condemn David in our minds as a hypocrite, we do entertain serious doubts about his common sense. Utilizing an outlawed substance in an experiment which *every* scientist in the galaxy will eventually examine with a fine-tooth comb is the height of academic insanity. More important, what if the planned experiment had taken place, and had not gone wrong until thousands of colonists had landed?

It would have been simpler (and better for David's reputation) if the script had simply stated that the Genesis Device had been designed to reform an existing planet, not create a new one, and that's why it was unstable. We then wouldn't have David's big confession, but we wouldn't have him looking like a fool, either.

It was nice to see the Klingons back in a Star Trek movie in full force. They are among the greatest villains ever created—ruthless, cold, violent, yet also charming, intelligent, and somehow likeable—and Star Trek never really made full use of them. (Yes, we too still yearn for the never-realized fourth-season plans to have William Campbell's Captain Koloth appear as a regular adversary for Kirk.) In *Star Trek III: The Search for Spock*, the Klingons are presented as well as they have ever been; the only thing lacking was the roguish charm which has always made Klingons so much fun to watch. Christopher Lloyd's Kruge showed flashes of it from time to time, but we yearned for one of the silkily smooth exchanges between him and Kirk that let us know they respected as well as feared and hated each other.

All in all, Lloyd's Kruge was quite effective, although there were several scenes in which he either overacted or was seemingly given things to do for no other reason than to show how mean and rotten he was. We would have preferred that a less well-known actor be given the part, as Lloyd, like most television actors, brings too much familiarity with his primary character to any subsequent part. If Nimoy was going to wax nostalgic, why didn't he cast John Colicos as Kor to head up the Klingons? Kor was evil and rotten enough to do the job, and we certainly wouldn't have minded seeing him die. Not only would it have been ironic for Kirk to encounter *two* old villains in the course of these two adventures, but it would have been somewhat of a surprise to us as well. No one, but no one would have expected to see Commander Kor in that Klingon ship.

However, perhaps the producers thought that the inclusion of Mark Lenard's Sarek was enough. It was nice to see that Lenard still has the same dignity and grace which so impressed us almost twenty years ago. Mark Lenard has always been one of our favorite actors, and his contribution to Star Trek, and *The Search for Spock*, can never be overestimated.

It is only fitting that it is Sarek who forces Kirk to recall the events of Spock's death, for this entire movie is about the need to accept feelings and realities, not to deny them. Lenard manages to convey a sense of sadness and tragic loss which would seem almost impossible, given the fact that his character is essentially emotionless and does not, ever, in this film lose his alienness.

Others of the supporting cast were up to the usual Star Trek excellence, but we feel that it was unfortunate that Nimoy instructed many of them to perform in a broad, sometimes almost farcical manner. Comedy relief is just that—a short burst of humor or incongruity in the middle of tension, suspense, or action which allows us to catch our breath and relax strained muscles for a moment. It is a classic movie form and movie tradition. And in *The Search for Spock* it worked as such, especially during the escape sequences. However, we feel that too much humor—too much downright *cuteness*, if you will—somehow worked its way into the film.

This tendency toward cuteness, even silliness, is becoming a raging epidemic among recent films, and has literally ruined quite a few for many viewers. One can only presume that it is "this year's fad," the old-fashioned Hollywood trick of following the leader, and thus it is all the more depressing to see such a trend surface in a Star Trek movie. Star Trek does not need to pander to current fashion or audience whim, and doing so, even in a small way, was Leonard Nimoy's biggest mistake.

All in all, however, *Star Trek III: The Search for Spock* is a splendid example of a Star Trek episode. We get to see a healthy dose of each of the major characters (though, as always, never as much as we'd like), we get some rousing and tragic-ending action, we get to know more about the characters and their world, and, most important, we get to see the total importance of the theme of friendship to the characters and to Star Trek itself. Not since the days of Gene Roddenberry's earliest shows has this theme been so eloquently stated and reaffirmed. It was, as one fan said when leaving the theater, "just like 1967 again!"

Well, maybe not exactly, but it was doggone close. . . .

The thanks and good wishes of all of us go out to Harve Bennett, Leonard Nimoy, Gene Roddenberry, and the entire cast and crew of *Star Trek III: The Search for Spock*. Once again, we have Star Trek continuity and consistency returned to us. We fervently hope that it will continue into *Star Trek IV* and into many, many Star Trek films to come.

# KIRK AND DUTY

### by William Trigg and
### Dawson "Hank" Hawes

*G.B. Love's article "Captain Kirk's Duties" (Best of Trek #2) gave us a fine overview of what the day-to-day duties and responsibilities of a starship captain are. Mr. Love's article was admittedly written in a rush to meet a deadline, and he is the first to admit that it is not nearly as comprehensive as it should be. With his permission, this article will expand upon his final original (in some instances using his phrasings), as well as update it to contain information in the Star Trek films. Moreover, we will attempt to show the ways in which duty and the necessity for obeying orders has affected Kirk personally and professionally—how a lifetime of adherence to duty, honor and the rules, regulations and traditions of Starfleet and the Federation have molded Jim Kirk into what he is today.*

James T. Kirk is undoubtedly one of the finest and continuingly successful officers ever produced by Starfleet. Surely, if nothing else is considered, he is one of the most experienced in terms of dealing with the unknown and unexpected, and probably the only starship commander to have returned from promotion and a ground assignment to retake command of the same ship from which he "retired" . . . and Kirk performed this small miracle not once, but *twice*. There is little doubt that Starfleet Command considered Kirk to be their number one line officer, for he is allowed to get away with things for which other captains would be court-martialed on the spot.

We know that much of Kirk's success comes from his willingness—indeed, even his need—to take chances, to bend the rules, to do it his way and no other. We also know that even with the edge offered by his innate skills and the famous "Kirk luck," he many times would have suffered defeat or disgrace without the help and support of his friends and subordinates, especially Spock, McCoy, and Scotty.

Throughout much of his career, however, Kirk was pretty much on his own, both personally and professionally. He was not a loner in the ordinary sense, for he had many friends and quite a few affairs, and we can assume that he was fairly popular in a quiet, respectable way. He also would have to have gotten along well with his co-workers and superiors, for no military man, no matter how gifted, can expect command to come his way if he is not able to work with people and both obey and command them. But from the time he made up his mind to attend Starfleet Academy to the present, James Kirk was and is his own man.

A person as independent and diligent as Kirk instinctually understands the necessity of duty. He feels dutiful not only to his country and his service, but to himself as well. Kirk knows that only by doing the very best that he can, only by doing a job as well as it can be done, can one feel satisfied and self-assured.

Although we know little about Kirk's early years, we do know that he is essentially a self-made man. This inner need to pull himself up by his bootstraps, if you will, and the greater, more pressing need to get into space, caused him to become the grimly determined, often unsmiling underclassman so many of his contemporaries remember. But the lack of smile would've been caused by distraction and determination, not through any grudge against those classmates who did not share his overriding desire to command. Kirk simply would not have had time for them; if they didn't want to get on with their careers, it wasn't his worry . . . he had too much to do.

We may assume that Kirk understood and accepted the concept and necessity of duty when he was still quite young, so the strictness of military life and the constant hazing by upperclassmen would have been much less surprising and disheartening to him than to a young man less prepared.

The unsmiling, determined young cadet was immediately targeted as a scapegoat by one Cadet Corporal Finnegan. Finnegan and his cohorts (such bullies always have sycophantic followers) made Kirk's life a living hell for the first two years at the Academy, but although he wanted nothing more than to lash out at the sneering Irishman's face, Kirk managed to hold his temper and channel his hatred and aggression into constructive areas. Thanks to Finnegan, Kirk became the most unflappable cadet at the Academy, able to think quickly and coolly under extreme stress (and occasionally under extreme pain, as well). Both of these qualities—controlling his temper and staying cool—would later help to make Kirk a successful commander, but at the time the future seemed far away. It was only strict adherence to duty which kept Kirk from retaliating overtly—for although he could have convinced himself that ignoring Finnegan was the best way to get along, just part of the process, Kirk was too stubborn to allow himself this mental "out." Finnegan was a superior officer, and even if he ordered Kirk to wallow in the mud, wallow Kirk would. For it was his duty to follow orders.

Kirk, of course, had other things to do at the Academy besides jump whenever Finnegan said "frog." He, like all cadets, was required to attend all scheduled classes and to keep over a minimum grade point average in those classes. He also had to go through rigorous physical training and a rating of his skills. Besides the curriculum, cadets were expected to stand guard duty, serve KP in the kitchens and dining halls, serve as functionaries for visiting dignitaries and civilian guests, act as aide-de-camp or secretary for instructors and officers, assist in routine maintenance and cleaning, and go through continuing and constantly varying military training and exercises ranging from the erection of a pup tent to starship maintenance.

It was a killing schedule, designed to weed out those whose strength and determination were not equal to the demands of serving as an officer in deep space. Fully half of Kirk's entering class was gone by the end of the first year, and something more than two-thirds by the end of the second year. Kirk, despite Finnegan, thrived on it, gradually loosening up as he became more self-assured. Now that Finnegan was gone and he was no longer subject to the onerous chores and humiliations of an underclassman, Kirk was able to concentrate solely on his studies and his self-improvement. As part of that self-improvement, he naturally sought out and gladly accepted a greater amount of duties. Kirk had been, from the very first, recognized by his superior officers and instructors as a cadet of promise, and now their hopes were fulfilled. Kirk was taking on unassigned duties and responsibilities—the mark of a dedicated and ambitious officer. Kirk was too sharp not to have very soon realized how this pleased his superiors, and although he was pleased at their approval, such favor really did not matter to him. He was only doing what he thought was right and proper, and although he was vain enough to enjoy the attention and perks which eventually came his way because of his hard work, he did not attempt to use his superiors' liking for him to curry easy assignments or promotion. If he deserved it and did his duty, promotion and credit would come his way.

As an upperclassman, Kirk found himself even busier than before. While his new duties were more pleasant than washing garbage cans or digging trenches, they were no less difficult or time-consuming. And they were considerably more important.

Kirk was now acting as an instructor in military history and basic tactics, the two classes in which he had obtained the highest marks in Academy history. He was also in charge of a crack phaser company, acting as both instructor and drill master. While completely uninterested in sports, Kirk found time to join teams which he thought would serve as invaluable experience. He belonged to the unarmed combat team, and although he placed in several tournaments in his weight division, he was never of championship caliber. He could never quite believe that skill alone could best a larger, tougher opponent and so tended more toward an eclectic roughhouse style which was not popular with judges . . . or with battered opponents. Kirk also joined the shooting team and the fencing squad. Through constant practice, he eventually obtained an expert rating on the range, and although he was not naturally proficient with the phaser, he did develop an unbelievably quick concealed-weapon fast draw. He was never more than a fair fencer; he simply could not relate to the mystique of edged weapons.

All of these duties and extracurricular activities Kirk performed with his usual skill and determination. This was in addition to his normal schedule of Academy duties which included, still, classes, drill, and physical training, plus running a squad of underclassmen (and necessarily hazing them, although Finnegan had planted a distaste for the practice within his mind), serving as officer of the guard, day officer, etc., and overseeing groups of cadets at work and study. By now, however, Kirk and his fellow classmates were more than used to the punishing schedule; indeed, they thrived on it, Kirk more so than most. Now he became almost the exact opposite of the solemn-faced, obsessively dutiful cadet he had been for the last two years. He easily commanded his cadet charges, winning their respect by his firmness and fairness; he made friends among classmates who until now had only been acquaintances. Again, however, Kirk was not trying to win any popularity contests. It was simply that he now felt that he was going to make it, and he could relax a little bit, enjoy life a little more. The thing which had concerned him the most, that he would not be able to rein in his independence and stubbornness and fit himself into the tight strictures of military life, was no longer a worry. He was not only surviving the Academy, he was conquering it.

Kirk's duty load increased dramatically during his senior year, but he took it in stride. Now added to his burden was yet another teaching assignment, plus the extra classes needed to qualify for Command School. Kirk had decided that he did indeed have "the right stuff" (as it had been called for uncounted years) and felt he could be one of those very few who were allowed to command starships. Most cadets by now realized either that they did not have within themselves the necessary tools to make it as a starship commander or that the responsibility of starship command was more than they were willing to accept. Even so, a larger number of cadets announced (as they were required to do) their intention to try for acceptance to Command School.

Kirk did not graduate from the Academy with highest honors, but he was in the upper 10 percent of his class and, more important to him, was accepted for Command. The only disheartening thing about the honor was that he would be required to spend two more years at the Academy while his former classmates would be out in space. Those accepted for Command, would, however, get "out there" first though they wouldn't stay long, for in lieu of a summer vacation they would take their first training cruise into deep space.

It was on this cruise that the first weeding-out process was begun. Cadets were required to serve duty watches for sixteen to twenty hours straight, then to rise and attend classes after only a few hours' sleep. They had to swab the decks, anti-frictionize the engines, cook the captain's dinner. Although full-fledged Academy graduates technically holding the rank of ensign, they were for all intents and purposes the lowest of the low on this cruise, subject to the same living and working conditions as the average crewmember—ordered around by every noncom, treated as deadheads and dunces by the regular crew.

The annual Command training cruise was known among Starfleet veterans as the "baby run," and it was considered privileged and very cushy duty. For when and where else could an able shipman give a good ranking-out to a fresh-faced ensign? Starfleet did not have the Command cadets treated this way just for the enjoyment of the crewmembers (although the practice was common knowledge throughout Starfleet and helped to boost overall morale), but rather to give them some practical experience in what it feels like to be a common crewmember in the service. The theory was (and Kirk agreed with it) that a man could not lead those whom he did not understand, nor order work done which he had not himself experienced.

Kirk saw the value of this and so uncomplainingly performed the onerous chores and good-naturedly endured the sometimes less than good-natured razzing from the enlisted crewmembers. He immediately saw the value of the plan, however, for the varied "scut" duties took the Command cadets to every part of the giant starship, and working with the crewmen, he learned things which he would not have learned in years of classroom simulation. Mostly, however, the cadets learned about themselves. Some who had breezed through the worst hazings and tensions which the Academy could offer them found themselves lacking the same poise or patience in real-life day-to-day contact with working crewmen. Others realized that there was just too much to learn, too much to be responsible for, when commanding a ship, and they too fell by the wayside. Although the attrition rate was not as dramatic as that of Kirk's first year at the Academy, a fairly large percentage of his classmates decided that Command School was not for them after all.

When the three-month cruise finally came to an end, Kirk and his mates immediately disembarked to a schedule of classes and training which tested them, mentally and physically, as they had never been tested before. Menial work and harassment were now forgotten; they had proved themselves as officers and gentlemen on the cruise . . . now it was time to begin molding them into commanders, and as such they were treated with the utmost respect and expected to comport themselves accordingly.

Each person was now on his own more than ever. Command cadets were expected to keep to a rigid schedule of classes and duty watches, just as they would aboard ship, but no one stood over their shoulders to see that their assigned work was performed properly—indeed, if it was performed at all. Cadets now stood watches in command of groups of enlisted personnel and civilian workers, and they were responsible for the results attained by their groups.

Such an environment was, of course, exhilarating to Kirk. Duty was now not a question only of obeying orders, but of taking charge of himself and his men to get a job done well. Kirk realized that if he could not command himself under such conditions, he could never hope to command others. So it was himself that he gave the roughest discipline, assigned the hardest, dirtiest chores, gave the most critical evaluations. It was not, to Kirk, a question of whether or not he would make it—he knew he would—it was a question of whether he would make it according to his own harsh inner guidelines.

As the months passed, the cadets' schedules became somewhat less hectic, but they were assigned accordingly more important duties. Many of these duties, somewhat surprisingly to Kirk, were at various locations on and around Earth. Thanks to the transporter and other high-speed people movers, Command cadets could report for duty to any Starfleet Earth station, any space-docked ship, any moon base, and so on. This not only gave them experience in an amazingly varied number of duties, it removed them from the somewhat cloistered confines of the Academy. With all of this experience, it seemed almost an anticlimax to make a second deep space cruise at the end of the first year.

This cruise, however, was quite different from the first. This time the class was not dumped aboard one ship, but broken into smaller groups and sent to a number of different ships going to different areas. Too, the cadets were now treated as officers, with the respect due their rank of ensign. Ensigns didn't rate all that much respect, Kirk soon found, but when serving midnight watches on the bridge, he consoled himself with the thought that at least he wasn't swabbing the poop deck.

As he did on Earth, Kirk thrived on this duty. Moreover, now that he occasionally had a little time of his own, he discovered that he was developing quite an affection for space and space travel. He knew that in time he would come to love space, and eventually, when given command of just the right ship, he would come to love it as well. More important, he also discovered that he loved command. Looking into himself as objectively as he could, Kirk decided that it was not the simple power to order men and machinery about that attracted him, but rather the continuing process of self-testing and self-assurance, the thrill of making a decision quickly and coolly, the satisfaction of having the respect of subordinates and a job well done.

To Kirk, duty was becoming life itself. Although he had to admit to himself, somewhat ruefully, that his ego was often larger than necessary, he was seized by a growing conviction that he could do just about any job, command any ship, better than anyone else. This conceit did not go unnoticed by his fellow cadets and superiors, but it was not only understood, it was expected. Each of them felt a similar conceit to one degree or another; how could a person in good conscience command a starship when he felt that someone else could do a better job? What it was necessary to instill in the cadets was acceptance of the knowledge that although perhaps no one could do the job better, there were many others who could do it just as well.

During the second year of Command School, Kirk and his mates were given more of the same duties as in the first year, the only difference being that they spent more time aboard starships and their classroom time was increasingly devoted to lectures and demonstrations by captains and first officers on or recently returned from space duty. Much of the time, these men simply sat and talked with the cadets, answering questions and relating incidents having to do with the cadets' current studies. Kirk, as cadets were intended to do, found these sessions to be overall more informative about what made certain people good commanders than technically rewarding. Some of the speakers were defensive about their work, others offhand. But those who impressed Kirk the most were those who obviously considered it to be nothing more than their duty. These commanders invariably gave credit for successes to their crews; just as invariably they took the blame for failures upon themselves. Also in each of them was a fierce pride, a determination to succeed, which Kirk found perfectly mirrored within himself.

It was under one such captain that Kirk gratefully found himself serving when he graduated from Command School. Charles Garrovick was one of the "old line" of starship commanders, having served in the United Earth Forces which were only now slowly coming completely under Federation and Starfleet command. He was considered something of a maverick by Headquarters, and generally ignored when it came time for promotion and assignment to the newer ships, but no one could fault his ability.

In Garrovick, Kirk found a mixture of adherence to duty and dogged independence which more than matched his own. Garrovick might gripe and rail and call Starfleet Command names that made even his grizzled old engineer blush, but he never hesitated one second to follow orders and perform his duty to the best of his, and his crew's, ability. Only once did Kirk see Garrovick disobey an order: He refused to leave an area where space mines were being tested until he'd succeeded in rescuing a crewman with a malfunctioning spacesuit.

What surprised Kirk more than Garrovick's disobeying the order was the fact that his bridge crew seemed to expect him to do so—nobody but Kirk so much as raised an eyebrow when Garrovick ignored the group admiral's order to leave the area. They also, Kirk discovered in later conversations, seemed unconcerned that the reprimand that Garrovick would surely receive would also be mentioned in their own permanent records.

Kirk, of course, understood Garrovick's reluctance to abandon a crewperson—he too would do the same thing for a person under his command, a person who was his responsibility—but what he didn't understand was how Garrovick and his crew could treat the whole thing so blithely. Duty was duty and orders were orders, and to ignore them, even for sufficient reason, even though he would have unhesitatingly done so himself, was not something to be proud of, certainly nothing to treat as an everyday occurrence.

Garrovick noticed the stiffness with which Kirk faced him for several days after the affair, and rightly surmised what was going on in the ensign's head. He called Kirk in for a talk and led the young man into opening up. In response to Kirk's questions, Garrovick explained that in his opinion, a commander held as much allegiance to his men as he did to his command. Duty, therefore, became a balancing act: what was best for the service versus what was best for the members of his crew. Garrovick always liked to tip the scales to the side of his men, but this was often not possible or prudent. Kirk would have to set limits within his own mind, his own conscience, and decide when he would and would not cross those limits.

It was the first good look Kirk had gotten into the head of a starship commander. He had heard other commanders talk about the occasional need to disobey orders—some of them had paid dearly for doing so—but this was the first time that he had been able to relate to it on a personal level. He knew that he would have made the same choice as Garrovick under the circumstances, but what of other times, other circumstances? He knew that he should do as his captain suggested and define within his own mind some limits, but he also knew that to set such limits now and cement them into permanency would be ultimately self-defeating. He decided that he would, as long as possible, simply "wing it," and take each situation as it came. He trusted his ability to think fast on his feet and knew that his subconscious would now be working constantly on the problem and would suggest the proper course of action to him at the proper time.

Of course, quick decisions and making choices are two of the most—if not *the* most important—aspects of command. They often go hand in hand, and more often than any commander would like, human lives are involved. Even if a person is as self-assured as was young Ensign Kirk, one split second of indecisiveness, or one wrong choice, can lead to a lifetime of recrimination and regret.

Kirk discovered this sad fact when Captain Garrovick was killed by a mysterious, malevolent "cloud creature" because— Kirk believed—Kirk "froze" and failed to shoot his phaser quickly enough. Kirk had enough self-awareness to know that he had not failed to shoot because of cowardice, and, indeed, he was not given any sort of reprimand, official or unofficial, by Starfleet, but Kirk did blame himself for not acting quickly enough. He saw it as a failure of will, of determination. The effects were devastating enough to cause Kirk to doubt his qualification for command for some while, but the assurances of his shipmates and superior officers that he still had "the right stuff," plus his natural self-confidence and desire to command, soon brought him out of his depression.

In fact, Kirk became a better leader after the untimely death of Garrovick. He steeled himself with the determination to never again "freeze" in a crisis, but more important, he began to see the importance of careful planning ahead. Kirk reluctantly admitted to himself that if the maverick Garrovick had taken a full security team of experienced veterans down to the planet with him rather than just raw ensign Kirk, he would probably still be alive. Preparation and following the rules were two things which Kirk, enamored of his ability to think on his feet, had previously given little attention to either at the Academy or on shipboard. He now knew why rules were rules, and why it was important to follow regulations.

Duty, Kirk realized, was more than just leading men. It was leading them in the proper fashion, utilizing the accumulated knowledge and experience of an entire history of military chain of command.

This lesson didn't stick all that well. Kirk was too much of a maverick himself to keep to the ordered, regimented style of doing things, but the knowledge that these seemingly stultified, outdated, hopelessly stiff-necked rules were often *right* had been permanently branded into his subconscious. Now the military history which Kirk had always so loved to read and study meant more to him than just battle plans and adventure. He developed an understanding of the problems of discipline, of supply, of ordnance. He now had the potential to become a better officer than Garrovick had been, a more rounded, better-informed officer whose maverick streak would be tempered by an appreciation of the necessity of military hierarchy.

Kirk's next assignment was to the *Exeter*, where the newly promoted Lieutenant Kirk served as relief helmsman. On this, his first full-time duty post, Kirk had drilled into him the necessity for keeping to a minutely detailed schedule, one infinitely more complex and demanding than those he had followed as duty officer or other such "watch" posts. He also learned to train himself to instantly obey any command from his captain or first officer. Helm was one of the most sensitive and demanding positions aboard a starship, and one to which promising young officers were often assigned to test their mettle. In times of battle or emergency, a helmsmen had to instantly translate his captain's verbal orders into commands to the controls of the ship. A moment's hesitation or uncertainty could result in the destruction of the ship. Although the active Kirk found it stifling to be sitting in one place for hours at a time, he learned to love the way in which the mighty ship responded immediately and smoothly to his slightest touch on the controls. For the first time, he felt in touch with a ship, almost part of it. (It was felt in the service that no person could be fit for command without experiencing this feeling, another reason why promising young officers were assigned to helm.) A real feeling of communion grew between him and the *Exeter*, and he was reluctant to leave the helm position when his captain decided he should have some firsthand experience in dealing with diplomats, semihostile aliens, and the bureaucracy, and took Kirk along as his orderly to the Axanar Peace Mission.

Diplomacy was one of the duties of a starship captain which Kirk had not yet experienced, and, to to truthful, had little desire to experience. He knew that he was too impatient, too unforgiving of duplicity, and too straightforward in speech and action to be a good diplomatic negotiator. He quickly changed his mind, however, for the negotiations which took place on Axanar were nothing like the soft-voiced, polite ramblings he had seen on occasion in the Federation Council or the World Government on Earth. These negotiations were a series of hotly contested bargaining sessions in which several parties vied for advantage or leverage. Occasionally things got a little loud, and once or twice diplomats from the opposing sides came close to blows.

Kirk realized that here were beings fighting—with words rather than weapons, but fighting none the less—for what could eventually be the very survival of their respective cultures. It was enthralling, it was exciting, it was the education of a lifetime. Kirk's captain, Chester Pao Ng, was there to represent Starfleet, whose constant threat of intervention in the Axanar crisis had brought the opponents to the bargaining table in the first place, and when the conference quickly bogged down under the leadership of a Federation diplomat, Ng made it plain that he was not just going to sit idly by and watch the opponents wrangle and waste everybody's time while a ruinous war still went on. He quickly took over, backed up by his own forceful personality and by the unstated but ever-present knowledge that his powerful starship was parked, guns ready, just a few thousand kilometers away. He intended to run the conference in, he snapped in his incongruous British accent, "Bristol fashion." This action, at first greatly resented by the parties at hand, later admired when Ng proved himself fair and firm, made more work for Lieutenant Kirk than he expected.

In fact, the work load was almost too much for one man: Kirk not only had to keep track of the computer notes and records of what was said, proposed, rejected, etc., but he was responsible for overseeing the lodgings, feeding, etc. of the diplomats and their large and often unpleasant staffs. Kirk also was in charge of security, a constant headache, for there was not yet peace, and the threat of terrorist activity or even Klingon intervention was always present. In addition to all of this, Kirk was constantly at loggerheads with the staff of the official Federation Diplomatic Corps, who (rightly) resented Ng's intervention in a mission which was expected to be their show. With them, however, Kirk did not have to be polite, and he made it plain that he backed up his captain to the hilt and if the Diplomatic Corps couldn't run the show, then they should get out of the way and let someone who could do so get the job done. Kirk's bluntness made him many enemies among the younger members of the legation, who did not have the experience or aplomb, as did their elders, to overlook internecine rivalries and bickering, and with the eventual success of the mission, all of the resentment felt against Ng and Starfleet focused on Kirk. He gained a reputation of being "antidiplomat," a reputation which he did little or nothing to destroy in the ensuing years.

Starfleet, with the grudging concurrence of the Diplomatic Corps, awarded specially struck medals to Ng, Kirk, and their staff for their efforts at the Axanar Peace Mission. More valuable to Kirk were the lessons in diplomacy he had learned, and the ways in which those lessons tied into starship command.

Diplomacy, Kirk discovered, was as much a part of the duties of a starship captain as was the day-to-day running of a ship. Often during a lull in the negotiations, Ng would take the time to point out to Kirk similarities to other disputes and disagreements he had had to settle in his role as Federation representative in deep space. A starship captain, Ng explained, *is* the Federation when venturing into unknown and unexplored territory. A starship captain is automatically appointed military governor of any colonies, outposts, or expeditions in his space sector. In this capacity, he is the final arbiter of the disbursement of materials, persons, or facilities to and from these outposts, etc. He is also authorized to settle any disputes over claims or territorial rights. If he feels the need is dire enough, a captain may severely restrict the activities of these outposts, etc., or even go so far as to completely shut them down.

Kirk, of course, had learned all of this at the Academy, but it took on more meaning now that he had experienced first-hand just how difficult it could be to deal with fiercely independent beings fighting to retain their rights and property, especially since those beings often felt their fight was right and just. He also gained an appreciation of just how hard it could be to be fair to all sides involved in a dispute. The truth or the right was not always clear-cut, and Kirk realized that diplomacy, like command, was a series of tradeoffs, a balancing act between duty and immediacy.

This would be more and more of a problem in the coming years, Ng pointed out, for space travel was growing at almost a geometric rate. By the time that Kirk and others of his generation became starship commanders, there would be literally hundreds of thousands of vessels, outposts, colonies, etc. spread all over the galaxy. Space was becoming less and less the property of the military, and as a larger number of private citizens made their way into space in one way or another, a feeling of resentment and an attitude of ''So who needs you anymore?'' would inevitably rise against Starfleet.

Too, each newly discovered inhabited planet would bring problems of its own. Some would prove resolutely hostile, others unbendingly resolved to have nothing to do with outsiders. Many would fall under the protection of the Prime Directive, and as such would have to be policed against interference by Klingons, other alien races, and unscrupulous citizens. Inevitably, a starship captain would find himself in the middle of disputes, sometimes even open war, between newly discovered planets or systems, and in each of these cases, a captain was under standing orders to make his best effort to bring hostilities to an end and offer the good offices of the Federation to settle disagreements peaceably.

Each captain had to decide for himself how best to carry out such duties. Many captains went strictly ''by the book,'' but Ng had discovered that although the book was generally right in a given situation, he was rarely given that particular situation. Often a captain had to make decisions quickly, without time to give a fair hearing to all sides of the question.

This is where instinct, experience, and plain old-fashioned luck came into play. Ng had given Kirk a start on the experience, and he believed that the junior officer's instincts were good as well—but was he lucky?

Kirk felt he was; in fact, he had always counted on his luck to aid him to a certain extent throughout his career. But what Ng was telling him now was that any officer who trusts solely to luck is courting disaster—there is no substitute for intelligence and knowledge. Kirk had to remember that "chance favors the prepared," but also "fortune is always on the side of the largest battalions."

So impressed was Starfleet Command with the record Kirk had so far compiled and with the glowing recommendation Captain Ng had given him that he was jumped several grades and made first officer aboard the pocket destroyer *Chesty Puller*. Once again, Kirk was confronted with an entirely new set of duties. As first officer, he was responsible for the smooth running and maintenance of the ship; in other words, for the thousand and one details with which a captain cannot be bothered. Now more than ever, Kirk had to learn to deal with subordinates and crewmembers in shipboard routine. He quickly learned that such routine is deeply ingrained, and even ambitious, young, spanking-new first officers find such routine almost impossible to change.

Frustrated at first by his inability to implement what he saw as badly needed reforms in the operation of the ship, Kirk began to resent the people under him who, seemingly, were either too stubborn or too stupid to understand what he was trying to do. He became especially frustrated with the endless necessity of following the chain of command with every order he gave. When he wanted something as simple as a new kind of cleanser in the toilet areas, he found that just calling down and ordering the steward to change cleansers was impossible. The man could not act without approval from his chief, who could not approve the request without orders from his section head, and so on. And this, moaned Kirk, was on a relatively small destroyer. What must things be like on a starship?

More frustrating, however, were the reams and reams of paperwork which confronted Kirk as first officer. He knew that much of his duty involved relieving the captain from such mundane chores, but it seemed to him that the captain handled just as many papers as he did. (The term "paperwork," of course, does not refer to actual sheets of paper, for such had long since been replaced by computer-terminal and hand-held displays, but rather to the flood of often meaningless and endlessly repetitive *words* with which Kirk had to deal each day.)

Most irritating to Kirk were the everpresent fuel consumption reports, an archaic practice which nobody ever seemed to be able to stop. On the *Chesty Puller*, there were thirteen different computer stations which monitored fuel comsumption, and a readout of fuel used, remaining, etc. was continually available on the main screen. But still yeomen came up from belowdecks every hour on the hour with the official report, which had to be signed by the officer holding the conn. None of the other paperwork was as omnipresent or as irritating as the fuel reports, but a never-ending stream of relatively useless facts, data, and trivia crossed Kirk's desk each working day.

This, then, was the dull, repetitive side of command which Kirk had been warned about by many commanders, a surprising number of whom had been burned out not by the responsibility or pressure, but simply by the never-ending routine. Kirk, confident as ever, thought that he could change things once he was in charge—streamlining, cutting red tape, eliminating the endless rounds of duplication and rubber-stamping which needlessly complicated any order or request. Like so many others before him, he failed.

What he learned from his experience with onboard bureaucracy and paperwork was not the kind of thing of which Starfleet officially approved; Kirk decided that whenever possible, he would simply skip the inner workings and do things himself. This decision did much to negate his earlier vow to work through channels and "by the book," but it served to make him a more independent and efficient officer. Of course, by doing so he took upon himself an immeasurably greater amount of personal responsibility, but he figured that ultimate responsibility came with command anyway, so what was the difference?

This final phase in the battle of rules versus independence

which had been going on in Kirk's mind since his Academy days marked his maturation as an officer. He now spent less time worrying about whether or not he was doing the right thing and instead did what he *thought* was right. If he was wrong, he would find out soon enough; if he was right, then it was one less problem to worry about, leaving him available to go on to the next chore or problem. Kirk began in this way to see facets of command separately, and learned the necessary trick of compartmentalizing his mind and organizing problems in order of their importance and urgency.

All of this Kirk had known before, or had been lectured about it at the Academy, but now he was beginning to do it easily, instinctively. He was beginning to think like a captain, and, as a result, he began to act like one as well. A certain maturation took place in Kirk about this time: He no longer let his impatience with things beyond his control affect his work; he became less critical of others who were less gifted or less dedicated than he; he became somewhat more introspective and broadened his reading habits to include philosophers, poets, and novelists, for whom he had previously not found time. Mostly, however, he learned how to relax, rather than play hard. Without realizing it, Kirk was responding to his broadening experience which had taught him that a good commander is more than just a great tactician or crackling disciplinarian. A good commander realizes that duty flows both ways, up and down the chain of command, and a commander must be as responsible *to* his ship and crew as he is responsible for them.

Kirk got his first taste of actual battle not long afterward when a Klingon cruiser launched a sneak attack against the *Chesty Puller*. Badly outgunned, the ship suffered massive damage from the first blast, including the complete destruction of the bridge with all hands. Kirk fortunately had been on the way to the bridge at the time, and although suffering from a serious head wound taken when his turbolift shuddered with the impact, he managed to make his way to auxiliary control. With only two crewmen available, Kirk had to man the helm himself while issuing orders to the rest of the ship. Kirk brilliantly managed to evade the Klingon ship (and another which arrived thereafter), and succeeded in getting his badly wounded ship into Federation space without further incident. He was rewarded with the Medal of Honor and command of his own ship for his gallantry and quick thinking.

While recovering from his wound at a Starbase, Kirk was offered a chance at which any ambitious young officer would normally jump: to participate in an experimental officer-exchange program with the Klingons. Kirk, however, was having none of it. Klingons had just killed his captain, ruined his ship, and put him in the hospital. Now Starfleet wanted him to delay his promised command to live and work with a Klingon. Kirk adamantly refused.

A com-link ''visit'' from the widow of Captain Garrovick caused Kirk to change his mind. It was his duty to join the exchange program, she insisted. Not only could he perhaps learn something about the Klingon mind and personality which might someday help to preserve lives, it was possible that this program could be the beginning of a rapprochement between the Federation and the Klingon Empire which would end forever the possibility of war between them. She lashed out at Kirk. How dare he refuse when his duty was clear and the stakes were so high? Still, Kirk would not commit himself.

Kirk did not really believe that the program would have any lasting benefits. They would learn nothing about the Klingons which the Klingons did not want them to learn; on the contrary, the Klingons would probably learn more about the Federation and Starfleet and the people in it than would be advisable or prudent. Kirk also believed that any real peace between the Federation and the Klingons was a long way away, and would come only after the Klingons had decided they'd been beaten often and thoroughly enough. They understood fighting, not talking.

Mostly, however, Kirk was instinctively distrustful of any project which was fueled more by goodwill than good sense. It seemed to him that mankind would never learn that good intentions and high hopes were no substitute for fair and firm resolve. If anything, he believed that his duty not only compelled him not to participate in a program which he believed to be foolhardy, but to actively speak out against it.

Kirk was not out to destroy his career by becoming another Billy Mitchell, however, and he refrained from making public statements, instead confining his comments and objections to interservice memos and letters to friends and associates. Many of the higher-ups in Starfleet agreed with Kirk—the project had been instigated and insisted upon by the Federation Council—and they admired the courage with which he voiced his convictions. The program had to go through, however; major funding for the next few years was inextricably tied to it. But it was now also a must that Kirk join in the program. He had become a rallying point for opponents, and continuing criticism of the project could only be stifled by his active participation.

It was left up to Captain Ng to convince Kirk. The *Exeter* was "coincidentally" rerouted to the starbase where Kirk was just about to be released from hospital, and Ng paid him a visit. He pointed out that no one, not even Kirk, was more philosophically opposed to the program than he, but that they must, as soldiers, follow orders and make the best of it. If the program had not been publicly announced as voluntary from the start, Kirk would have been ordered to participate, objections or no. Now, because of the furor he'd stirred up, he had to take part, or the long-term effects could be much worse than anything the program could cause.

Kirk ruefully had to agree. His stand was beginning to hurt the service; if that wasn't enough of a consideration (and it was), the service would soon lash back at Kirk and his career would be over. Kirk had to swallow his pride and agree to participate. A bagain of sorts was struck, however, before he would finally agree. He would not have to travel to a Klingonese planet, nor would he promise to remain silent if he thought the program was a complete fiasco. Starfleet Command agreed, and Kirk signed on.

Kirk's time spent in the exchange program was not as bad as he feared it would be. He was assigned a charming young Klingon officer named Kumara as a roommate, and while they never became friends, they developed a grudging respect for each other. The main benefit of the program to Kirk was the acceptance of his book-length report on the program (and the events preceding it) as required reading at the Academy, as well as the attention and respect which the entire affair, and his behavior during it, gained for him among the Starfleet hierarchy. For diplomatic reasons the exchange program was termed "a complete success," but Starfleet knew it for a failure and it was never repeated.

For Kirk, the affair had marked the first time that he had felt strongly enough about something to be willing to put his career on the line, and take on all of Starfleet if necessary. He knew that it would probably not be the last, but he also realized that the action had made him a stronger, better officer. He also had a new conception of duty: His loyalty would be given unquestioningly, as he had sworn, but he would reserve to himself the right to question and even protest against Starfleet and Federation policy when he thought it wrong. He'd follow orders, yes, but he would also resign rather than violate his conscience and his convictions. As the goals and beliefs of Starfleet and the Federation generally paralleled his own, Kirk saw little chance for conflict, but he had learned that both people and governments change. Kirk would go a long way before he would allow things to reach a point at which a line must be drawn, and he believed Starfleet would as well, but he mentally prepared himself for a possible time when he would have to resign his commission.

This decision marked the final maturation of Kirk as an officer and a creature of duty and honor. To simply, unthinkingly obey orders, any orders, Kirk believed, is not what makes a good officer. Indeed, it makes a very bad officer indeed. Kirk had finally learned that what was required of an officer in the performance of his duty was the intelligent carrying out of orders. With foresight, planning, reliance on skills and procedures, and a little bit of luck, it would never come to a pass where he would have to refuse to follow orders. He must be a thinking captain, not one who simply reacts to events and depends on "the book" to get him out of trouble when in over his head.

Kirk was given his first command shortly after the completion of the exchange program, and he proudly and prudently began to apply all that he had learned. Now it was his responsibility to represent Starfleet and the Federation when venturing into new, uncharted space. Kirk took on his duties as commander, administrator, lawmaker, and diplomat. As he took his vessels deeper into almost unimaginable reaches of space and became responsible for more crewmembers and more colonists, miners, explorers, etc., Kirk was often called upon to exercise his almost unrestrained powers in areas of dispute, conflict and even war. It was a mark of the highest confidence in Kirk as a commander that he was continually advanced in grade and assignment, eventually reaching command of a Constitution-class starship, the *Enterprise*. For above all others, a starship *is* the Federation in the minds of many and the practical experience of a few.

In his years of command, Kirk made mistakes, but he also, often by making those mistakes, discovered new things about command, himself, the ship, his enemies, and his men. He learned how to accept victory graciously and defeat unblinkingly; he learned to accept death—and the threat of death—as an everpresent companion. Mostly, he learned what it means to be alone.

James T. Kirk has the hardest job in Starfleet, and the loneliest—a job which has literally destroyed many good and brave men. But it is a job that he believes in, loves, and performs exceptionally well. It is somewhat wondrous, then, that when we realize the sheer number and weight of his responsibilities, we still think of him most for his humanity. Although it is James Kirk the captain we admire, it is Jim Kirk the man we love. That is why James Kirk has touched, and will continue to touch, our lives in so many ways.

# A DISCUSSION ON STAR TREK III:
# THE SEARCH FOR SPOCK

### by Rita D. Clay

*One of the very first articles we received addressing itself to* Star Trek III: The Search for Spock *was this one from Rita Clay. It is not as long and detailed as some of those we received a few days later; maybe the writing is not as polished as it could be. . . . Never mind. Rita's article is just the kind of thing we, and, we know you too, like to see. It is made up of the kind of unbridled enthusiasm and sheer love for Star Trek that used to typify* all *fan writing. More than that, it says a few things which others of us may have said at more length, but not half as well.*

Well, we waited patiently through the rumors and the hopes and at last we saw what became of Spock. What we were not expecting was the route it took to get us there.

The night I went to see *The Search for Spock* was a special night, one eagerly awaited, perhaps more so than the launching of the space shuttle. I was one of the few lucky ones who had passes to the premiere, who did not have to stand in line for hours or fight traffic afterward. Premiere night was an orderly affair, and as we waited there were many discussions on the upcoming movie, guesses, logical insights; a few knew inside information but would not tell.

The movie started.

Even the beginning said that this movie was going to be different. Were we ready for it?

*Yes*.

There are many points to discuss about *The Search for Spock*, both technical and generic. Let us begin with the storyline and its development.

The first we see of Spock comes to us through McCoy. "Remember." One word can carry so much. Has Bones really lost his grip on reality after the death of a friend, or is there something more? We are asked to believe Spock survives beyond his death, tied to McCoy by a word. And we do believe it.

The confirmation Sarek seeks from Kirk during the mind meld is painful to watch because Kirk relives the incident word for word, emotion by emotion, all over again. We see complete devastation, perhaps more than ever before. And yet we see . . . hope, even as Sarek grieves, even as Kirk desperately grabs at straws. We go with Kirk as he challenges Starfleet, puts his career and those of his friends on the line, all to take the risk his soul demands he take. There is no Vulcan at his side this time to quote the odds against the task succeeding, but we know it is a long shot. We also know that to Kirk, odds do not matter.

We see the dedication of Spock's friends as they join Kirk on the quest. They all know that things will never be the same in their lives after this journey. They know this, yet go anyway. What they do not know, and cannot know, is the extent to which their friendship will be tested.

It seems—and it's quite a shock, actually—that Genesis was a bit more involved than even David suspected. We see now a David Marcus who is more like Kirk than he (or we) thought possible, who is rash and forceful when it comes to getting his own way, and whose impulsiveness ends up costing him his own life. David admits to having stacked the deck (more than slightly), and the outcome was a mutated world with a dangerous secret.

David's death was fitting in that he gave his life heroically, and he died on the world that he had created. It was upsetting mostly in that it was such a futile death. That futility made his son's death doubly hard on Kirk. It was a terrible thing for us to see yet another part of Kirk ripped away; it was terrible, yet it was necessary to show what limits Kirk would face to find Spock. At this point, we might well ask, what more could he lose? He has lost Spock, lost his career, lost his son. He is a man being torn into small pieces, who must yet face more—including the loss of the *Enterprise*. It was certainly not his choice; it went out gloriously, but to see it streaking across the sky in a trail of fire was to watch the end of an era. It was as though the fire reflected all the turmoil and anguish in Kirk's soul.

There is much to learn about Kirk in this film—perhaps more than even he cared to know. There is not one facet of his being that is not called upon to make a sacrifice, a sacrifice he willingly, but painfully, makes. (McCoy, too learns much about himself, as we see in his speech to the unconscious Spock: "I don't think I can bear to lose you again.") When Kirk finally pushes the Klingon off the cliff, we cheer because he is finally fighting back, not only against Kruge, but against all that fate has thrown at him. We see once again the old Kirk who will not accept defeat. After all that fate has thrown at him, the human will does not concede. It is the one single statement we must hold on to.

And if we do, there is yet hope that Spock can be saved.

Kirk stands alone, having lost everything, and waits for the outcome. Like the rest of us, he is helpless in the aftermath. When we see Spock walk by his captain and start up the steps, our heart sinks. For now it seems that Kirk has lost not just everything, but everything that matters.

. . . and Spock turns . . .

Hearts leap. Breaths are held.

"I have been, and ever shall be, your friend."

It has not all been for nothing. He is not the Spock we lost, but he is Spock—and when it comes to a certain Vulcan, we take what we can get.

I have heard many opinions about this movie. Some fans are of the mind that it is a disappointment. In my view, these people were expecting more *Wrath of Khan* excitement, and were displeased when it did not occur. *The Search for Spock* is more a study in the psychology of the individual, more a view of life after death and loyalties, more than could be expressed by a simple adventure.

Other fans are of the mind that *The Search for Spock* serves as a logical extension of character and possibilities. With some joys and more reservations, I share this view. I was not disappointed by *The Search for Spock*. I was . . . words fail me in the short run. What must be said cannot be expressed in one or two adjectives.

Leonard Nimoy is a good director. Because he is "Star Trek-oriented," he saw characterizations as no one else could have seen them. His camera angles and shots are technically perfect, a little too television-biased, but workable. He almost went too far with large-screen closeups of a single eye or mouth, but it did work in the one scene where it needed to.

Shatner's Kirk was perfection; every time I see him, he gets better. And Dee Kelley stold the show . . . the scene where McCoy tries the Vulcan nerve pinch on the security officer was perfect! Surely Nimoy must have come up with that.

There is an entire gamut of Star Trek in-jokes in this film—a revelation that Star Trek and Star Trek fans do not take themselves too seriously. McCoy speaking in Spock's voice is eerily effective, enough to send chills down your spine hearing it. The Klingons are, at once, super-nasty and incredibly amusing. Kruge seems to care more for his pet than his men; and his disregard for life (his own included) reflects a complete lack of human morals which Kirk finds almost impossible to combat. Klingons represent the atypical, the very essence of evil, the very opposite of what Kirk and Spock stand for.

There was a tendency to rely too much on *Wrath of Khan* as a visual basis. We hear the words "I have been and always shall be your friend" one too many times. The editing could have been sharper. We should have experienced more with David's death—as shot, it was simply too quick, too common-place. This was probably intended, as death, even a hero's death, is both quick and common. However, much of the shock of it came through Kirk's reaction.

Saavik, in *The Search for Spock*, not only lacks the controlled passion Kirstie Alley's Saavik had, but is a block of ice. I cannot find fault with the performance of Robin Curtis—although her voice wasn't pleasing to my ears—because, in all honesty, it was the director who gave her character its dimension. This Saavik walks through what could have been a fantastic preformance. There is no awe in her at the discovery of her teacher. There is no desperate savagery of temper, barely leashed, when the *Grissom* is destroyed or when David is killed. The savage, Romulan half of her seems more easily controlled than Spock's human half ever was. Sadly, where Saavik is concerned, Nimoy and company completely missed a great opportunity. Instead, she is virtually nonexistent.

The mischaracterization of Saavik is only one major flaw requiring mention. Another mistake is the portrayal of Starfleet personnel as incompetent, boorish, childish, and crude. However straitlaced the military is, I do not see them this way. I do not believe that Starfleet would turn down a request by Kirk or Sarek of Vulcan to return to Genesis if there was even the slightest possibility that Spock could be alive, in any form. We have all known since the beginning that Spock was more than an ordinary officer, or an ordinary Vulcan.

(As you have probably surmised by now, the novelization of the screenplay of *The Search for Spock*, by Vonda McIntyre, is a must read. She has an extremely personal view of Star Trek and the characters who inhabit the *Enterprise*, and to read her word pictures is to know the true Kirk, to see what could have been with Saavik, to want so much more from the film than it is possible to get. I shouldn't fault the film in comparison to the book—as always, the detail possible in the written word will win the contest every time.)

All in all, the movie was thoroughly Star Trek and satisfying. It did, however, leave a great void for a final statement. One cannot help wondering: Where can they go from here? Kirk says it himself: "I intend to recommend you all for promotion . . . in whatever fleet we end up serving."

It seems we are left with a shambles. The *Enterprise* is gone for good. Kirk's son, and therefore the line of continuity, is dead. Kirk and his officers have jeopardized their careers and cannot help but be on the extreme outs with Starfleet. (But remember, Vulcan holds great power in the Federation.) And although Spock has been found and returned to us, he is not the Spock we lost. We must ask, was it all worth what it took from Kirk?

Everything lost, including, it would seem, the relationship Kirk and Spock shared. It seems obvious that they will have to begin again, Spock because he has no memory, and Kirk because he has lost all his past. A clean slate for one, a difficult decision for the other. Will there be any going back?

Of course not. There is only forward, always forward. And the future must be that much better.

Remember . . . the human adventure is just beginning.

# THE BLACK AND WHITE COOKIE EPISODE

## (A Star Trek Parody) by Kiel Stuart

*Okay, already! We know there was no Kiel Stuart parody in* Best of Trek #7! *So stop with the threats and angry letters and bricks through the windows already, okay? Hokey smokes, we promise that it'll never happen again! This time around, Kiel takes on one of everybody's favorite episodes (what? You mean it isn't your favorite?) and, not surprisingly, manages to do it the full justice it deserves.*

The stolen shuttlecraft had been missing for weeks, but now the *Enteritis* was hot on its trail. Why can't some other starship have the pleasure of picking up petty thieves once in a while? thought Captain Jerk as the starship drew alongside the shuttle. Bad enough to have to rush to the planet Aramis, he reflected, where accumulated tons of bachelor laundry awaited decontamination.

"When she passes, throw a ViseGrip beam on her and haul the sucker in," said Jerk. "Shmuck, I suppose you and I had better see who we've caught. Uwhora, have Dr. McCrotch meet us there." He and Shmuck languidly rose and sauntered to the lift.

The being who stumbled out of Hangar 18 was quite unlike anything they had ever seen before. The bizarre, painted humanoid mumbled a few words and collapsed at McCrotch's feet.

"Ah'll be hornswoggled," he said, "Guy looks jess lahk a black-'n'-white cookie."

"Say, those are really good," said Jerk. "I remember a little bake shop just outside the Academy where we used to—"

Shmuck tapped him on the shoulder. "Captain," he said, "Should we not convey this creature to sick bay?"

"Ohhh . . . right! Good idea!"

When the alien thief had been encased in one of the cots, Jerk shook him awake. "Hi there, fella." He beamed at the captive. "This is the *USS Enteritis*, I'm Captain Jerk, and you are in big trouble."

"*Enteritis*," said the alien. "I've heard of it. Belongs to United Space Movers or the Army or the Confederates or . . ."

"Jeez," said Jerk, "don't you even know whose property you've stolen?"

"I am no thief!" The bicolored alien shook with indignation. "You are jumping to conclusions, making accusations, putting the horse before the cart."

"Oooh, pardonnez-*moi*!" mocked Jerk. "Now who the hell are you, and why are you wearing that ridiculous makeup?"

The alien bristled. "I am Locus, from the planet Cheroot."

"They're not part of the Fodderation," said Jerk. "That means I could hang you and nobody would notice, so watch it, bub." He narrowed his eyes. "And what are you doing so far from home, eh?"

"I would have returned it as soon as I'd incited half the galaxy to . . . oops, I mean I'm tired and I think I'll go to sleep." Locus began to saw the wood.

Jerk wished fleetingly that he really *could* hang the lout. Unable to discover anything more about the alien at the moment, he and Shmuck headed back to the bridge. Locus's snores echoed through the ship's corridors, the sound mockingly follows them all the way back.

"Captain!" cried Ensign Wackov as they exited the lift. "Alien wessel approaching, sir!"

"I haven't even had a chance to sit down!" complained Jerk.

"It's invisible, too," chirped Lieutenant Lulu.

"Fabulous," said Jerk. He sat, chin in hand, waiting for the inevitable crash. "Brace yourselves, gang," he said wearily.

"Hey," said Lulu. "Nothing happened. What gives?"

Schmuck referred to his Science Panel. "It disappeared."

"Aww, how can it do that when it's *already* invisible?" said Jerk.

Ignoring him, Shmuck went on, "And it has deposited an alien life form."

"Where?" asked Jerk.

"Right here on the bridge, Captain," said a voice from behind them.

They turned to look.

"Oh, crud," said Jerk, "Not another one."

The alien who stood before them was smeared with the same garish makeup that Locus wore.

"Hey," said Lieutenant Lulu, "We used to get cookies just like that in a little bake shop outside the—"

The alien interrupted, "I am Jeel, from the planet Cheroot."

Jerk tapped his fingers impatiently on the arm of his chair. "And what are you doing all the way out here?"

"Oh, a little of this, a little of that," said Jeel blithely. "Actually, I've come for that bag of alien slime you've got in your sick bay."

"Ah," said Jerk, "I see. You are in need of some sort of exotic medication which McCrotch keeps on hand."

"I don't know who this McCrotch is. I was referring to Locus. Hand him over, will you?"

Jerk rose, advancing until he faced the painted figure. "No one throws his weight around like that on *my* ship!"

A twenty changed hands.

"But if you're really sincere . . ." Jerk coyly hesitated.

A fifty was produced.

"Right this way, Mr. Jeel. Come along, Mr. Shmuck."

They crowded onto the lift. "By the way," said Jerk, "what do you do for a living, eh, Jeel?"

"I am the commissioner of FIJAGDH on my home planet, Charon."

"Hah?"

"Fandom Is Just A Goddamn Hobby," said Shmuck. "Third floor: Notions, Complaints, and Sick Bay."

Locus was somewhat taken aback by Jeel's appearance. "Yaaah!" he shrieked, leaping into McCrotch's arms.

He was hastily deposited on the floor. "I am not going back to Chartreuse with that Nazi!" he snarled, rubbing his posterior.

"No, you're going back to Starbase Four to stand trial," said Jerk. He faced Jeel. "I only said you could *see* him, not haul him off."

"And you observe how this perverted leader of FIAWOL repays your kindness," said Jeel.

Jerk looked mystified. "Fandom Is A Way Of Life," whispered Shmuck into his ear. Jerk remained mystified.

Locus stood on the cot, pointing a quivering finger at Jeel.

"You! You raised the postal rates, raided our conventions, banned our favorite zines!"

"Horse feathers!" Jeel retorted as passionately. "We tried to expand your consciousness, to teach you to appreciate classical literature, to get you to watch something else other than *Battlestar: Ponderosa*." Jeel seethed.

"Ahh, who needs all that highbrow crud?" Locus bounced on the cot. "You just wanted to feel superior."

"You spray-painted graffiti on our office buildings!" said Jeel. "And talk about us being elitist—You had your own secret language!"

"Hah!" Locus's eyes blazed. "Were we free to wear *Misplaced in Space* costumes to work? Were we free to play with life-size models of the Multilinear Falcon? Were we free to talk like D.T.?"

"Perhaps if you grew up, you'd stop wanting to. You personally even went so far as to write pornographic B/R stories!"

Again mystified, Jerk leaned to Shmuck. "B/R?"

"Batman/Robin," whispered Shmuck. "You know, like those rumors they used to tell about us."

"Those *unfounded* rumors, Mr. Shmuck," added Jerk quickly. He turned back to the arguing aliens, who had moved their argument onto a considerably lower intellectual plane.

"Yeah?"

"Yeah!"

"Oh, yeah?"

"Yeah!"

"Oh, Yeah?" Locus began to flap his arms. "Sez *who*?"

"Sez me! You . . . you . . . you . . . I can't *stand* it!" Jeel leaped across the room and grabbed Locus in a stranglehold.

"Hey," admired Jerk, "that's a pretty good Kirk Douglas impression." He peeled Jeel from Locus. "Awright, fellas, show's over."

"Captain," panted Jeel, "it is imperative that you return Locus to . . . ummm . . . ah . . . Cheryl, to stand trial."

Jerk yawned, bored with their bickering. "Forget it, you don't have enough money on you." Ordering Shmuck to keep the two separated, he ambled back to the bridge.

As he exited the lift, Jerk was annoyed to see that technicians were asprawl all across the deck. "What now?" he griped.

"Malfunction" said Lieutenant Lulu. "Don't worry, we'll have it fixed in a jiffy."

Jerk settled down in his chair. He had just passed happily into a light snooze when Wackov shook him awake.

"Captain, ve are headed off course at Warped 8!"

Jerk shot a look at Lulu. "Jiffy, eh?" He pressed the Red Alert button and popped two aspirin down his throat.

"Oh, uh, gosh, duhh, Red Alert, me better stop guarding prisoner." Locus's security goon lumbered off to his assigned battle station (conveniently out of everyone's way), and the bicolored alien lost no time appearing on the bridge.

"Captain," said Shmuck, "the planet Charee . . . we seem to be headed for it on a direct course."

Jeel popped onto the bridge as well. "That's right, we *are* headed for Cheerio, and I'm in control of this ship. I'm gonna get that lousy Locus if it's the last thing I do."

Locus crept up behind him and slipped an ice cube down his tights.

"ARRGH! You scheming, filthy little mound of refuse!" Jeel whirled on Locus. "By the Ten Commandments, you shall not escape!"

"Say, that's a neat Burt Lancaster," said Jerk. "Who else can you do?"

"My cause is just!" cried Locus. "How would you feel if someone took away *your* fully functional model light saber?"

Jerk shook his head. By this time, he was quite willing to

stuff both of them into the antimatter chambers, if only he could be sure it would not plug up the choke.

"You're *both* fish heads," he marveled. "Might I remind you that we have a massive pile of laundry to decontaminate on Aramis? Release this ship!"

Jeel clenched his face.

"All right," muttered Jerk. "Security, throw these two in the fusion reactor!"

Both aliens threw off a shower of sparks as the security goon reached for them.

"Me scared!" he cried, and fainted.

Jerk scowled. "Sparks or no, this ship is going to Aramis!"

"Nope," said Jeel. "It's headed for, er, Chauffeur."

Jerk hitched up his trousers. "Wanna bet?" He rummaged through a tool chest and withdrew a hand grenade. "Once I pull this pin . . ." He tried twice to pull it with his teeth, then sheepishly gave up and pulled it by hand. "If I don't put it back in ten seconds . . . *Blooey*!"

"You're bluffing," said Jeel.

Jerk whistled Chopin's "Death March."

"Heh, heh," said Jeel, "Just kidding."

Jerk slid the pin back into the grenade. Shmuck relaxed in his chair. Uwhora heaved a huge sigh. Snotty took his fingers out of his ears. Wackov crept away to change his pants.

"Well," said Jerk, "now that that's settled and we're back on course to Aramis, let's go have a drink."

The ship's Happy Hour room was lavishly furnished (it even came equipped with a topless waitress), but Jeel was too busy proselytizing to notice.

"I'll tell you," he sighed, putting down his boilermaker, "I'm so cool that sometimes I even scare myself. So when will Starfleece hand over Locus for trial and hanging?"

Before Jerk could answer, the intercom beeped. "Lieutenant Uwhora here. I got a message from Starfleece at Starbase 4: 'Jeel, you're out of luck. Sorry.' Uwhora out."

Jeel slammed his fist on the table, upsetting everyone's drinks. "Curses! So that juvenile bucket of drool has succeeded in brainwashing Starfleece! Next thing you know *they'll* be going to conventions! Why, that little snotnosed brat! It's all lies, loathsome perversions and foul . . . stuff!''

"Oh," said an exhausted Jerk, "shut up, willya?"

"You fool!" Jerk snarled. "Locus is an inferior breed!"

Shmuck spoke gravely. "You *both* look like black-and-white cookies to me, just like the ones we used to get at that little place—"

"Are you nuts?" cried Jeel. He stood up. "*Look* at me!"

"You and Locus are both wearing equal amounts of black-face and clown white," shrugged Jerk. "So what?"

"So I wear blackface on the *right* side," said Jeel smugly.

"So *so what*?" Jerk was at the end of his rope.

Shmuck smoothly interjected himself between the sputtering Jeel and Jerk. He inflated his lungs to the limit and said:

"Perhaps the history of my planet, Vulgaris, may set a shining example for those of you on the planet Chivoom, for many years ago we were quite as silly as yourselves. Yes, it is true; that is why I know what those bizarre acronyms mean. We Vulgarians, too, were long ago split into those two noxious groups. We behaved abominably, going to conventions and beating one another up. We espoused opposing points of view, leading inevitably to death, destruction, and hangnails. Some of us even wore garish makeup, but we saved ourselves in time by the disciplines of logic and common sense, and I am sure that you will no doubt be pleased to listen as I impart this philosophy to you, and . . . Jeel? Jeel? Wake up, Jeel!''

"Yeah," said Jerk, himself hastily awakening. "Maybe Locus can change, eh?"

"Never," said Jeel. "How can you expect anyone who plasters his living room with Dr. Hoot posters to ever grow up?"

The intercom buzzed again. "Captain," said Snotty, "we're orbiting Aramis."

"Right," said Jerk. "Clean up that laundry." He went back to his lite beer.

The trio, having consumed whatever recreational liquids they could pour down their throats by the time the laundry was finished, sauntered back to the bridge. Jerk stretched out in his command chair. "Okay, gang. Time for Starbase Four. We got a date with justice."

"Not so fast," said Jeel. He made a few passes in the air, pulled a rabbit out of his hat, and lit some sparklers. "We're going to Charvon. And don't look for the hand grenades; I've hidden them."

Locus barged onto the bridge. "Kill him! What are you waiting for? What's the matter with you, anyway? Hell, he broke my lasergun!"

"But ve are not killers," said Wackov, "except vhen ve feel like it."

"Talk is cheap," said Locus. "Let's see some action."

Jerk squared off in front of him. "You look mighty damn healthy for the fugitive leader of a band of hunted renegades."

"Undoubtedly, many of his gophers are somewhat the worse for wear," Shmuck pointed out. "So throw no bricks at us, and call no kettles black."

"Hahahahooo!" sniggered Jeel. "Know what we've done to your kind back on Chirop? We stuck them in civil service jobs! We have confiscated their comic books! We have forced them to give up their pocket protectors!"

"Captain," said Shmuck, "we are within scanning range of Charoo. My Feeler Gauges indicate . . . no life forms remaining." He looked up. "There are corpses stacked everywhere."

"All the people . . . dead?" whispered Jeel.

"You got it," said Shmuck.

Jeel began to inflate; he staggered stiffly over to Locus.

"You . . . you dirty rat! You killed my brother!"

"Hey, great," said Jerk. "Jimmy Cagney, right?"

Locus slammed Jeel on the side of the head, then they grabbed each other and fell to the deck. They rolled around, scratching, yelping.

"You effete intellectual!" screeched Locus. "You and your kind have trashed my entire collections of Duck Rogers videotapes!"

"You worthless piece of mangy flesh!" growled Jeel. "This is what you do when confronted with anything beyond your fifth-grade mentality—you murder it!"

"Hey," said Jerk mildly, "not on *my* bridge, guys."

"Oh, goodness," said Shmuck loudly. "The transporter room seems to be unattended at the moment."

"Say," drawled Jerk, "why, that means if a couple of unauthorized personnel were to wander in there in the hope of beaming to, say, Sauron, well, no one could stop them. Pretty interesting, eh?"

Locus gave Jeel a quick chop and sprinted off the bridge. Jeel, wiping blood from his mouth, staggered to his feet and ran after Locus.

"Gosh," said Jerk, leafing through his travel orders, "where do you think *they're* headed?"

"Why, just look at this," said Shmuck, face deep in his computer hood. "It appears that the transporter is being activated. And there it goes again. This is indeed a surprise."

"Migosh," said Jerk, buffing his nails. "What could that be?"

"Humm," said Shmuck, fiddling with some knobs. "It seems that there are now two life forms on Charreau, where none previously existed."

Jerk raised his voice slightly. "Oh, Jeel, Locus, where are yooooou?" He cocked an ear, deliberately. "Ohhh, no answer. Well, I guess that means they aren't interested. I can't *force* them to come back and stand trial, now can I?"

"In fact, Captain, I would extrapolate that those two life forms we observed materializing on Moron were Locus and Jeel themselves." Shmuck idly computed a course to Starbase Four.

"Gee, it's a shame, but since Chargon isn't a member of the Fodderation, I have no extradition authority there," said Jerk.

He and Shmuck looked steadily at one another. After a minute or two, Jerk spoke. "Starbase Four, Mr. Lulu."

Uwhora wriggled up behind him. "Captain, them two sure hated each other's guts. Why, seems like that's all they ever lived for. Sure behaved in a disgraceful manner and all, seeing as how they really weren't different in no true sense, comin' from the same species as they did." She leaned closer to Jerk, batting her inch-long eyelashes. "D'you suppose we could learn something *significant* 'bout ourselves from all this?"

Jerk closed his eyes. "God, I hope not," he said and swallowed a handful of painkillers.

# STAR TREK MYSTERIES SOLVED . . . AGAIN!

## by Leslie Thompson

*Leslie's back and Trek's got her! And if you're old enough to remember the movie that line is paraphrasing, then you'll probably be very glad that we wouldn't allow Leslie to call this edition of the Mystery series "Abbot and Costello Meet Star Trek Mysteries." (We were holding out for "Star Trek Mysteries' New York Adventure.") Yes, folks, your favorite little mystery solver is an old movie buff. None of this has anything to do with Star Trek, of course, but the following article does. Once again Les has painstakingly read, sorted, cursed, ripped, and—finally—answered your questions about those nattering Star Trek Mysteries. As of this moment, Leslie is at Happy Acres Rest Home, preparing for the onslaught of* The Search for Spock *mysteries that are already beginning to flood in. Until then, enjoy these.*

Many thanks to each and every one of you who have sent in your mysteries or have just written to say "Hi." Your kind words and interest in these continuing articles is appreciated, and G.B. and Walter have informed me that I can keep to this every-other-*Best of Trek* schedule for as long as I wish. I'm not bored yet, folks, and as long as you keep sending in questions that start my poor tired little brain thinking again, I'll keep finding the time to do these articles.

At the request of their majesties the editors, I'm going to include a lot more excerpts from your letters; on my own initiative I'm going to include a number of letters in which readers have done my job for me and supplied their own answers to some Star Trek mysteries. I'm simply going to present these explanations this time, and not (as I've done infrequently in the past) accept or reject them. Instead, I'll ask you readers to comment, and perhaps even supply answers to these questions and still others of your own devising.

This, of course, is a cunning if transparent ruse to get *you* to do all this work and thinking *for* me, so the next time I sit down to do a Mysteries article, all I'll have to do is quote from your scintillating letters.

Not really. But I do love to hear from you, and I will be looking forward to the next batch of letters.

Now, to begin: Our first question comes from Debbie Mark, of Warren, Ohio. Debbie rightly points out that when Ambassador Kollos arrives aboard the *Enterprise*, only Spock is on hand to greet him, for the transporter room, the halls, etc. have all been cleared of humans, who will go mad at the slightest view of Kollos. Debbie wonders why, when the story is over and Kollos and Miranda are ready to leave, Kirk stays in the transporter room while they beam down and why Kirk didn't go mad when seeing Kollos.

The reason for the security when the ambassador beamed up was the possibility of an accident. The antigravs could have failed, dropping the box and spilling out Kollos where a crewperson could have accidentally seen him. Also, one must never discount human curiosity. Even such intelligent and highly trained personnel as those in Starfleet might have one or two among them who couldn't resist the urge for just "one quick peek." It was obvious that even the unemotional Mr. Spock could hardly wait for his first look at Kollos, and Miranda Jones was so curious about "what does he [Spock] see when he looks at you?" that her jealousy and insecurity almost destroyed them all.

Kirk stuck around in the transporter room because it was fairly safe for him to do so. Kollos was on the pad, and the transporter effect "dissolves" *all* of the component parts of a being at once, not from the outside in, so Jim wouldn't have been able to see, even for a split second, through Kollos's box.

This person leaning over my shoulder just pointed out that perhaps Debbie got the impression that it would drive a human mad to simply be in line of sight with Kollos, box or no. Could be. If so, sorry, Debbie . . . it was clearly stated that the box was for transportation and protection (both ways) purposes only and besides hiding him, had nothing to do with Kollos's appearance.

Lynda King, of Schofield, Wisconsin, sent in several questions. The first is more of a *Trek* mystery than a Star Trek mystery: Lynda says, "Will someone please print a list of the titles and authors of Star Trek books in one of the future *Best of Trek* books so that those of us who are collecting them know what we're missing?"

I asked Walter and G.B. about this and they explained that they get a request for such a list at least once a week. But they're reluctant to do one because it would be so out of date by the time it appeared in print as to be virtually worthless; more important, they feel (and I agree with them) that such a list could possibly cause fans more trouble than help, for it might drive up prices of books which collectors can still get relatively cheap at used-book stores, etc. Most readers know by now that various Star Trek publishers have rereleased many of the ST fiction titles, and these include lists of other titles available from the same publisher.

Lynda also wants to know, "How did James Kirk meet Dr. Carol Marcus?" I'm going to dodge that one—don't you folks think some things are better left to the imagination?

"Why were Christine Chapel and Janice Rand present in the novel *Wrath of Khan*, but left out of the movie? I refuse to believe that Christine Chapel would not be present for Spock's funeral. Did her feelings for Spock disappear during the time lapse after the last television episode and between movies?"

The old Movie Versus Novelization bugaboo again! Okay, since Vonda says so, it's gotta be true: Christine and Janice were aboard the ship, we just didn't see them in the movie. (G.B. says they did get one letter in which somebody claims to have plainly seen Christine Chapel in sick bay during the aftermath of Khan's attack. Hmmm.) It's entirely possible for them not to be seen—weren't there plenty of episodes in which Chekov or Sulu or even Uhura weren't seen?

As far as Christine's feelings for Spock: Even in *Star Trek: The Motion Picture* we weren't sure that she was still in love with him; her pleasure at seeing him could have been just that which anyone would feel greeting an old friend. Even if she had managed to forget him, wouldn't her hopes have revived once Spock had his "revelation" from V'Ger? What if he could've then felt a "simple feeling" for her, too? Since Christine is not around, and certainly not married to or living with Spock in *Wrath of Khan*, then we must assume that she either again gave up on him or resumed her former life of hopeless longing. I prefer to think that Spock, with his expanded set of emotions after V'Ger, finally found the words to convince Christine that it was not to be between them, and she gracefully accepted this, and eventually went on to happiness of her own.

As to why she wasn't at Spock's funeral . . . Well, different people face grief in different ways, and perhaps Christine just couldn't face it, even with the help and support of her friends. Why Janice wasn't there is easier to explain: There had to be one or two experienced officers on the bridge, even at such a solemn time, for the ship was badly crippled. Even with the reduced cadet crew, we saw only a few of the onboard personnel at Spock's services.

Lynda also asks, "Why was there no reduction in rank for Admiral Kirk when he took command of the *Enterprise* in *Wrath of Khan*?"

The reduction in rank in *Star Trek: The Motion Picture* was a sacrifice Kirk was willing to make to regain command of the ship; we do not know if it was required by Starfleet regulations or was insisted upon by Admiral Nogura as a sort of "punishment" for Kirk's boldness. In *Wrath of Khan*, Kirk only assumed command because (1) he was senior officer there and (2) it was with Spock's permission and full approval. It was understood to be only temporary, and therefore no reduction in rank was needed.

Lynda's last question is: "What happened to the awful computer voice that screamed 'red alert' in *Star Trek: The Motion Picture*, but was nowhere to be heard in *Wrath of*

*Khan*?'' It was probably ripped out because someone, most likely Kirk, agreed with Lynda that it was indeed awful.

All the way from his post in Spangdalem, Germany, Air Force crewman Kevin Wandick asks several questions:

"When the *Enterprise* was leaving drydock, a dock worker did a flip. What kept that person from flying out into space?" Internal stabilizers in his suit, most likely, augmented by his own sense of balance. Remember, these workers spend as much time in weightlessness as we do at our jobs, so they would be entirely comfortable and conditioned to moving about without worrying about the effects of opposite and equal reaction.

Also referring to the suits, Kevin asks, "The emergency thruster packs are of what use? If a ship is going to explode, escaping from it into deep space is no good."

The emergency thrusters in the suits are not designed for escape from a damaged ship, but for "escape" from sudden dangers encountered while working in space. This could include onrushing meteors, small ships, even damaged equipment which is flailing about or about to explode. The main purpose of this device is to get somewhere—or away from somewhere—fast.

Kevin also wonders about the use of impulse engines when the *Enterprise* left Earth orbit in *Star Trek: The Motion Picture*, wondering how the ship reached the area around Jupiter so quickly at the slower-than-light impulse speed, and why the crew didn't feel the effects of the almost instantaneous acceleration from zero to .5 lightspeed. The *Enterprise* really didn't get from Earth to Jupiter so quickly, the movie simply cut from Earth to there to indicate the ship's progress. Kevin mentions inertia dampers, but says they would not be enough to overcome the effects of sudden acceleration. Not alone, but you have to consider the ship's artificial gravity and the fact that the crew were old hands at this—they'd have so subtly braced themselves against any pull as to make it virtually unnoticeable. It's only in times of unexpected acceleration that everyone gets a good tossing around.

Kevin's last question is: "In *Wrath of Khan*, the Genesis machine rearranged matter. Is it an advanced version of the transporter?" Several persons have wondered if the Genesis

Device operates on the same principles as the transporter, and, if so, why the transporter hasn't been used in the past to, for example, create "new" duplicates of deceased crewmembers. It's been definitely stated that (under ordinary operating conditions) the transporter cannot create living duplicates, nor can it create life, even simple life. The Genesis Device is more likely an advancement upon the materializers around the ship, which recreate dead organic and nonorganic materials in any form or bulk desired. The big advance in Genesis, of course, is the ability to create extremely complex and interlocked eco-and metabolic systems. It is probably this ability which results in the formation of "life" as we define it.

Tim Shumate, of Winston-Salem, North Carolina, has a question about an article which appeared in a past *Best of Trek*. Why, he asks, does Bill Krophauser's biography of Montgómery Scott state that he was one of the designers of the *Enterprise*, when in "Is There in Truth No Beauty?" Scotty says that he considers it "a rare opportunity to meet one of the designers of the *Enterprise*," Larry Marvick.

Biographies of crewmembers, etc. which appear in *Best of Trek* are not intended to be "official" by any means, Tim. They are simply "what-ifs," a bit of fun speculation about the forces and events which shaped the characters of the Star Trek regulars. However, as Scotty has been firmly established as one of Starfleet's top engineering men, it is only natural that he should have at least been consulted about, if not an active participant in, plans for the *Enterprise* and other Constitution-class starships. If so, he would continue to be active in new, more advanced starship design, and we can assume it is only his love of space and actually working on his beloved *Enterprise* that keeps him from accepting a berth at Starfleet Fleet Operations.

Tim also asks, "Whatever happened to the Gorns? I enjoyed your articles about the Klingons and the Romulans; why don't you write one about the Gorns?"

I'd like to, Tim, but we simply don't know enough about them to enable me to extrapolate a history, psychological motives, culture, etc. As they were never seen again, we can only assume that the Federation took their—admittedly violent—warning to heart and left that particular sector of space alone.

After all, the Gorn *did* feel they were being invaded, and although they are certainly warlike and aggressive, we and the Federation really have no way of knowing whether or not they are truly evil. It is not the Federation's job to destroy and supplant every form of government which is not exactly like their own or to their liking. It is their job to expand peacefully throughout space, making the galaxy a safer, happier place for everyone. As long as the Federation is not again attacked by the Gorn in Federation territory, they will gladly leave those icky old Gorns to their own business. (And good riddance! Lizards and snakes! Ugh.)

Michael Wertheim, of Plantation, Florida, sends in a number of what I call "gnats:" Little things, but they'll drive you crazy. Michael asks:

"In 'The Deadly Years,' how was the aging disease reversed? The adrenaline compound caused the aging to stop, but I doubt it would cure the effects of the radiation."

The adrenaline was not the cure, but the clue to the cure that Dr. McCoy needed to make his previously formulated serum work.

"In 'Shore Leave,' how did Sulu's gun fire seven shots? Was he thinking, 'Boy, I'd love to have a Police Special that shoots seven bullets'?"

No, but the mental image that antique gun collector Sulu had in his head probably included a few extra loads.

"In 'Mudd's Women,' Eve McHuron came up with the brilliant idea of sandblasting the pots and pans. Hadn't the miners ever heard of nonstick cookware?"

The cookware probably was a nonstick formula, one which would certainly be more advanced and efficient than anything we now have available. But nonstick is understood to be a help in *cleaning* as well as cooking. When you don't clean at all . . . well, the miners, probably from one of the wilder colonial outposts, couldn't be bothered with such niceties as wiping out a pan. Eventually, it was too late, and the food leavings were so thoroughly baked on only a long, good soak (which wasn't available) or sandblasting could loosen them.

"Also in 'Mudd's Women,' Kirk tells Childress that the miners need starship protection, implying that Rigel XII is pretty isolated. Yet, in other episodes it is stated that Rigel II,

V, VI, and VII are populated and that the Rigel system is a major trading center.''

Michael is right; in terms of how quickly a starship can get around a solar system. Rigel XII is hardly isolated—we're talking about around the block, here. Obviously, what Kirk was actually saying was that the miners needed starship protection to keep their valuable ore safe from pirates, claim jumpers, etc. And in terms of other people on the same planet, the miners were very isolated indeed.

''What did Jose Tyler mean when he told the survivors of the *Columbia* crash on Talos IV in 'The Menagerie' that the time barrier had been broken? Captain Pike also used the term 'time warp' as an indication of speed.''

When the Enterprise's first visit to Talos IV took place, warp drive capability had been around only a relatively short time, and it is possible that most Starfleet officers (and maybe even the ship designers and physicists) had only a vague understanding of how it worked. Since they were able to travel vast distances which would normally take years to cover in a few days at most, it is easy to see why they would think of warp speed as a ''time warp.'' Later on, a better understanding of the process and how it operated filtered its way down through the ranks, and it began to be simply (and more correctly) referred to as ''warp drive.''

''In *Star Trek: The Motion Picture*, if the *Enterprise* was beaming up Lori and Sonak, why did Kirk tell Starfleet to boost its matter gain and that more signal was needed?''

When the malfunction developed in the *Enterprise* transporter, a redundant system at Starfleet transporter control attempted to lock onto their signals; so, in effect, both transporters were working in concert to beam the people to the *Enterprise*. As the trouble had developed on the *Enterprise*, it was only natural that Kirk should ask Starfleet to override his signal.

''In 'Whom Gods Destroy,' when confronted with two Kirks, why didn't Spock simply shoot them both with a light phaser stun?''

Spock had no way of knowing whether or not Garth's powers were extensive enough to preserve the illusion in a lightly stunned condition, and time was of the essence. He naturally went with something he *did* know, and that was the personality of James T. Kirk.

"In 'Where No Man Has Gone Before,' why does Kirk's tombstone read James *R*. Kirk? Couldn't Gary Mitchell spell?"

Apparently not. This told us two things: One, that Gary Mitchell was not the good friend he pretended to be to Kirk all those years; and, two, that even a "god" was fallible. We know that Kirk would never give up, but have you ever stopped to think that it might have been the sight of that little mistake by the "god" which enabled Jim to make that extra effort which resulted in victory?

Tom Lalli, of Orange, Connecticut, asks three questions, the third of which is, as he says, "a toughie." But first:

Tom asks, "Since it is so dangerous for Kirk in 'This Side of Paradise' to make Spock angry, why didn't Kirk first rid McCoy, Uhura, etc, of the spores, and then they could all gang up on Spock if necessary?"

You'll have to remember that Kirk had just thrown off the effects of the spores himself, and might not have been thinking too clearly. Even muddled, however, the uppermost thought in his mind would have been to get Spock cured; he needed Spock.

Alternatively, Kirk could have feared the effect upon Spock had he been angered and confronted by anyone but himself. A group could have so angered and frightened Spock that it would have been impossible to calm him down before someone got seriously hurt. Kirk may have figured that he and he alone stood a fair chance of escaping damage at the hands of an enraged Spock.

"Why, in 'Who Mourns for Adonais,' did Scotty disobey a direct order from Kirk and rush Apollo when he returned without Lieutenant Palamas? Was he on drugs?"

Not drugs, Tom, but something a lot more powerful—love. And, no, Kirk wouldn't have disciplined Scotty for his impulsive rush. Chances are Kirk's done a bit of impulsive rushing in his time, don't you reckon?

Now for Tom's "toughie:" "If Star Trek is assumed to be real, then the crew's journeys into Earth's past must be equally real. If this is so, then why hasn't there been a real Edith Keeler, or a real Captain Christopher, or a real Roberta

Lincoln? And please don't say parallel universe. I'll understand if you want to cry foul on this one, but it certainly is a mystery.''

I won't cry foul, but I *have* to say parallel universe. Not only has the existence of such universes been established without doubt in the series itself, it is accepted fan doctrine that ours *is* one of those universes which coexists alongside that of Star Trek. Some even say that it coexists at the same time; that while it is 1985 here, it is 2285 there. While it woud be possible to make a case for the existence of the people you mention on our world, it is impossible to reconcile the events which have been documented as being in Star Trek's past with our present. For example, there were no attempted nuclear weapons space platform launches in 1968 in our world; there was in Star Trek's. So while I hate to disregard your plea and use the parallel universe theory, the only other thing I could do is to simply say that Star Trek and everything having to do with it is just sheer fiction. And we all know better than that, don't we?

Bill Mason, of Glenolden, Pennsylvania, has questions about ''Turnabout Intruder:'' ''Why did Janice Lester (as Kirk) reveal in the Captain's Log that she had taken over Kirk's body? How did Kirk get access to his Personal Log record while in Janice Lester's body?''

It really doesn't make sense for Janice to admit her crime in a permanent record, but then switching bodies with Kirk didn't make much sense, either. We all know that Janice was mentally ill, so why should we be surprised that she would do the irrational? In his own convoluted logic, however, one can assume that it wasn't enough for her to have taken over Kirk's body and assumed command of the *Enterprise*—she had to tell someone or something about it. It was too much of a triumph not to crow about. While Janice was cunning enough not to openly reveal the switch, she did succumb to the compulsion to gloat into the Log. And, of course, since *she* was now the captain, she used the Captain's Log.

Kirk, in Janice's body, knew that his situation was desperate, and that he could be killed or silenced at any time. His training, plus his own desire to see justice done, required that he keep a record of what was going on. As Janice, he used the (restricted) access to the computer which everyone, even visitors, aboard the *Enterprise* has, and opened a file. As he still thought of himself as Jim Kirk, Captain, he naturally logged observation etc. into what he called his Personal Log, although this was not the true Captain's Personal Log, which Janice was making use of. Another reason Kirk may have logged his reports in this fashion is, should he have died, Spock or someone else might have noticed the curious fact that Dr. Janice Lester entered so-called Captain's Personal Log reports in which she claimed to actually be James Kirk. If nothing else, questions would have been raised which might have eventually led to the truth, and Kirk would have had his vengeance, albeit posthumously.

Bill also included a couple of questions about *Star Trek: The Motion Picture*.

"Why does Sulu (in the movie and on TV) control the magnification and direction of the main viewer, rather than Uhura?"

Bill is assuming here that the viewer is an adjunct of communications, which is incorrect. When Kirk or Spock tells Uhura to engage the viewscreen to display an incoming message, she's just tapping that message temporarily into the screen display. The primary purpose of the screen is to picture what is going on outside, in, and around the ship; as such, it is usually controlled by the helm. To put it simply— would you want a ride on a bus in which the driver's view of the road was controlled by someone sitting in the back, facing the rear? No? Well, Starfleet feels the same way about its starships.

"When (in STTMP) Decker meets Ilia in the corridor, why is she off the bridge while she is on duty, and why does she go into her quarters?"

Each crewmember, even those on the bridge, would get a break of several minutes every hour or two, and probably a longer break about the middle of their shift. Call it a coffee break, a go-to-the-can break, lunch, whatever. Ilia was probably headed for her cabin anyway, and dodged in there hurriedly to get away from Decker.

This is a good time to mention a few other puzzles which have cropped up in questions and in conversations with fans over the past few years. Because we see the limited number of crewpersons which a television budget allows for, it is easy for us to stop thinking and to always envision the same people at the same positions on the bridge all the time. But if you do think about it, you realize that these people are just putting in their daily duty shift, and a few hours from now, someone else will be at the helm, communications, etc.

In actuality, a ship the size of the *Enterprise* would have a second officer, probably also with the rank of lieutenant commander, who would run the bridge when neither Kirk nor Spock was on duty. Say, one eight-hour shift to each man. Two or more of them would be on the bridge at the same time only when their shifts overlapped, or in time of emergency. (Kirk and Spock, being the workaholics they are, probably stay on the bridge twelve or fourteen hours a day, causing their shifts to overlap quite a bit, explaining why we see them so often together.)

Regular members of the bridge crew would knock off after their shifts were over—and even if they were inclined to hang around, Kirk probably wouldn't let them. This would be true throughout the ship, which is why well over four hundred souls are required to run a vessel which, we have more than once seen, can run pretty efficiently on a tenth that many personnel.

The reason we so often see the same faces on duty at the beginning of a given adventure is that most of the important duties and nonaggressive action would take place while Kirk was on duty (overlapping with Spock). Kirk would naturally want his best people on hand for such events, which is why Sulu, Uhura, and Chekov are usually at their stations, and Scotty is on duty either on the bridge or down in engineering. (We may assume that Scotty also works long, loving hours, too.)

Leanne Gentry, of Churchville, Maryland, wants to know why Spock could not simply use the mind meld to erase memories of the *Enterprise* from Captain Christopher's mind in "Tomorrow Is Yesterday" as he did for Kirk in "Requiem for Methuselah." Spock knows Kirk very well, and has mind-melded with him on a number of occasions, so he is "familiar" with Kirk's mind, making it easy for him to locate and erase the hurtful memories of Reena. Christopher was a stranger to Spock, which would have made it immensely difficult to enter his mind and perform an erasure of memory. Not only would it be potentially harmful to both Christopher and Spock, it might not have worked completely, leaving Christopher with, at the very least, disturbing half-memories, or, at the very worst, enough full memories to drastically change the future.

Patricia Dunn, of Bradley, California, has a few words to say about the Indians in "Paradise Syndrome:" "Why were [they] living in tepees and wearing buckskins, when none of the tribes they were supposedly descended from had ever inhabited the Great Plains? The Delawares and the Mohicans were Eastern Woodland tribes, and usually dwelt in earth-covered lodges. The Navajos were nomadic sheepherders from the Southwest, whose traditional shelter was the hogan, not the tepee. Personally, I suspect that the Preservers transported a colony of Hollywood Indians, perhaps in order to save the vanishing Western."

No, Pat, that's not right. Had they been Hollywood Indians, they would all have been Italian, Spanish, or Jewish. Seriously, this is one case where history need not be insulted. The Preservers obviously took natives from a number of tribes, from a number of areas across the American continent. This makes sense. Not only would the mixture of cultures prove an interesting experiment, but a wider range of bloodlines would help to ensure the continuing health of the transplanted Indians. Once reconciled to their state, the Indians would have begun to intermarry and either accept or reject customs and life-styles as suitable to their present needs. After a few generations, a new culture would have been firmly in place, and their origins forgotten.

Also, as nothing was said about other tribes or other inhabitants on the planet, the Preservers must have designed a birth-control system of some sort to keep the Indian population at a set level, for they would have had to have been on the planet for at least five hundred years, possibly longer, and there would have been many more of them around had they multiplied at a normal birthrate. Control of birthrate would also have prevented the eventual rise of other, competing tribes, which the Preservers obviously wanted to avoid. Warfare, apparently, was one facet of Indian culture which the Preservers felt did not need to be preserved.

While we're discussing the Preservers, I'll answer a question from K. Johnson, of New York City: Yes, it is possible the Preservers took samples of other human cultures. Perhaps one day the *Enterprise* will encounter thriving examples of cultures which are even now vanishing from the globe: the Bantu, the Eskimo, the Zuni, maybe even the great whales. I certainly hope so.

Back to Pat Dunn, who asks, "If the Romulans and Vulcans are supposed to share a common root, as seen by their racial features and languages—Spock understood the meaning of the female commander's name in 'The *Enterprise* Incident' —then why was one of the officers on the Romulan ship in 'Balance of Terror' named Decius, which has a Latin ring to it, and would apparently be of Earth origin?"

It's a well-known fact that Romulan culture and Earth Roman culture share many facets. This is a fine example of how humanoid cultures develop in similar fashion. It is entirely possible that the Romulan's name was Decius, although it is less likely that it meant the same thing as the Roman translation. More likely, however, is that the universal translator built into the *Enterprise* viewscreen took the closest equivalent of the Romulan's name—which, like Decius, apparently had something to do with "ten"—and translated it into a Roman-sounding name. This would be why Romulan military terms would translate as "commander," "officer," etc., and the even more Roman-sounding "centurion."

Nancy Stoll, of Santa Cruz, California, says, "Has Spock been promoted to admiral or merely captain? Both he and Kirk have white shirts. Also, why, when the *Enterprise* had just been refitted for Decker's command in *Star Trek: The Motion Picture*, was it to be used as a training ground in *Wrath of Khan*? Why do you suppose being killed by a phaser beam is now painful? Do you suppose it was just too tempting to commit murder when it was so sterile? Fourth and final: Do you care to speculate on the circumstances and/or method of Spock's resurrection?"

To answer the fourth first, *no*! I have a feeling I'm going to be busy enough offering solutions to mysteries about *The Search for Spock* without putting myself out on any limbs this early. To Nancy's other questions: (1) All command-grade officers wear white shirts. (2) The *Enterprise* had been refitted, true, but that was something on the order of ten or twelve years earlier, Star Trek time. Ships of the *Enterprise*'s class are obviously being supplanted by those of the *Reliant*'s class, yet even though the *Enterprise* is no longer a state-of-the-art ship, she is still a valuable vessel for both training and active duty. (3) I always thought that being dematerialized by *anything* would be painful. I think you're referring to the mournful cry which Captain Terrell gave when he committed suicide rather than kill Kirk. I suspect that was more a cry of rage and anger than a cry of pain, and consequently more touching. Murderers will use anything they can get their hands on; they usually couldn't care less how painless and sterile is the death of their victim.

From Leah "Trekkie" Horton, of Lamesa, Texas, comes the question: "What does the NCC in the *Enterprise* registration number stand for?"

Now I'm embarrassed. I know that the NCC prefix was one used on airplanes a few years back, and was chosen for the *Enterprise* by pilot Gene Roddenberry, but I don't know, and can't discover what if anything the letters are an acronym for. If any of you readers can help me with this, I'd appreciate it very much, for now Leah's question is bugging me!

Leah also wants to know: "Is there, anywhere, a document, list, writing, or compiling of any kind of Starfleet Rules and Regulations, and if not, would you or someone else on the staff kindly compile one?"

*The Star Fleet Technical Manual* compiled by Franz Joseph has a section dealing with "Articles of Federation," but not specific Starfleet Rules. The *Tech Manual* is long out of print, and I understand it commands healthy prices on the back-issue market. If anyone out there knows of such a list of rules and regulations, please let us know about it, even send a copy if possible, for it would sure come in handy for solving mysteries!

Now once again comes the nagging question of Spock's name. Pam Ward is joined by Sharon Moody, of Matthews,

North Carolina, in pointing out that Spock tells Leila Kalomi (in "This Side of Paradise") that she couldn't pronounce his *first* name, while in "Journey to Babel." Spock's mother, Amanda, tells Kirk that he couldn't pronounce her *last* name.

I'll have to admit I don't know what's going on with those crazy Vulcans. Is "Spock" Spock's first name or his last name? If it is his first name, why did he tell Leila she couldn't pronounce it? If it is his last name, why did Amanda think Jim couldn't pronounce "Spock"? All fun aside, this is something which bothers readers, for it has been mentioned before in letters to us. (Notice the sneaky way it becomes "us" when I'm stumped for an answer, and "I" when I've got it right off?)

You've noticed by now that I'm stalling. The only explanation I can offer for this mystery is that "Spock," "Sarek," and other such Vulcan names are what we humans would refer to as "middle" names. The situation is different on Vulcan, of course, where the first and last names symbolize family antecedents and perhaps place of origin, and are probably sentence-long (and therefore while not completely unpronounceable for a human, it would be boring and difficult for a Vulcan to hear his own name being mangled in a dozen different ways by one speaker). So let's say, for instance, that Spock's real name is something like, "He who is of our family and the eldest son of Sarek, Spock, holding the property of his fathers at the place of hidden fires." Sounds kinda romantic, doesn't it?

Herb Swartz, of Granby, Missouri, wonders why, if Sulu has been promoted and will soon take command of his own ship, he wears the insignia of a commander throughout *Wrath of Khan*.

Sulu's well-deserved promotion was never mentioned in the movie, as we all know, but it is understood to be a fact. So the only question remaining is why he did wear commander's insignia when it seemed he was entitled to wear that of a captain. After all, Kirk himself called him "Captain Sulu."

Sulu hadn't yet taken command of the *Excelsior*, and so wasn't wearing captain's braid for one of two reasons: One, his promotion might not have yet been official; or, two, it may be against Starfleet regulations for anyone but the captain of a particular vessel to wear the insignia of a captain while serving duty on that vessel. (Kirk, you'll remember, wasn't on duty, he was just along for the ride.) Anyway, I'm sure that Sulu felt more comfortable wearing his commander's insignia for his one last time at the helm of the *Enterprise*.

Herb also points out, "In the movie and novel, Khan states, 'You see here all that remains of the crew of my ship *Botany Bay*, indeed all that remains of the ship itself, marooned here fifteen years ago by Captain James T. Kirk.' Yet, at the end of 'Space Seed,' Spock asks, 'What shall I do with the *Botany Bay*?' Kirk replies, 'You'd better dump it into—no, on second thought, let's keep it in tow. I suppose there are still things aboard that the historians will want to see.' "

What Khan was referring to on the surface of the planet was the gear and supplies which had been taken from the *Botany Bay* to supply his company. It was, for them, all that remained of the ship itself. Even though now just a ragtag collection of *Enterprise* cargo containers and fittings (intended to be quite temporary), it was still probably referred to by Khan and his people as "the ship"—perhaps even as *Botany Bay*—as a constant reminder of their marooned status.

Finally, before we get to the promised section wherein I'm going to let some readers have a crack at solving Star Trek mysteries, we'll have a look at a number of questions submitted by Ida Wheeler, from right here in Houston, Texas. Amazingly, Ida's letter consisted of questions which were echoed in about two dozen others, which means that Ida must really be in tune with other fans.

Ida leads off by wanting to know why in *Wrath of Khan*, Klingon ships were present in the Neutral Zone. As did many others, Ida points out that it was established in the series that Romulans were using Klingon ships, but this does not explain the mystery. The ships are clearly identified as being *Klingon*. The most likely explanation is that in the ensuing years between the series and *Wrath of Khan*, a Neutral Zone had been set up between the Federation and the Klingon Empire. If you want to be more obscure and dig a little deeper into the psyche of Starfleet Command, it could be assumed that the unexpected appearance of Klingon vessels in the *Romulan* Neutral Zone during the *Kobayashi Maru* test was intentionally planned to confuse and disorient the testee. Or perhaps it's just that Starfleet considers the Klingons to be the greatest threat, and so Klingon vessels and tactics are used in every battle simulation.

Also like many, many others, Ida was confused by the fact that Kirk and Spock called Saavik "Mr." She points out that Uhura was never called "Mr. Uhura," so why Saavik?

The use of "Mr." to refer to an officer is an old naval tradition. (Ever wonder why the play was called *Mister Roberts* and not *Lieutenant Roberts*?) It is, however, just a tradition, and it's possible that Uhura simply requested that she not be called "Mr.," preferring "Lieutenant" or, more informally, "Miss." That tough little cookie Saavik, on the other hand, certainly could not object to "Lieutenant" but I bet nobody (except maybe charming old McCoy) could get away with calling her "Miss."

Next, Ida brings up the question of Sulu's first name. In Vonda McIntyre's excellent novels, she gave us the fine name of Hikaru for Sulu, but other sources, including reportedly George Takei himself, have confirmed that Sulu's first name is Walter. Most folks seem to have settled on Hikaru Walter Sulu, so that's the way it'll be around here from now on. (Interruptus: And Uhura's first name is inarguably Penda. No compromises there.)

But what puzzles Ida about Sulu in *Wrath of Khan* is this: "Where in the galaxy did [he] get the Southern accent?" That's not a Southern accent, Ida, but good old George Hikaru Walter Sulu Takei's own casual way of talkin'.

Ida then asks, "If the *Reliant*'s sensors could pick up preanimate life on Ceti Alpha V or IV, why oh why couldn't they pick up Khan and his people?"

The sensors on the *Reliant* probably suffer from the same complaint as an increasingly large part of our own electronics fields—they're too doggone specialized. When told to seek microscopic life forms on the planet, that's exactly what they did—to the exclusion of anything else. Terrell and his people can't be blamed . . . they thought they were inspecting a completely lifeless planet, one where it was not necessary to run even the most casual check for larger life forms.

Ida wants to know why the turbolifts on the *Enterprise*

suddenly require the pushing of buttons to start, stop, etc. Apparently, the voice-operated and automatically opening lifts of the past were scrapped in favor of more old-fashioned but probably more reliable button-operated ones. A turbolift which is always down for repairs isn't very efficient, is it? And after all, Starfleet personnel are big, healthy folks who can probably push buttons all day long and not get tired, and it takes only a fraction of a second longer to push than it does to say "Bridge" or whatnot.

Ida asks, "How could anyone, even Admiral Kirk, enter Spock's meditation room without asking permission?"

The answer is implicit in the question: No one but Admiral Kirk *could* have. There are no secrets and no barriers between Kirk and Spock by this time, especially in times of emergency. And after all, Kirk didn't come barging in, he entered quietly and respectfully, as a friend.

Ida's final question concerns the new planet which was formed by the Genesis Effect. "Where did that planet come from? I never saw anything [in the Mutara Nebula] large enough to become the planet."

Several people have asked about this, and I believe the confusion stems from the "presentation tape" which Kirk views earlier in the film. There, we see what appears to be a lifeless moon transformed into a beautiful planet, fully capable of supporting life. What must be remembered, however, is that the moon was only transformed, not created whole. The Genesis Effect which took place in the Mutara Nebula actually created an entirely new planet (and a small sun to shine on it) from the dust and gases of the nebula itself. The Mutara Nebula contained enough mass, albeit in particle form, to construct the planet, so no planet-sized chunk of mass was necessary. This planet formed from what seemed to be nothingness was, of course, what so amazed and enthralled the *Enterprise* crew even in the midst of their grief. Changing the surface of a planet is wonder enough—*creating* one fulfills the promise of the word "Genesis."

The next letter is from Jennifer Weston, whom you will remember as the author of "Of Spock, Genes, and DNA Recombination" from *Best of Trek #5*. Jennifer offers two mysteries and a partial solution for each, asking me to comment on her conclusions. Which is as good a way as any to ease into the promised section wherein readers offer their own solutions to Star Trek mysteries.

Jennifer writes, "In 'Court Martial,' it was established that Captain Kirk had served as an ensign aboard the starship *Republic*, along with Ben Finney. Then, in 'Obsession,' he stated that his first deep-space assignment had been as a lieutenant aboard the USS *Farragut*. Does this mean some by-the-book bureaucrat demoted Kirk in the aftermath of the *Farragut* disaster? Even if that unjustifiable break in rank was repaired shortly after Jim's falling-out with Finney, the remembered stigma may help explain Kirk's uncharacteristic damn-the-risks (to the ship as well as himself) drive to redeem himself in 'Obsession.' And also Kirk's oft-expressed contempt for 'chair-bound paper pusher.' "

That sounds like a good theory, and would surely explain Kirk's obsession about and disdain for headquarters personnel, but is not likely. Kirk definitely wasn't busted in rank, for if he had been held responsible enough for the disaster to be demoted, surely he wouldn't have been able to overcome the stigma and rise to command of a starship. Memories are long and unforgiving in any service. Kirk's obsession with the cloud creature grew from his inner need to negate failure, and a desire to revenge the crew of the *Farragut* and Captain Garrovick, who had been a friend and a father figure to Kirk.

The official solution to this mystery can be found in the phrasing: Kirk says that his first "deep space" assignment was on the *Farragut*; therefore the incident involving Finney on the *Republic* had to have taken place on a training cruise, or a similar mission which Kirk did not consider being into really "deep space."

Jennifer then asks, "How did such a doubly formidable creature as Vulcan's *le-matya* ever evolve? A large, fast, powerful animal should have no need to develop a potent venom-injection apparatus, and conversely, an animal with potent venom shouldn't have any need to become large and strong. Even if this convergence of predatory traits is written off as an 'evolutionary fluke' (this phrase being merely a diplomatic way of indicating that the evolutionary origin is unknown), it leaves a more important question unanswered.

Why didn't the appearance of such an invincible beast (capable of killing a *sehlat*-sized animal with one scratch, and superbly equipped to administer that scratch) create a cataclysmic imbalance in the predator-prey populations?

"The answer to the latter question must be that some environmental factors keep the *le-matya* population so firmly limited that they never become numerous enough to be overly effective predators. Perhaps some species-specific disease, or parasite, kills most of the offspring before maturity. Or maybe they're their own worst enemies, staking out very large hunting territories and routinely killing off any trespassers of their own species. (In fact, that's probably the only way any large carnivore could get enough food to survive on a desert world.) But none of this explains why the species originally became deadly enough to require such severe checks on its population potential. Any theories, Leslie?"

I wholeheartedly agree with your assumptions about why the *le-matya* population remains small—why it would develop as it did is another question. Perhaps its prey was equally large and powerful; the only edge it would then have was the venom. If *sehlats* were your diet, you'd want a quick and effective way of killing them, right?

Next comes Chris Rassmussen, who offers solutions to several mysteries:

"In *Star Trek: The Motion Picture*, it is stated that Admiral Kirk has been Chief of Starfleet Operations for two and one-half years, but the *Enterprise* has only been in the redesigning and refitting stage for eighteen months. Why?

"Answer: The original *Enterprise* which Captain Kirk and crew brought back from the five-year mission had to be almost completely disassembled before the refitting could begin. Also, much of the equipment was still being tested before finally being put into service. All of the crew members had to learn how to operate the sophisticated new equipment while it was being installed onboard the *Enterprise*.

"In *Star Trek: The Motion Picture*, why do Spock's eyes squint in the bright sunlight of Vulcan when he should be used to it?

"Answer: Vulcans have an inner eyelid, which as mentioned in the episode 'Operation: Annihilate' saved Spock from permanent blindness when McCoy tried to rid him of the parasite with extremely bright light. But the experience, added to the fact that he is only half Vulcan, left Spock very sensitive to bright light, such as that on Vulcan. However, this condition did not develop immediately, or we would have seen evidence of it in "Amok Time" when Spock visited Vulcan.

"In *Wrath of Khan*, why didn't Spock's 'coffin' disintegrate during its entry into the atmosphere of the newly formed planet?

"Answer: The planet was in the early stages of development and the atmosphere was not entirely present when Spock entered it, so it did not cause as much friction against his tube as the fully formed atmosphere of a normal planet would.

"In 'Mudd's Women,' after pursuing Mudd's ship through the asteroid field, why must the *Enterprise* go to Rigel XII to get lithium crystals? Shouldn't they have some extra crystals in storage aboard the ship for emergency situations?

"Answer: Lithium/dilithium crystals are very unstable and must be stored in electromagnetic stasis fields to keep the particles of matter/antimatter separate so as not to cause an explosion. When five of the six crystals in the assembly are strained past the point of recovery, the stasis field does not fail completely, which would cause the destruction of the ship, but it makes the extra crystals deteriorate rapidly (as they did in "Alternative Factor" and "Elaan of Troyius"). This does not happen often, since most of the crystals in the converter assembly do not fail unless a tremendous amount of strain is put on them. Currently, there is no other way to store dilithium crystals.

"Why is there a dilithium cracking station on the Tantalus V penal colony in 'Dagger of the Mind'?

"Answer: Tantalus V was established many years before sensors were widely used. At the time the penal colony was built, they had no idea that the planet was a rich source of dilithium crystals, even though they had been used in starships for years. It was not until a drastic shortage of crystals developed that many planets within the Federation were thoroughly investigated. After discovering the abundance of crystals under the surface of Tantalus, a crystal mining and cracking station was constructed. The station, operated by inmates under the close scrutiny of therapists, helped to pay the enormous cost of running the penal colony.

"In 'Devil in the Dark,' when the *Enterprise* crew discovered hand phasers wouldn't stop the Horta, why didn't they use the more powerful phaser rifle to hunt it?

"Answer: The phaser rifle seen in 'Where No Man Has Gone Before' was recalled by Starfleet Command because of major design flaws. After reevaluation, Starfleet decided that only members of the Starfleet Marines and other similar task forces needed so much hand-held firepower."

Nicholas C. M. Armstrong, of Toronto, Ontario, Canada, sent quite an informative letter commenting on past mysteries, which I will reproduce below almost in full:

"To start off, concerning the direct phaser hookup seen in the ship after 'Balance of Terror,' it is unlikely that Kirk and Scott would have initiated the work themselves. It is more likely that they would have submitted the idea to Starfleet for approval. Starfleet would then have had all the starships docked and rewired (if wire is not obsolete by this time). However, try answering this: Why did it take until the twenty-third century to think of a direct hookup, from bridge to banks, when it is quite apparent that any other arrangement would be disastrous to the fighting efficiency of the ship?

"In regards to future Earth, since many of the crew have accents, this would suggest that most old languages still exist. Would this not suggest too that countries also still exist, perhaps in some cultural form? However, a nuclear war as the reason for a unified Earth should be questioned, due to the fact that the *Enterprise* actually went back in time to the 1960s to discover how man *avoided* a nuclear war in 'Assignment: Earth.'

"You suggest that Number One taped her voice into the ship's computer. However, by the twenty-third century, I would think that the computer voice would be synthesized. She may have submitted a voice sample for the synthesized voice of the computer, but most navies have always had a tendency to standardize all components of their ships. Thus we should assume that it is only a coincidence.

"Concerning whether the primary and secondary hulls can

separate, Gene Roddenberry has stated as much. I also agree that it probably would be a permanent separation (by small explosive charges or some such device), and it would require a dockyard to rejoin the two hulls. The warp nacelles, however, would in all probability also be separable, for to lose the entire secondary hull would be an expensive proposition indeed. Remember, engineering is located down there.

"You mentioned that in both 'The Menagerie' and 'Where No Man Has Gone Before,' both Pike and Kirk had only two rank stripes. Rather than suggest that Starfleet changed the ranking system (the Royal Navy and the United States Navy haven't done so for over eighty years), I suggest that it is more likely that they were both of the rank of commander at the time. All ranks from lieutenant to admiral have been known to officially command ships. They are referred to as 'captain' because that is their appointment—captain of the ship. Later on, Kirk attained the *rank* of captain, which is something else again. In *Star Trek: The Motion Picture*, Kirk became an admiral, but was the *captain* of the *Enterprise* at the time, and was thus called captain.

"Time paradoxes are always fun. The reason that Kirk was there to perpetuate Edith Keeler's death in 'City on the Edge of Forever' was that this event was a part of history. Even before McCoy or Kirk had seen the planet of the Guardian of Forever, Kirk had watched Edith die in the 1930s, three hundred years before. I justify this explanation by referring to a statement Spock made in 'Assignment: Earth': After a renegade ballistic missile had just been prevented by the *Enterprise* from exploding over the U.S.S.R., Spock said there was a record in the memory banks of such an event on that date (in the 1960s).

"The reason that so many names appear to be used for Starfleet Command is most likely that there are many different names for SFC. An organization like Starfleet could not survive if it were bureaucraticized to the extent you suggest. It would need a strong, *central* command.

"Concerning the aging of Spock, it is unlikely that he would age as anything other than a full Vulcan. For a being such as Spock to exist, he must have been produced artificially using his parents' genes, since they are not only of different species, but of entirely different planetary origin. Unassisted fertilization would be impossible. Obviously, his genes have been selected for life on Vulcan. In any case, evidence in 'The Deadly Years' states that he, as a half Vulcan, would live much longer than a human. Perhaps his genetic makeup accounted for his early maturity, thus the apparent difference in age between him and T'Pring. Or maybe Vulcan males naturally mature faster?

"This next topic is the subject I really had in mind when I began this letter. It concerns the former first officer of the *Enterprise*, Number One. No offense taken, I hope, but I found all the complex explanations concerning her apparently odd name and 'cold' nature quite amusing.

I myself am involved with the military and can offer the solution, which is quite simple to those who are familiar with naval matters. In Commonwealth navies, the first officer of a ship is commonly called 'number one' by his/her captain and fellow officers. (Look for the old 1950s version of Nicholas Monsarrat's *The Cruel Sea*. The term is used often in this film.) Obviously this old nickname for the first officer has not died out by the twenty-third century.

"Regarding her cold nature, I cannot understand why you feel this is so. To me, she merely appears competent, and perhaps a little career-conscious. In any case, we never saw her off the job, did we? She was probably quite different then. Thus, Christine Chapel's name is just that, and her 'estranged' sister's name (if they are indeed sisters) is unknown simply because no one bothered to use it during the mission. The two are not necessarily estranged, either. Maybe it (the fact they are sisters) is such common knowledge aboard the *Enterprise* that nobody bothered to mention it. Perhaps her sister even arranged a place on the *Enterprise* for Christine?

"In 'Journey to Babel,' I believe it was stated, or at least implied, that Spock was an only child, so siblings can be ruled out. How about human cousins, then?

"Onboard ship, junior officers are often placed in 'command' —*irrespective* of their section—they are all spacegoing officers and must be able to take command if all other senior officers are killed. They must also share the watchkeeping duties with the senior officers. However, they would never be placed in command over more senior officers during emergency conditions for 'training purposes,' as the safety of the ship is the highest priority at such a time. DeSalle would never have been put in command in an emergency, as you suggested.

"Regarding the use of a weapons control station in *Star Trek: The Motion Picture* for efficiency, I would like to point out that the entire ship is inefficient in terms of manpower. The whole of the vessel could be run by a half-dozen men, if it were so modified. In *The Making of Star Trek*, the large crew was explained in terms of the fact that this helps them exist closed away in the ship for the long periods of time necessary. The *Enterprise* is not only a ship, but a community. The people that make her run not only work within her, but live within her as well.

"I shall finish with two questions: First, why, in 'Where No Man Has Gone Before,' was the edge of the galaxy shown to have an actual, physical barrier, and why was it two-dimensional rather than three-dimensional like the rest of the galaxy (i.e., why no top or bottom?)? It appeared as a solid band of light which the *Enterprise* could maneuver above or below.

"The other question is this: How is it that the *Enterprise*'s arrowhead uniform emblem has now become standard throughout the fleet, when before all ships had their own identifying badges? (The command emblem, too, has also become standard, with its central star, whereas before Engineering had a stylized nut and Science a sphere.) Please do not say that this is because the Federation recognizes the *Enterprise* as such a worthy ship she ought to be honored in this manner. Don't laugh—its been suggested to me more times than I like to remember."

To drop back a bit to your question about the phaser hookups, I don't find it the least bit unbelievable that it would take any organization with a built-in bureaucracy over two hundred years to make any commonsense decision.

I see the barrier at the edge of the galaxy as being composed of many kinds of energy, only a few of which are visible, and only then in the form of a band which seems to be in front of the ship whichever way the ship is facing. In other words, an optical illusion. Surely if it were possible to go above or below the barrier, the *Enterprise* would have done so, and twice avoided great danger.

You yourself mention the military's mania for standardization when discussing the computer voice, so why should it surprise you that insignia were standardized? I don't think the *Enterprise* emblem was chosen for any special reason; perhaps it was thought to be the most attractive or meaningful; perhaps it was always the standard Starfleet emblem (or a close variation thereof), and it was other ships' emblems which were unusual. I'd agree that with elimination of the uniform color scheme which differentiated ships' services, varying designs on the emblems would be seemingly even more necessary, but apparently Starfleet didn't think so. Perhaps they felt that in a closed community such as a starship or starbase, everyone would at least recognize everyone else and know where he belonged, so identification via emblem was superfluous.

In closing, I'm going to take a whack at the mystery which, to judge by my mail, you readers consider to be the most vexing of all: Just how, in *Wrath of Khan*, Khan recognized Chekov, when we all know that the Russian didn't show up onboard the *Enterprise* until the season following 'Space Seed.'

Bill Mason opines that Chekov wasn't seen during all of the first season because he was suffering from a spacegoing form of "Montezuma's Revenge" and spent most of his time in the, ahem, head. Having been kept impatiently waiting by the ensign, Khan warned as he dashed inside, "I shall never forget you." Yeah.

All foolin' aside, I'll give you a few thoughts from Margaret Dickson, of Pueblo, Colorado, whom I think has come closest to what I believe is the solution of this mystery.

Margaret deduces that we *must* accept the fact that Khan actually saw Chekov. Because it is difficult to believe that he served on the ship for an entire year without us seeing him (and because we are a number of times led to believe that he has just reported aboard the *Enterprise* at the beginning of the second season), the only other explanation is that Khan saw

Chekov on Ceti Alpha V. The trouble with this is: when? Margaret suggests that Pavel may have been part of an expedition sent by Starfleet to check up on Khan and his folks. This would seem to be disputed by Khan's claim that Kirk "never" bothered to check up on them. Margaret abandons this, and ruefully returns to the premise that Chekov was actually on the *Enterprise* during "Space Seed."

I can't buy it. Sure, we know there were dozens of junior officers and trainees we never even got a glimpse of, but we also know that Kirk has a special fondness for young Chekov, so he'd have been at least visible for that entire year had he truly been around. I have to theorize, then, that Chekov was part of a small, previously unmentioned force which met the *Enterprise* at Ceti Alpha V when Khan and his folks were marooned. (Perhaps it was a medical team; perhaps they wanted to get as much cultural information as possible; perhaps a fleet officer came to inspect the situation and second Kirk's judgment that Khan and his people were too dangerous to be allowed to roam freely around the universe.) In any case, Chekov certainly had some personal contact with Khan; and it proved chilling enough so that over fifteen years later, he was openly frightened by the very thought of Khan's being near. It could have been during this mission that Kirk first noticed Chekov, and seeing much in the ensign that reminded him of young Jim Kirk, he decided to have the Russian assigned to the *Enterprise* as soon as possible.

Not a very neat explanation, I am afraid, but one which I like and I think we can live with.

That's about all for this issue, friends. I will be looking forward to reading your comments about this Mystery article (and earlier ones). And, as always, I urge you to send in your favorite Star Trek mystery. I'll do my best to solve it for you. Thanks again so very much, and my love to you all. See ya next time!

# THE TREK "FAN ON THE STREET" POLL

Several years ago we ran a filler page which was a simple series of questions about our readers' major likes, dislikes, and attitudes about Star Trek. We expected enough of a response to this poll to fill another page or two, providing our readers with some insight into how their peers felt about the same things. Were we surprised when literally hundreds of responses to our poll began pouring in! We were forced to devote a full-length article to the results of the poll (Best of Trek #1), and it itself drew almost as much mail as did the poll.

Several years have passed since then, and readers have continually asked if we were ever going to take another poll. Well, we already did. Earlier this year, we pulled out the list of questions from the first poll, added a few new ones, and set out with clipboards and tape recorders to talk to the general public about Star Trek. We talked to people in shopping malls, theaters, schools, etc., and our only criterion was that they know a little something more about Star Trek than just "a TV show" and "pointed ears." We were not surprised at the number of people who did have a fairly intimate knowledge of the show, along with (naturally) strong opinions about it, for it's long been our contention that the Star Trek characters are about to enter (if they haven't already) that shadowy realm of folk heroes. In any case, here's what the average person thinks about Star Trek. And if you think you know what's coming, well, think again. . . .

The questions in this poll were asked of people halted at random and asked: "Are you familiar with Star Trek?" "Do you like it very much?" "Can you remember any of the shows?" If an affirmative answer was given to these questions, then the subject was led into the poll questions. Each question was stated in a conversational manner, and while every effort was made to keep answers specific, it was not always possible to do so. The results of this poll, then, are quite unscientific, but damned revealing and a lot of fun.

All of the responses are given in percentages, with the exception of the most-liked and most-disliked shows, which were given weighted point values . . . again, unscientifically. If the subject gave several responses, they were put in order of like or dislike; if only one was given, the fervor of the like or dislike was considered. Also, as most of the general public does not know and would not recognize the titles of the episodes, we always accepted a brief, but fairly accurate, description of the episode instead. For instance, if someone said that he really loved the show "where Mr. Spock's parents came on the ship and Spock and his dad argued," we put "Journey to Babel" as his response. However, when the subject obviously was confused, we overlooked his response. For example, if that same person had said, "I really liked that show where Spock went home to get married and saw his father and mother," we put no response at all. As the average viewer remembered only a few episodes with any clarity at all, whether liking or disliking them, the listing of ten "favorite" and "most disliked" episodes are listed in the order in which they were the most mentioned.

A bit dissimilarly, because all of the characters on the series are so familiar to viewers, we accepted such responses as "the engineer" or "the black communications lady" or "the guy with the pills that made women beautiful" for questions asking about favorites. We feel that to have insisted upon proper names would have defeated the spirit of the poll, for, again, the average person is not nearly as involved or interested in Star Trek as we are.

Several questions were discarded from the poll. They were judged as being either too esoteric for the average person (for instance, "Who is your favorite Star Trek writer?") or else no longer valid or of interest (such as "Do you think that Arex and M'Ress should be included in the Star Trek movie?")

We also decided to have a little fun and start the poll off with a rather unusual question:

## 1. What do you think of immediately when you hear the words "Star Trek"?

Overwhelmingly (87%), the respondents answered, "Mr. Spock." Captain Kirk accounted for a minuscule 3%, and the remaining 10% was broken up among such responses as "the Starship *Enterprise*," "space travel," "Khan," "pointed ears" (which was not accepted as Spock), and "the future."

## 2. Name your favorite episodes in the order of your preference.

1. "Space Seed"
2. "City on the Edge of Forever"
3. "Journey to Babel"
4. "Arena"
5. "Mirror, Mirror"
6. "Charlie X"
7. "Balance of Terror"
8. "Shore Leave"
9. "The Menagerie"
10. "Amok Time"

We found this result very interesting. Seven of the episodes which made this "top ten" were in our readers' poll ten favorites, and the remaining three are all excellent episodes. This should not be surprising, for excellent shows should be, and often are, viewers' favorites. The fact that "Space Seed" tops the list is also not surprising, for it may be assumed that many viewers' memories of it were refreshed by *Star Trek II: The Wrath of Khan*, and most of those who named "Space Seed" their favorite admitted they'd watched it again since the movie premiered.

What makes this list so notable (and somewhat different from our readers' poll list) is that each episode named is a particularly memorable one: One has a Gorn; Spock dies in one; Spock's parents appear in one; a boy with superpowers is in one; etc. We feel that it is these striking images, as much as the quality of the episodes themselves, which have made them fondly remembered favorites of the average viewer.

### 3. Who is your favorite Star Trek character?

Sorry, Spock fans, but Captain Kirk won this one overwhelmingly with a whopping 73% of the vote. Spock did, however, finish second with 20% of the vote, leaving a scant 6% for Dr. McCoy, and a vote of 1% for Uhura, the only other crewmember mentioned.

Why this result would be so lopsided is a mystery to us. Perhaps the average viewer, who is not as involved with the mythos and inner workings of the show as is the dedicated fan, finds it harder to relate to the Vulcan. It could also be simple chauvinism, a reluctance on the part of people to express a preference for an ''alien.'' Upon reflection, however, we feel that it boils down to the simple fact that the average viewer does, and wants to, identify more with Kirk than with any other member of the crew. Kirk is a hero in the classic mold, a spiritual and dramatic descendant from years of hard-jawed, fast-talking film and TV heroes—private eyes, soldiers, adventurers, and so on. Add to this the fact that William Shatner is by far the most recognizable and prolific of all the Star Trek actors, and the result seems almost inevitable.

Spock had his followers, as always, and they were indeed vehement: ''Star Trek would be just another show without Mr. Spock'' was a typical comment. Just as supportive were those who chose Dr. McCoy as their favorite. Not only were we treated to cherished snippets of McCoy dialogue from several of his supporters, his was the only instance in which *everyone* who picked him remembered his name and at least one episode in which the good doctor had a pivotal role.

### 4. Which actor is your favorite? Which do you think contributed the most to the show?

William Shatner won the first half of this question by a margin only slightly smaller than that by which his characterization of Kirk won ''favorite character,'' 65%. Leonard

Nimoy finished with 30%, and DeForest Kelley got the remaining 5%. Again, the familiarity of Shatner and the popularity of Kirk probably accounts for the large lead.

More interesting, however, was the response to which actor contributed the most. Here the results were more even between the two leads: 51% for Shatner and 47% for Nimoy, with 2% for Kelley. Apparently, even many of those who prefer Shatner as an actor appreciate the contributions of Nimoy's Spock to the success and popularity of the series. This is due, we feel, primarily to the immense amount of media coverage which the Spock character and Nimoy have received (you'll remember the overwhelming response to our first question), causing the average viewer to appreciate a little more the difficulty of creating and maintaining such a character.

## 5. Which villain from Star Trek do you remember best?

As would be expected from the first-place finish of "Space Seed" in the "favorite episode" category, Khan Noonian Singh finished well beyond any of the other villains. What surprised us the most, however, was the sheer number of villains recalled fondly by the respondents to our poll. We expected, at most, four or five, including Khan and Harry Mudd, but the eventual number was sixteen. (This would have been seventeen, but several people named *T'Pring* as their best-remembered villian, and we just can't bring ourselves to put her in such company. T'Pring was misguided, yes, but hardly evil.)

Harry Mudd, as one would expect, finished second with 18% of the vote, followed by the Gorn captain with 3% and 1% (or less) each for Charlie X, the Mugato, the Tholians, the Ultimate Computer, Trelane of Gothos, the Horta, Kor and/or Kang, the Talosians, Gary Mitchell, the Salt Creature, Janice Lester, and both the male and female Romulan commanders.

## 6. Which male guest star do you remember best?

Again, Khan came most to mind, and almost every respondent mentioned Ricardo Montalban by name. So overwhelming was the response for Montalban, in fact, that just about every respondent was asked to name a second guest. It is these which are listed below, with the understanding that the majority of them were second choices to Montalban.

William Campbell was mentioned by most of those polled for his portrayal of Trelane. He got a substantial 31%. Second was Mark Lenard, with 21%, mentioned for both his roles, the Romulan commander and Spock's father. (It is interesting to note that many of those polled did not realize that Lenard played both parts.) Third in the balloting was Roger C. Carmel with 13%; it seems that although his portrayal of Harry Mudd was loved and remembered by quite a few respondents, he himself was not as popular. Finishing with 8% was Jeffrey Hunter, a number substantially higher than his finish on our strictly fan poll. The remaining 23% was divided among a long list of male guest stars, including David Soul, Robert Lansing, William Windom, John Colicos, Gary Lockwood, and Robert Walker, Jr. Weirdly, we found that a number of respondents had somehow gotten the impression that Henry Winkler had guest-starred in a Star Trek episode, and that many firmly believed that the fellow in the Gorn suit was a very young Tom Selleck. How in the world do these rumors get started?

## 7. Which female guest star do you remember best?

As she did in our fan poll, Joan Collins led the pack by a wide margin. We feel that this is due not only to Miss Collins's fine performance in "City on the Edge of Forever," but also to her current scintillating appearances as the evil Alexis in *Dynasty* (not to mention her even more scintillating appearances in *Playboy*—part of this poll was taken in the month that Joan's photo layout appeared in that magazine). Miss Collins garnered a hefty 58% of the vote, and no one else was even close.

What is most interesting about Miss Collins's votes is that the percentage of those who voted for her as "the woman who played Edith Keeler" or "the woman that Kirk fell in love with back in time," etc. came out to just about 20% of the total . . . which is uncannily close to the 21% which Miss Collins got as favorite guest actress in our fan poll.

Finishing second with 23% of the vote was Mariette Hartley, who has also become considerably more well known since her appearance on Star Trek, thanks to the popular series of ads for Polaroid cameras she did with James Garner. Third-place finisher, with 11%, was Arlene Martel, memorable for her role as T'Pring. Sharing almost equally the remaining percentages were Teri Garr, Susan Oliver, Joanne Linville, and Madlyn Rhue, who didn't receive any votes in our fan poll, but apparently rode in on Khan's coattails in this one. One somewhat startling result was that the lovely Jane Wyatt did not receive even one vote for her performance as Spock's mother, Amanda. In our fan poll, she finished second.

## 8. What do you think was the most believable piece of equipment aboard the *Enterprise*?

The overwhelming favorite, 57%, was the phaser. Most respondents pointed out the phaser's similarity to a laser beam (or simply believed they were the same thing), and noted that we have laser beams now, which are doing more and more things every day. Several respondents actually have had laser surgery performed upon them; many others have had skills or services performed for them by lasers, and realize that the devices are coming into everyday use in many fields.

The shipboard computer was also a favorite choice, getting 22% of the total. We had suspected, with the recent rise in popularity of the personal home computer, that more respondents would choose this device, but perhaps computers have become a little *too* familiar.

The communicator, which tied for first place in our fan poll, perhaps also now seems rather a commonplace device, and this time around it got only 6% of the vote. Tying for that 6% was the warp drive; quite a few respondents also mentioned it as their second choice. Apparently the average viewer fully expects science to someday break the light barrier. Finishing with only a minuscule 2% was the transporter . . . . apparently the average person is not as convinced of the feasibility of matter transport as he is of the warp drive or other Star Trek devices. Also mentioned were the shuttlecraft and the various sick-bay devices.

**9. Which kind of Star Trek episodes do you like best, those which are primarily action or those which lean more toward ideas?**

Surprisingly enough, "idea" shows finished way ahead, with 61% of the vote. Many of those who expressed a preference for such shows said that they were "tired of chases and cops" and found many such shows boring, making a Star Trek "think" episode a refreshing change. Even those who picked action shows as their favorites said they liked the fact that Star Trek "always had something in it to make you think."

**10. Name your least favorite episodes in the order that you dislike them.**

1. "Spectre of the Gun"
2. "For the World Is Hollow and I Have Touched the Sky"
3. "The Way to Eden"
4. "And the Children Shall Lead"
5. "The Cloud Minders"

A couple of surprises here. "For the World Is Hollow" certainly would not appear on a fan "worst episodes" list; especially not on that of a McCoy fan. And "The Cloud Minders," while not generally acknowledged to be among the best episodes, is certainly not considered by fans to be one of the worst, either.

The terms used most often to describe those episodes chosen were "silly," "boring," and "unbelievable." Only the top five vote-getters are mentioned above, but the range of least-liked shows was much greater than that of most-liked shows. Apparently, *any* Star Trek episode can contain something which just rubs somebody the wrong way, for many of the best-liked and most famous episodes were mentioned as least-favorites, and a couple were even vehemently derided as "real stinkers."

**11. Would you rather Paramount keep making Star Trek movies or would you rather have Star Trek return as a series on TV?**

The majority of those polled (76%) would prefer that Star Trek return as a weekly series, but only "if they could keep the quality high." Several suggested that a monthly, or even semimonthly schedule might be the best, allowing more time for special effects and the like; a similar number thought that cable television could do the best job, providing us with four to six Star Trek movies each year.

Of those who wanted to continue with the practice of having Star Trek as an ongoing series of theatrically released motion pictures, most thought that the greater amount of time and money that could be allotted to a theatrical film made enough difference in quality to make up for a lack of quantity. Several also felt that it would be impossible to get the original actors to return to a weekly series, and rather than eventually have replacements in the roles, they would live with the biannual schedule. Just about everyone who favored feature films thought that they could be made and released at least once a year without any loss of quality or box-office appeal. Only a tiny number felt that quality would drop if the films were made more often. One respondent, however, was adamantly opposed to speeding up the schedule, claiming that the public would get "burned out on Star Trek" if the films appeared any oftener than every two years or so.

**12. Would you go to a Star Trek movie or watch the series on TV if different people played the parts of Kirk, Spock, etc.? Do you think you would like the show any less?**

Most of those polled (89%) said they probably would give Star Trek a try if other actors took the major roles, but that percentage dropped sharply at the second part of the question. Only 41% of the respondents said they thought Star Trek would be just as good with new actors; 27% thought it would be better ("depending on who they were" or "if it was somebody I really liked"); and something less than 30% thought Star Trek would be totally unsuccessful without the original cast. A few respondents had absolutely no opinion at all.

In general, however, most of those polled did not find the prospect of having new actors take over the roles to be repugnant. Several mentioned characters like Sherlock Holmes or Charlie Chan who had been played by various actors over the years; others bluntly pointed out the undeniable fact that the original cast members aren't getting any younger.

**13. Do you think that the producers should start bringing in younger people, playing new characters, who can take over Star Trek when the original cast retires?**

Surprisingly, this suggestion found less favor with most of our respondents than did the previous one: 65% of those polled thought that bringing in new people was a bad idea; 31% per cent thought that it would improve the series, as well as be smart planning for the future. (The remaining percentage, again, had no opinion.)

Those who were against new characters cited disappointing experiences with new characters being introduced into favorite television shows. They felt that in most cases, such replacement characters were only pallid copies of the originals, and that the same thing would happen with any new characters brought into Star Trek. Those in favor of the practice pointed to the popularity and presence of Kirstie Alley's Saavik and Merritt Butrick's David as evidence that it could, and should, be done.

**14. Do you think that it was a good idea for Spock to die in *Wrath of Khan*?**

Respondents were about evenly split on this question at 46% on each side, with the remaining percentage having no opinion. Those who felt that it was a good idea for Spock to die thought that the act provided some needed realism to the series. "After all," said one person, "people die in real life. It's kind of silly to have us believe that none of the officers would die in [a voyage of] ten or fifteen years."

A smaller number of those favoring the death stated that it

made for a natural progression of making room for new people and plots.

Those who opposed Spock's death were more mixed in their opinions. Many felt that it had been done as "a cheap publicity stunt" and had hurt the series' overall credibility. Others felt that Spock was a symbol of the series (again, see question 1), and to kill him off was to kill off a part of the series itself. Still others thought that Leonard Nimoy was at fault, and blame him for callously disregarding the wishes of fans. And a tiny number blame William Shatner, claiming that he "pulled strings" to get rid of the Spock character and grab all the glory for himself.

Most of those opposed, however, simply felt that Star Trek just would not be the same without Mr. Spock. Not as a symbol, but as a beloved and admired character.

## 15. Do you think Spock should be brought back to life?

Again, the voting was about evenly split on this one: 52% felt that, yes, Spock should be brought back to life in the next film. (This question was asked several months before the release of *The Search for Spock*.) Most of those voting yes felt that the Star Trek series would benefit from having Spock back; again, many cited a simple belief that Star Trek would not be the same without Spock, and they were willing to overlook just about any breach of film logic to have him return. One respondent said, "Sure they can bring him back. It's science fiction, isn't it?" Indeed it is.

Several others, while in favor of bringing Spock back, made sure to put a caveat on their yes vote. Most of them felt that if the resurrection was not logical and dramatically effective, it should not be done at all. Said one lady, "If they bring him back the Star Trek way, all right. If they do it like some of those other movies, I won't like it." We agree; "the Star Trek way" it should be.

Those opposing the return of Spock were more adamant. "No way!" was a typical reaction. The great majority of the 45% who felt that Spock should rest in peace said that they thought having him revived would stretch the bounds of credibility a little too far. Many also believed that the Spock death storyline was such a strong and effective one that to effectively negate it by having Spock brought back to life would be a shame. "Spock died a hero," said one respondent, "why not leave it at that?"

A vociferous few took the position that it would be "a cheat" to revive Spock, both from the standpoint of invalidating the series' integrity and as a somewhat sleazy way to get patrons into the theaters. "If Spock can die, then come back, anybody on the show can. So who cares if they die?" said one person polled. Another took the other tack: "First the big deal was to see him die. Now the big deal is to see him come back. What's next . . . a sex change?"

## 16. If you could change any one thing about Star Trek, what would it be?

This question, of course, cannot be expressed in percentages, nor can a consensus of opinion be reached. Many respondents to our poll had no answer to give to this question; most simply said they had never thought about such a thing. Those that did have an answer, however, were most definite—they know what they'd do with Star Trek if they were in charge:

"I'd put in more laser-beam battles and action like that."

"Kirk and Spock should retire from the service and go off in a ship of their own. Be explorers or something."

"I'd like to see everybody in the crew have a chance at running things; Kirk does too much himself."

"I'd like to see Saavik and Uhura do nude scenes."

"I'd hire Michael Jackson to be the new captain."

"The show should be more accurate. The captain wouldn't go on missions, he'd send people. And ships would go out in bunches, convoys if you will. Make the show more like the real navy."

"If I was in charge, I'd have Kirk and his people quit the Federation and steal the ship and go off and be soldiers-of-fortune."

"Kirk, McCoy, and Spock should retire."

"I'd have more aliens on the ship, and have everything look more futuristic, weirder."

"Uhura should get a chance at being captain."

"I'd redesign the *Enterprise*; it's been the same for too long. And I'd show more of Earth and Vulcan."

"The main thing that Star Trek needs is new blood. Why not bring in a second crew, on a second ship, and kind of cut back and forth between them? As a matter of fact, you could have movies about Captain Kirk and the *Enterprise*, and a television show about this new ship and captain and crew. Every once in a while they could meet or fight the same villians. That would be neat."

"I'd like to see some pets aboard the *Enterprise*. I think Spock would be a cat person."

"Give everybody a drink from the Fountain of Youth."

"I'd go way back to the original premise of the show; Let Kirk and the ship be out there all alone, cut off from everybody and having to make decisions and deal with things without help or interference from the government."

"Have more romances."

"Have more comedies."

"Have more action."

"Have more drama."

"Don't dare change a single thing!"

And, finally, our demented favorite:

"I'd kill everybody off and start all over again with trained monkeys."

So what does it all mean? When all of these responses are put together, what have we learned about how the average "fan on the street" feels about Star Trek?

Well, we see it like this:

The average viewer most clearly recalls with fondness those episodes which had a strong, active villain or overt threat to the *Enterprise* crew, contained a goodly measure of action and suspense, and put the crew or a particular member of the crew in an unusual situation, while also being colorful, visually exciting and fast-paced. All of the episodes which made it to the top ten favorites contain one or more of these elements, and every one of them is noted as a particularly memorable episode by the average viewer and hard-core fan alike.

The average viewer did not seem as concerned with the moral viewpoint or message of an episode as were fans, but it's interesting to note that every episode in the top ten is a show with a strong moral viewpoint, and each carries an extremely strong and effective message. Many respondents made it a point (either at this question or when naming least-liked episodes) to give an example of how a particular episode had a bearing on their lives, and how real life experiences helped them relate to Star Trek. In several instances, we were told how a Star Trek episode helped that person relate to something in his or her real life. The magic of Star Trek can, apparently, work both ways.

We quickly learned in the course of taking this poll to ask the "favorite episode" question again about three quarters of the way through; invariably, the questioning and the respondent's own growing enthusiasm had led to his remembering more and more about the show, which occasionally led to a change or addition to the "best shows" list. (As the average viewer can hardly be expected to remember every Star Trek episode, we felt this was quite fair.)

The average viewer is far more partial to Captain Kirk than to Mr. Spock (or to any other member of the crew, for that matter); but although respondents followed in this vein and chose William Shatner as their favorite actor, they feel that Leonard Nimoy's portrayal of Spock is the most important contribution to the series. As we stated above, we feel (and several respondents came right out and said so) that they felt more comfortable liking a human character with whom they could identify more easily. The most intriguing thing about this question, however, was the number of people who, later in the poll, changed their mind and switched from Captain Kirk to Mr. Spock (or William Shatner to Leonard Nimoy). Frankly, just about *everybody* leaned toward Kirk when the question was first asked—typically: "Well, I guess the captain . . . no . . . it'd be okay if I said Mr. Spock, wouldn't it?"—and only chose Spock somewhat reluctantly and, we were amused and amazed to see somewhat embarrassedly.

Those who favored other characters and other actors had no such qualms of conscience—they (especially the McCoy/Kelley fans) came right out and said so, loud and clear. Perhaps they feel part of a small and somewhat persecuted minority, and proudly and unashamedly bear the banner of their favorite. One young man told us, "I just like that little devil Sulu. . . . Most people like the captain or Spock, and they look at you kind of funny when you give Sulu as your favorite. Lots of people don't even remember him right off."

As stated above, there's no mystery why Khan finished so far ahead of everyone else in the "favorite villain" category: the immense popularity of *Star Trek II: The Wrath of Khan* and the subsequent flood of rebroadcasts of "Space Seed" made the Eugenic Prince a certain winner, as it did Ricardo Montalban in the "favorite male guest star" category.

What's most notable about the villains chosen by our average viewers is that each of them is colorful and bizarre, definitely memorable. Harry Mudd, thanks to Roger C. Carmel's fun-filled, larger-than-life portrayals, is always a favorite, and we feel that he'd have won this category easily if not for the influence of *Wrath of Khan*. The relatively high finishes of such creatures as the Gorn captain and the gorillalike Mugato tells us that the average viewer remembers monsters clearly; but the presence of Janice Lester and Gary Mitchell tells us that the average viewer will remember and appreciate a strong character as well. It was a pleasant surprise to find Jeffrey Hunter finishing fourth in the guest star balloting. We feel that this fine actor is being sadly forgotten, even by Star Trek fans to an extent, and we were heartened to see that a number of viewers remembered him as "the first captain" of the *Enterprise*.

Joan Collin's victory was no surprise. What interested us most was seeing who would finish second. Sad to say, most viewers don't remember female guest stars as clearly as they do male guest stars. The nature of the medium has a lot to do with this, as, unfortunately, a female guest star is often relegated to playing "the girlfriend of the week" or a victim or a walk-on yeoman. Star Trek offered more strong female roles than most series of its time (and of today, sad to say), but there really weren't that many of them. The three top finishers in the poll, Miss Collins, Miss Hartley, and Miss Martel, had perhaps the three strongest and most developed female roles on Star Trek. It is heartening, however, that the average viewer remembered each of them with fondness, and many expressed a desire to see similar roles for women in programs made in the future.

As we stated, it was a surprise to us that viewers expressed a preference for "think" shows over "action" shows. What is strange, however, is that *all* of the shows which made the top five on the "most disliked" list are "think" shows. Maybe its just that they're *bad* think shows, for fans aren't overly fond of a few of them, either. What we thought of when we looked at this short list is that in none of these shows "Spectre of the Gun," "For the World Is Hollow and I Have Touched the Sky," "The Way to Eden," "And the Children Shall Lead," and "The Cloud Minders"—is there a particularly strong and colorful villain; indeed, in none of them can a particularly strong performance be found from anyone, including the regular cast. As these elements are invariably found in those episodes named as favorites by our respondents, we can only assume that the absence of a strong central character or villain and/or an outstanding performance will not make for a memorable show—unless, of course, it is remembered as a *bad* show.

As do fans, the repondents to our poll feel that you can't get enough of a good thing, and they overwhelmingly want Star Trek returned as some kind of television series, even if it appears on pay cable. The movies, while extremely popular, don't seem to be satisfying enough for the average viewer, especially at the present rate of release. As we saw, even those who prefer feature films over a new television series feel that they should be released more often, preferably at the rate of two a year.

A majority of those polled thought it would be a good idea for the producers of the Star Trek films to start bringing in new, younger actors, but not to replace the original actors in the original roles. This seems pretty clear-cut. Fans have always been divided in their opinions about whether or not new actors would be acceptable as Kirk, Spock, etc., but the average viewer, probably because he is less involved with the mythos and background of the series, feels such substitution would be a major mistake, although a majority of them say they'd give a new series and new stars a chance anyway.

Respondents were just about evenly split when asked whether or not Spock should have been allowed to die; and they were evenly split again when asked if he should be brought back to life. The most interesting aspect about these questions when considered in tandem is that there is not a one-for-one overlap in opinion. In other words, those that felt it a bad move to kill Spock are not always those in favor of bringing him back, and those who thought it a good idea to have Spock die don't automatically feel it would be a mistake to bring him back. We found this not so curious as one would think upon first consideration, for the resurrection of Spock is an event which would prove so dramatic in intent and form that it really has little bearing on his death or the intent behind that death. Mostly, respondents' feelings about whether or not Spock should come back were colored by their expectations of how such an event would take place, and not by how they were affected (or not affected) by his death.

The opinions expressed about if and how to change Star Trek ranged from the ridiculous to the sublime, but most of those questioned simply wanted to see more shows of quality similar to that of those they enjoyed and remembered from the past. One typical comment was, "If they can keep making shows as good as those I remember, then they don't have to change anything." A good many subjects stated that the best thing a new series could do is to "get away" from the "garbage," "preaching," and "crappy junk" of the third season, and return, in spirit and practice, to "the neat kind of shows" Star Trek presented during its first season. (This seems like a good place to note that in conversation, many fans admitted that they stopped watching Star Trek during its final season, and that if they can recognize one as such, they still refuse to watch most third-season episodes in reruns.)

It seems to us that the average viewer knows what he wants and likes from Star Trek: He likes fast-moving, involving episodes with a strong storyline and a colorful villain. He likes lots of action and strong, involving characters (and does not mind if they are women). He dislikes shows which offer an overly obvious or awkward message or viewpoint. He prefers and identifies with Kirk, as a rule, but appreciates the contributions of Spock and the rest of the cast. He'd like to see Star Trek return to television, but only if the quality returned to the high standards of the first season. He is not opposed to change, even supports the introduction of new characters, but doesn't want to see new actors play the main characters.

All in all, the average viewer, who watches Star Trek only occasionally but harbors many fine memories of the series and individual episodes, feels much the same as we hard-core fans do. We all want the same thing and it's really very simple: We want good, enjoyable, involving Star Trek, and we want it just as often as we can get it!

Now you didn't think that we'd publish this article without giving you readers a chance to speak your piece, did you?

Yep, here it is, your chance to participate in our brand-spanking-new Trek Fan Poll #2! You'll notice the questions are somewhat different from those asked of the "Fan on the Street"; we feel that you readers are more involved in Star Trek and therefore more willing to talk about it.

1. Please list your name, address, age, marital status, profession, and sex. (All of these except your name are optional; we just want to get a statistical overview, and the information will be kept confidential if you choose to include it.)

2. Please list, in order of preference, your ten favorite episodes.

3. Please list, in order of dislike, your five least-favorite episodes.

4. Who is your favorite Star Trek character?

5. Who is your favorite Star Trek actor?

6. Which character do you feel is the most important to Star Trek?

7. Which actor do you feel contributed the most to Star Trek?

8. Who is your favorite villain?

9. Who is your favorite male guest star?

10. Who is your favorite female guest star?

11. Which do you think is the most believable piece of equipment aboard the *Enterprise*?

12. Whom do you consider the best writer of televised episodes?

13. Do you prefer "action" shows or "think" shows?

14. Do you think that the major characters should die, marry, or otherwise undergo major changes?

15. Would you prefer to have Paramount keep making Star Trek movies or would you prefer to have Star Trek return to television (commercial or cable) as a regular series?

16. Would you go to a Star Trek movie or watch a television series if new actors played the parts of Kirk, Spock, etc.?

17. Do you think the producers should start bringing in new, younger actors, playing new characters, who can take over when the original cast members retire or move on to other things?

18. If you could change any *one* thing about Star Trek, what would it be?

19. Who is your favorite Star Trek writer?

20. Which is your single favorite episode?

21. Which is your favorite Star Trek movie?

22. In which episode do you think each of the major actors gives his or her best performance?

23. Which episode do you consider to be the best-written?

24. Which episode was the very first you saw?

25. Which episode so interested you that you became a Star Trek fan?

26. Which Star Trek novel is your favorite?

27. Who is your favorite Star Trek fiction writer?

28. What is your favorite Star Trek merchandising tie-in (posters, toys, comics, etc.)?

29. Give a brief (very brief, please!) description of your "dream episode"—the Star Trek show *you'd* make if you had the chance.

Please don't worry if some of your answers seem to contradict one another. This isn't a test, and we probably won't even read them in sequence anyway. We'd appreciate having your response typed or at least written as neatly as possible, for we'll be reading lots of them. We'll try to have the totals and comments in our next *Best of Trek*, so if you're going to respond, please do so as quickly as possible. Send your responses to:

Trek Fan Poll
2405 Dewberry
Pasadena, TX 77502

Thanks, and we'll be looking forward to hearing from you very soon.

# WHITHER STAR TREK? ON POSSIBILITIES PAST AND FUTURE

## by Barbara Devereaux

*Sometime around last May, Barbara inquired of us whether or not we would be interested in a slightly humorous article discussing some of the ways in which Mr. Spock might have been resurrected. We immediately answered yes. A few days later, we received a letter from Barb thanking us for our permission. She also rather sheepishly admitted, "Maybe I'd better wait to see* how *they bring him back before I finish the article." Well, it wasn't long after the release of* The Search for Spock *that the promised article arrived. We immediately scheduled it for inclusion in this collection, and we think you'll understand why when you read on. . . .*

As our beloved friend Mr. Spock is fond of saying, "There are always possibilities." Star Trek has not only managed to explore the realm of the possible, but in creating an exciting series of films from a dead (but not forgotten) television series and in bringing back Spock from the valley of death, it has managed to do the impossible. In *The Search for Spock*, was saw our pointed-eared hero reunited with his friends with dignified, Vulcanly logic. With cheerful, human illogic, Kirk responds to Spock's astonishment by saying, "The needs of the one outweighed the needs of the many." A beautiful moment.

However . . .

Given the endless alternate universes of Star Trek, there

are a zillion (precisely 2,787,547,007.4) other ways they could have brought Spock back to life, of which we shall examine five.

In ''Spock Resurrectus—Or, Now That *They've* Killed Him, How Do *We* Get Him Back?'' (*Best of Trek #6*). Pat Mooney examined several ways in which Spock might return and cut them into small ribbons on the basis of scientific fact and simple logic. But Star Trek has never allowed the laws of science to get in the way of a good story. Thus, our five alternatives will tend toward dramatic, rather than scientific possibilities.

Concerning the past . . .

### 1. The "Who Are We Going to Discover Next?" Theory

If Spock was brought back to life by the Genesis Effect, then why couldn't that effect have resurrected others who died in the same neighborhood—like Khan and his nasty band of cohorts? One could argue that Spock's ''primary matrix'' was preserved in his body (in fact, was his body), whereas Khan's was blown to smithereens. True enough, but what if the supercharged Genesis Effect had been strong enough to act on even one molecule of Khan's remains that were still sailing around the nebula?

Remember, too, that Khan cursed Kirk with his dying breath. In fiction, these things have a way of getting back to a person. Imagine a scene (in a film that would have been entitled *The Curse of Khan*) wherein Kirk beams down to the Genesis Planet, finds a mysterious figure (robed in black, of course), and suddenly is looking into the face of his old enemy, Khan! Just when we thought the galaxy was safe!

### 2. The "Out of Time, But Not Out of Mind" Theory

A time warp! Even David Marcus didn't suspect that the Genesis Effect would create a time warp in the fabric of space. In this scenario, Spock would be trapped somewhere in the past where he would be broadcasting SOS signals to McCoy. Life could become even more interesting if Spock was trapped on Vulcan at a point in its history before they had discovered the advantages of life ruled by logic. Kirk and company could attempt to rescue Spock via the Guardian of Forever (from Harlan Ellison's "City on the Edge of Forever"), but would be thwarted in their efforts when it turned out that the ancient Vulcans liked to eat humans for breakfast. In this film version of *Star Trek III* (entitled *Breakfast of Champions*), the admiral's mission, should he choose to accept it, would be to find Spock, persuade him that humans are okay guys and not a substitute for corn flakes, and then persuade him to return with them to the present—not an easy task, even for J. T. Kirk.

### 3. The "He's Lost, Jim" Theory

It is possible that Spock could have been misplaced in space, rather than time. After all, they *are* relative. He might have wound up in a far-off, unexplored sector of the galaxy. Once more, Spock would be broadcasting his SOS signals to McCoy. Kirk and crew would then have to use a never-before-tested method of ultraspace travel through a black hole in order to make the great leap through the galaxy and rescue Spock. This version of *Star Trek III* would be called *The Black Hole*. [Sorry, Barbara, it's been done—the editors.] After Kirk went to all that trouble to find him, Spock might not want to come back. Problems, problems.

### 4. The "Everybody Makes Mistakes" Theory

It would take only a minor change in the old genetic structure to transform Spock from a Vulcan to a Romulan. The Genesis Effect could have made a mistake—especially if David has been playing around with protomatter again. If a Romulan scouting party found Spock, they might decide to rescue him first and ask questions later. No doubt they would whisk him off to the Romulan Empire, where Spock (the complete Spock, not just the body of Spock) might very well end up serving in the Romulan fleet. The situation in this version of *Star Trek III*, *The Empire Strikes Back* [Get serious, Barbara!— exasperated editors], would then begin to unravel very quickly and we wouldn't be able to tell the good guys from the bad guys. Another fine mess you've gotten us into, Mr. Spock.

## 5. The "May the Spook Be with You" Theory

As Pat Mooney pointed out, most fans immediately rejected the idea of Spock's existing on a higher plane of consciousness. This is assuming that the spirit of Spock would necessarily exist on a higher plane than we. Maybe not. Pure consciousness may not be all it's cracked up to be. If Spock the spook, like the ghost of Hamlet's father, had been doomed for a certain term to walk the galaxy, he might have suffered a bit in the transition. In *Star Trek III: A Ghost Story* [Why fight it? exhausted editors], Kirk is trying to persuade a group of aliens to join the Federation. "Swear!" thunders the Spook out of thin air. "Yeah," says Kirk, "Swear!" "Swear on your swords!" says the voice from nowhere. "Your phasers will do," says Kirk, getting embarrassed. "Swear on your phasers that you'll be loyal to the Federation." If this goes on for very long, the problem might not be how to get Spock back—it will be how to get rid of him.

The most important question, of course, is where do we go from here? Whither *Star Trek IV*? There are a few obvious course headings for Kirk and his loyal crew. There are also an infinite number of directions in which the Star Trek saga could continue now that Spock is back in the land of the living. But for the moment we will be content with five versions of the future.

1. They could be court-martialed. Stealing a starship, sabotaging the *Excelsior*—those have got to be felonies in anybody's book of rules. Even though Kirk did manage to save Spock, and even though Vulcan will no doubt try to intervene in Kirk's behalf, the truth of the matter is that Kirk is guilty. So are Sulu, Chekov, and Scotty. McCoy, of course, can plead temporary insanity, or, perhaps, temporary possession by a Vulcan. Uhura will get off, assuming that she did get "Mr. Adventure" to eat out of her hand.

If they are convicted and sent up the river for a stretch in the Federation pen, it will be up to McCoy, Spock, and

Uhura to break them out in the most daring escape of the century. McCoy and Spock will have to have the getaway ship warmed up and ready to go while Uhura distracts the guards and our heroes run for it.

Once the guys are out of prison, their troubles will just be beginning, because they'll be wanted men. The Federation will put a price on their heads. *WANTED* posters will appear all over the galaxy. Or maybe *WANTED* holograms will appear in Federation post offices. From this point on, Star Trek will become *Fugitives in Space*.

2. On the other hand, no one says that the guys have to turn themselves in to the authorities. And they do have the Klingon Bird of Prey. Granted, it's a goofy-looking ship with none of the grace and dignity of the old *Enterprise*, but it does fly. It is a little conspicuous, though. Perhaps Kirk would want to visit a used spaceship lot and trade it in for a better model. We can imagine the spiel that Kirk would give to Mr. Sam, the friendly spaceship man. "Hey, listen, Sam, I'm here to tell you this bird is loaded! I mean, it's got all the extras. It's got a cloaking device, front and rear photon torpedos, fully automated shields, and standard warp transmission. My man Scotty reconditioned it himself and it runs like new. We even gave her new filters and spark plugs."

Perhaps Kirk will trade in the Bird of Prey for a spiffy little foreign model, painted bright red with a chrome-and-leather bridge and tinted windows. However, if Spock, with a voice reminiscent of Ricardo Montalban, ever starts to talk about luxury models upholstered in rich Corinthian leather, we could be in *serious* trouble.

3. Then again, the crew could just stay on Vulcan for a while. We have just glimpsed a bit of that mysterious planet, and every Trekker would love to see more. The television series implied very strongly that everyone on Vulcan is a pacifist. What would happen if this peaceful planet was attacked? Would the Vulcans defend themselves? Would Kirk defend them? Would Spock choose to fight at the side of his old captain or would he bow to Sarek's wishes and maintain a pacifist position? *The War for Vulcan* could be one very exciting movie.

4. And then there is the reaction of the crew to Spock's

resurrection. Once the initial shock has worn off, how will they react to Spock's presence among them? Would they tend to be overprotective? As McCoy commented in *The Search for Spock*, the idea of losing Spock twice is more than any of us can stand.

Would word of Spock's miraculous return get around the Federation? Would the crew have to contend with autograph seekers and Vulcan groupies? Living with a legend can be very hard on the rest of the family.

5. Finally, what of our favorite Vulcan? What of the *pon farr* and the mind meld with Saavik? Does this mean that they're engaged? What of the mind link to McCoy? Will the link continue to bind them in some mysterious way—much to McCoy's annoyance?

Has Spock really survived his experience of death unchanged? Truly, he has gone where no man has gone before—and returned. Have his telepathic powers increased? Is he physically stronger, or more vulnerable? We note that the scars from his terrible exposure to intense radiation have disappeared. What lies across the gentle bridge of death, and what has Spock brought with him from the other side? There is a wealth of material here for writers to explore, and endless possibilities for Kirk and his loyal crew.

# A LETTER FROM PEGGY GREENSTREET

*When we first plucked out one of the longer and more interesting letters addressed to Trek Roundtable and featured it as a separate article, we had no idea how popular a feature it would be. It seems as if you readers just can't get enough of these letters. So here is another, this time from Peggy Greenstreet of Lebanon, Missouri. Peggy has something to say about almost everything in Star Trek, the movies, and the Best of Trek books. We think you'll enjoy reading her letter; and, as always, you'll find more than a little bit of yourself reflected in Peggy.*

I have been a Star Trek nut since its inception, though it was only during the last couple of years that I found out there were others like me. Everyone I talked to about Star Trek, and my love for it, thought I was totally insane, living in my own little dream world. Well, if I was, I was happy there. Now I am even happier knowing that there are thousands of others with the same love for the *Enterprise* and her crew.

Just a few days ago I found out there are *Best of Trek* books. A fellow Trekkie found she had two copies of the same issue and gave me one. I have found the book very interesting; most of the articles were informative and enlightening, not to mention the variety of views from the many pseudo crew members of the *Enterprise*.

Each person, in his or her own uniqueness, has a right to

private views and opinions. Very seldom will two people see the same thing, and be able to agree on what they've seen, or the motives behind it.

I found Joyce Tullock's article, "The Alien Question," well written, though I must disagree with many of her thoughts. I found many of them sounded rather insensitive to what she had been watching.

In "The Man Trap," we find an alien who is the last of its kind, and needs salt to survive. Joyce claims this alien is "not so dumb"; it has found the one human who can, and does, understand its plight and provide the salt it needs. If one human can understand, why not two, six, or even ten? The crew of the *Enterprise* have compassion not only for each other, but for other life forms as well. When I first viewed "The Man Trap," I felt, and still feel, that if the salt creature had sat down and talked to Kirk, Spock, and McCoy, it could have had all the salt it needed, and continued to live. As Kirk has said many times, "We don't look for fights, but we will fight when left no other choice." Put in the same position, with my crew being murdered, I would do the same thing . . . get rid of whoever or whatever was doing the killing.

The Vians of "The Empath" are ugly only if one sees them as ugly. They are different, they don't look exactly like us. So does that make them automatically ugly? Their actions left a lot to be desired, albeit they were trying to bring Gem out of her shell enough so that she would give of herself willingly to help others. The path they chose to do this was, to say the least, misdirected and cruel. That makes their actions ugly, not their appearance. Surely they could have found a more pleasant way to teach Gem to give of herself, one that would not inflict so much pain on other beings.

The Vians are ugly, while the Horta is simply unusual in appearance. That sounds a bit contradictory, doesn't it? The Vians at least were humanoid; the Horta looked more like a moving blob of rock. To protect her babies, mother Horta did just what she had to do, just as any mother would. Spock was able to use his abilities to understand and communicate, because mother Horta allowed it. The salt creature did not leave any room for such communication. If it had, I'm sure that a solution to its predicament would have been found.

*Webster's Encyclopedia of Dictionaries* defines ''alien'' as one of another country; foreign; different in nature. Thus, an alien can be anyone different from ourselves. Is their coloring different; is their language different; is their life-style different? All such differences, and many more, can constitute an alien. ''Alien'' does not automatically mean ''monster''; nor does it define a being who is unhappy just because it is not human. Tellerites, Andorians, Vulcans, Romulans, and even Klingons are not human, yet as races of beings unique unto themselves, they seem to be content and happy.

The Companion in ''Metamorphosis'' was not forced against her will to take on human form. And the human Zefrem Cochrane couldn't have changed form even if he had been willing to do so. It was the Companion's love for Zefrem which caused her to make the choice to merge her essence with that of Nancy Hedford.

When the Companion took over Nancy's dying body, that body was healed and allowed to ''continue.'' This action did more good than just saving the commissioner's life; Nancy was also able, through the addition of the Companion's essence, to find the love she craved. The Companion also benefited, for she was then able to let Zefrem know more completely of her love for him, and to finally have that love returned. No one told the Companion that she must become human in order to be happy. Her choice was made out of love and concern for Zefrem. In the end, all were happy and content—*not* because the Companion had taken human form, but because love was being given and returned.

Taking on a human form, or reasonable facsimile of one, however, does not always work out as expected. In ''Return to Tomorrow,'' Sargon and Thalassa held no animosity toward anyone. As advanced as they were, they felt that they needed humanoid bodies to be happy and productive. Soon, however, they finally realized that they didn't *need* human bodies to be happy; the time had come for them to move upward and onward.

Most Star Trek episodes work out to the benefit of all concerned; very few people end up losers. In order to be a loser, however, you have to have something to lose. It doesn't really matter how much or how little, just something which affects that person on a personal level.

For instance, Dr. Adams of "Dagger of the Mind" ended up losing all of the years of work and effort in his brilliant career when he let his delusions of grandeur rule him. By attempting to use the neural neutralizer for his own ends, Dr. Adams ended up losing far more than he ever dreamed of gaining.

Then there's Harcourt Fenton Mudd. Harry Mudd—will that man never learn? He's always looking for the pot of gold at the end of the rainbow, and if he thinks there's an easy way to that pot, he'll take it—and anything else that strikes his fancy, as well. Mudd's "borrowing" a ship and ending up captive of all those beautiful androids in "I, Mudd" is a perfect example of his luck: What started out as heaven turned out to be a living hell, and eventually the path to the loss of Mudd's ill-gotten freedom once again.

We have Mudd's kind of loser among us today. Is it possible that we'll have Mudd's kind of loser among us forever? I suppose it's possible that the Harcourt Fenton Mudds of humanity are a product of civilization, and a necessary nuisance that we will forever be coping with.

The innocent loser is something else entirely. Take for example the Tribbles of "The Trouble with Tribbles." Through no fault of their own, those sweet, furry little Tribbles caused a lot of havoc. They're a perfect example of the dictum that doing what comes naturally is not always the best thing to do. They were innocently brought aboard a space station filled with a huge supply of what was to them food; you can't blame them for eating, can you? I feel a little sorry for them, as it was a number of their deaths which proved the grain was poisoned. And being beamed aboard a Klingon ship was almost too cruel to the Tribbles, although the sure havoc they caused served the Klingons right—you know what the Klingons eventually did with them. . . .

Running the risk of losing, however, is one of the ways in which people grow. If the Star Trek characters did not grow, the entire concept of the series would diminish and eventually fall apart. Of all the Star Trek characters, it is Spock who has grown and changed the most. In the three years that Star Trek was on the air, Mr. Spock was coping with an inner battle between his Vulcan and human halves. After failing to achieve *Kolinahr*, he returned to the *Enterprise* in *Star Trek: The Motion Picture* still at odds with himself. Disappointed and frustrated with himself for failing to reach his Vulcan goal, he did the only thing he could do—he retreated within his own being until he could sort things out, and come to terms with his own feelings.

In *Star Trek: The Motion Picture*, V'Ger was looking for more, the reason for its existence. To become one with its Maker would give V'Ger the whole, complete, satisfied feeling it, as a now sentient and immensely knowledgeable being, needed and was searching for. V'Ger was missing emotional contact, be it human or otherwise. Like any other alien, V'Ger needed understanding and compassion. Spock's meld with V'Ger not only communicated V'Ger's needs and questions to the Vulcan, but allowed Mr. Spock to gain the insight to come to terms with his own human half. Spock then finally understood that the feelings within him for his friends are not something to be buried or camouflaged; the simple feeling of one friend touching another is, rather, something to be cherished.

Spock's learning to accept his human half and understand it does not mean that he has lost his usefulness or his credibility as a Vulcan. The fact that he is finally able to begin abolishing the turmoil that has been raging within him for years can only eventually make him more free—free to do those things which are most important to him, unencumbered by a crippling inner battle. This will not make him any less Vulcan, nor will it make him any more human. Spock will always be Spock—his history, his heritage, and his choice of career and culture says that loud and clear. Spock's love of science and logic and his dedication to Starfleet, the *Enterprise*, and his friends will not, and cannot, change. If anything, a better understanding of himself will only deepen those feelings.

If you stop to think about it, the only time you are truly yourself is when you are around friends you know love you for what you are, not for the masks you wear. When dealing with strangers or the public in general, we are always polite and considerate, whether we really feel like acting that way or not. But when with friends we know are friends, we can be a little flippant or even snappish, if we feel like it. They will understand; we are free to simply be ourselves with friends who love us.

This is certainly true of Spock's and McCoy's beautiful, loving battles. They remind me of brothers, different as night and day, but if anything happens to one of them, the other is right there to do what he can to help. Kirk is the mediator, keeping peace in the family whenever needed. Granted, in quite a few of their spats they seem more like two mischievous boys insulting each other than like grown Starfleet officers, but usually their comic, lovable bickering lends a touch of reality to what might be some pretty boring situations. Many of their debates, though, are intended to make each other think in a sensible or logical manner. In ''All Our Yesterdays,'' if McCoy had just left Spock alone and not badgered him, they might never have returned. It was McCoy's prodding—to the point that Spock grabbed his throat and McCoy said, calmly, ''Are you trying to kill me, Spock?''— that finally made Spock take a logical look at what was happening to him.

In any being, alien or not, the metabolism can be put out of balance by illness, lack of proper diet, a drug effect, or any of a number of things. The waterborne virus of ''The Naked Time'' caused everyone who came in contact with it to act irrationally, letting out his deep-seated emotions. In Sulu it was his love of adventure and perhaps his samurai heritage; Kevin Riley became an irresponsible boob; Captain Kirk feared that he was losing his ability to command; Spock bemoaned his inability to say ''I love you'' to his mother.

Why should we find Spock's reaction to the virus any more shocking that that of anyone else? It shouldn't be difficult for us to understand, if we understand Spock. Under all that Vulcan teaching about how to control his emotions and all that schooling in logic, Spock does love his mother; but from childhood on, he has been unable to tell her so, and this tears him apart deep inside, in his human half.

In ''This Side of Paradise,'' it is the effect of alien spores which must be dealt with. The spores induce a feeling of irresponsible happiness and goodwill within humans and Vulcans alike. With all inhibitions gone, and nothing in your soul but happiness and joy, who would not sing, laugh, and play games? How exhilarating it must have been—especially for Spock—to have all care and responsibility removed and be set totally free. . . . But when the spores' effect is banished, personalities return to normal. Again, why should Spock be any different? This glimpse of paradise, memorable though it might be, does not permanently change Spock—even though he admits to Kirk that it was the only time in his life that he had been truly happy.

As a Vulcan, Spock is naturally immune to many things we humans must endure. But he is not a god, nor an emotionless robot; Spock is flesh and (albeit green) blood, and cannot be immune to all things he meets in the universe, be they disease, drug, spore, or simple emotional experience. If Spock were not affected by these things, then his character would be unrealistic and unbelievable.

In the years that the bridge crew have been together, they have come to form an unflappable and unshakable unit. There is among them a special bonding which just cannot be broken. When trouble comes, there is no other group of people who work together as well as do Captain Kirk and his bridge crew (which, to me, includes Scotty).

Everyone talks about the Star Trek trio of Kirk, Spock, and McCoy. It is as though Scotty is out there somewhere in left field. In reality, however, Scotty's contributions to the *Enterprise* and to the success of her missions cannot be over-estimated.

For example, in "Bread and Circuses," it was Scotty, on the ship, who figured out a way to help his comrades stranded on the planet below. In a manner which did not disobey the Prime Directive, Scotty gave the landing party the chance they needed to escape further battles in the arena.

In "Metamorphosis," it was Scotty who had to go looking for Kirk, Spock, and McCoy; in "A Piece of the Action," it was Scotty's finesse with the phasers, then the transporter, that allowed Kirk and Spock to bring the two warring gangs to a cooperative state.

The *Enterprise* herself is Scotty's baby, and he knows her

like the back of his hand. No one, not even Kirk, has a surer touch at her controls. Scotty can get more out of that ship than a mother can usually get from her child. In fact, Scotty thinks of the ship as a child; on more than one occasion, he has been heard to call the engines "my poor bairns."

Time after time, Scotty has been right there, whenever needed, to offer his services, to give them freely, unasked.

So, in actuality, we do not have a Star Trek trio, we have a quartet. If you want to get down to the nitty-gritty, it would be rather thoughtless to leave out Uhura, Sulu, or Chekov. Thus, we have a seven-sided, bonded unit. For they are all a part of the wonderful exploration of Star Trek and give their all for Kirk, the *Enterprise*, and Starfleet's ideals.

James Tiberius Kirk, captain of the USS *Enterprise*, has led us through many exciting explorative adventures. Adventures not only on other planets and systems, but adventures within the soul and body, as well.

In "Return of the Archons," for example, the people of Beta III were static and unproductive, held in a kind of bondage that withheld their individuality and restricted their growth. Captain Kirk and his landing party freed these slaves of Landru, returning them to a normal way of life which allowed them to grow and learn at their own pace.

In "By Any Other Name," the Kelvans have indeed accomplished much. They have outlived their planet, and have traveled far looking for just the right system to be their new home. Kirk's offer of help was refused; he was politely told that "Kelvans conquer," and he, Spock, and the landing party were locked away and kept until needed. The Kelvans had hijacked the *Enterprise* for their own purposes, and thoughts of damage to the ship or its human occupants didn't faze them in the least. Is it any wonder that Kirk, or anyone else for that matter, never bothered to ask what it was like to be a Kelvan? Who would want to?

It takes caring and compassion to offer help when someone else is in need. Doing so, then being kicked in the teeth and watching your people be reduced to blocks of chemicals has a way of making a person want to fight back. If the use of human emotions (which the Kelvans know little of) will help to free the crew, then using emotion would be the most logical retaliation.

In "The Enemy Within," Kirk discovered for all of us that we need both our good and our bad halves to be complete. None of us like to look at our bad side, but it's there just the same; it's the side that gives our softer side strength and courage. Thanks to one of William Shatner's better performances, we were able to see clearly how, apart, neither side was worth two cents, but together, the whole man is priceless.

Another fine performance by Shatner is in "Turnabout Intruder." As we all know, even the most masculine of men have a trace of femininity, and vice versa. It helps the sexes get along more harmoniously. In this episode, however, we are dealing with more than just a soul transference. We are dealing with a woman who never came to terms with her own sexuality and sexual identity. She has lived her life full of jealousy for the (perceived) superiority of the male, and scorn for her womanhood, while never realizing that she could've reached any heights she wanted through her own ability.

The story and the situation were handled very well. Although Kirk had excellent reason to be more than a little vindictive after the return of his own body, again we see his compassion for all beings emerge as he offers to help Janice Lester find the help she truly needs.

In *Star Trek: The Motion Picture*, we see Kirk facing a problem that we all will eventually share with him, one that cannot be escaped by anyone—encroaching middle age. He has also lost command of his one true and lasting love, the *Enterprise*. He has to find a way to come to terms with himself, and although he manages to regain his ship, he has to accept his age as something he cannot change.

Decker, too, loses the *Enterprise*, but it is not the most important thing to him, as it is to Kirk. Decker's great love is Ilia, the Deltan, and for a while he thinks that he has lost her too. When Decker decides to join with V'Ger and Ilia, he is not under any order of any kind. He follows his heart and mind, doing what he feels is best for all concerned, including himself. So, while V'Ger's search comes to an end, Decker and Ilia begin a new existence.

Spock, having left Vulcan and *Kolinahr* in search of the

pure logic he felt from V'Ger, instead learns something more of himself, and of the value of friendship and emotion.

In *Wrath of Khan*, we see a Spock who is more at peace with his human half. Since we don't want to lose the Spock we have come to love and respect over the years, we must allow the character to grow psychologically as well as spiritually. Kirk is also making strides. He is coming, finally, to terms with his age, and learning that life is renewable, and is only over for you if you let it be. Having defeated death in many ways, Kirk has never really faced the possibility of his own or, more important, his friend's death. In the end, he grows enough not only to accept Spock's death, but to find a certain peace in it—not only for himself, but for Spock as well.

As a full-fledged Star Trek nut, I am full of hope that *Star Trek III: The Search for Spock* will return the Vulcan to us hale and hearty. (Anything is possible with the Genesis Effect still in progress when Spock's coffin landed in that beautiful glade.) Though I fervently hope that Spock is returned to us, I don't expect any great change in him. To have Spock change too much would not be believable.

And, if nothing else, Star Trek, its stories, and its characters are believable. What was science fiction yesterday is science fact today, and what is science fiction today will be science fact tommorrow.

As long as Star Trek continues to grow, and the characters continue to grow with it, we need never fear losing our vision of Starfleet and the United Federation of Planets. We must all grow to continue living. If we can do so, we will be able to appreciate similar changes in the cast and crew of the *Enterprise*. Although we may drift away from each other, we will never lose them entirely. Thus, may we all live long and prosper!

# MYTHOLOGY AND THE BIBLE IN STAR TREK—PART 1

## by Mary Hamburger and Sarah Schaper

*When Gene Roddenberry first created Star Trek, he knew that his futuristic format would allow his writers a great amount of freedom. The number of episodes which address social ills and moral conventions show that the writers took advantage of this freedom, but what is surprising is how many of them went all the way back to our earliest roots of literature— mythology and the writings of the Bible—to enhance their futuristic morality plays and social commentary. In this article, the first of two, Mary and Sarah not only examine the incidences of mythological or biblical references in Star Trek, but tell us a few things about the originals as well. And we will guarantee that you'll be amazed by some of the surprising parallels—we certainly were.*

Why should any television show spark the interest that Star Trek has generated? Why should this particular show so capture the hearts of fans? This is a question many people have tried to answer over the years since Star Trek was first aired. There is no single answer. Yet our separate interests in mythology and the Bible, combined with our mutual love of Star Trek, have caused us to look deeper into the world of Star Trek.

All the classics that have existed in western societies have some quality about them that touches the heart and soul of each generation. Although each generation produces new works, the underlying themes are common to our human interests. They live within us all, and we react to them daily. Many of these themes from mythology and the Bible were in episodes of Star Trek.

Myths are traditional stories that helped to explain to ancient societies the mysteries of themselves and the world around them. Some of these myths were religious in nature, dealing with the origin of the cosmos and man, and explaining the phenomena of nature. Other myths were stories of heroes or gods responding to their human nature and dealing with their emotions.

The Bible is a collection of writings composed over many centuries. It is divided into two sections known as the Old Testament and New Testament. The Old Testament begins with Genesis and the six-day creation of the heavens and the earth. It tells of the events which followed the creation of man, the actions of God, and the lives of the House of Israel. The New Testament deals with the life, teachings, death, and resurrection of Jesus Christ. It is also a record of Christian philosophy and belief through its beginning centuries. Both Testaments tell of God's promises of life and the hope of future generations.

Both myths and the Bible influence not only our lives but also our entertainment. Star Trek is no exception. Let's examine, in theme-by-theme reference, how these influences can be seen in Star Trek.

## Spaceflight

Interestingly, the possibility of space flight is allowed for in the Bible. In Deuteronomy 30:4, Moses said, "If your outcasts are at the ends of the sky, from there the Lord your God will gather you, and from there he will fetch you." Moses was talking about ordinary mortals like you and me. If your translation of the Bible says "earth" or "world" instead of "sky" or "heaven," it is a mistranslation, because the translators did not believe that Moses could have meant "the ends of the sky." An increase in travel and an increase in knowledge are predicted for the end times in Danial 12:4, where an angel said to Daniel, "Many will go here and there to increase knowledge."

The *Enterprise*, on its five-year mission to go where no man has gone before, is a modern-day example of these quotations. Every time we watch the opening credits, we see the *Enterprise* going to the ends of the sky. She and her crew seek out and search for knowledge. Captain Kirk also fits into this. In a sense, he is a kind of Prometheus, for he is indeed eager to learn from the universe. To the ancient Greeks, Prometheus was the giver of knowledge from the gods to man. Prometheus stole fire from the gods and brought it to man.

## "The Cage"

Daedalus, in Greek mythology, was a skillful inventor, architect, and sculptor who built the famous Labyrinth for King Minos of Crete as a cage for the Minotaur, a monster half man, half bull. The Labryinth was a huge maze with hundreds of hallways and passages opening into one another, and seeming to have neither beginning nor end. Any creature put into the Labyrinth was unable to find its way out. The island of Crete was guarded by the bronze giant Talos, also made by Daedalus. Talos walked around the island three times a day and kept strangers out by throwing rocks at them, making Crete a forbidden island.

Eventually King Minos became angry at Daedalus and imprisoned him and his son Icarus in the Labyrinth, and even Daedalus could not find his way out. To escape, Daedalus made large wings out of feathers and wax for himself and Icarus. They flew out of the Labyrinth and over the sea toward Greece, but Icarus flew too near the sun (spaceflight), and the heat melted the wax in his wings and he fell into the sea and drowned. (The comet in "Balance of Terror" was named after him.)

In "The Cage," the first pilot film of the Star Trek series, the people of planet Talos IV, which was a forbidden planet to Federation ships, made cages for creatures captured from all over their part of the galaxy. The Talosians developed their own mental powers and used them to create mental images that seemed just as substantial as the statues made by Daedalus.

To the Talosians, dreams became more important than

reality; they gave up building and creating, and eventually they found their life system threatened because they could no longer produce for themselves. They too were trapped in a labyrinth of their own making. Their only means of escape was to find a race who could run their planet. Unfortunately they chose humans, who have a distinct hatred for slavery.

## Good and evil

The humans, and most of the aliens, of Star Trek were capable of doing good and of doing evil. In "The Enemy Within," when a transporter malfunction made two Kirks out of one by separating his good and evil halves, we saw that the two halves were genuine parts of his total personality. Spock said, "We have here an unusual opportunity to appraise the human mind or to examine in Earth terms the roles of good and evil in a man—his negative side, which you call hostility, lust, violence, and his positive side, which Earth people express as compassion, love, tenderness."

St. Paul was aware of the two parts of his own personality, too, for he wrote, "When I wish to do good, evil lies near me." Good and evil are within us all as integral parts of our human nature, but the evil needs to be properly controlled and disciplined by the good. This episode of Star Trek allowed us to see these two very real sides of ourselves and to examine them safely in our living rooms.

## The Klingons

The Klingons are prime specimens of evil. In "Errand of Mercy," they invade Organia, the only Class M planet in a strategic location between the Klingon Empire and the Federation. Organia appeared to be inhabited by very peaceful, friendly people living in primitive villages with no fields, livestock, or goods. They seemed to have no defenses, but there were large ruins on the planet. The Klingon occupation army came in and set up a military dictatorship on Organia.

The biblical parallel is Ezekiel's prophecy against Gog, of the land of Magog, the prince of Rosh, Meshech, and Tubal (Russia, Moscow, and Tobolsk):

"On that day thoughts will come into your mind and you

will devise an evil scheme. You will say, 'I will invade a land of unwalled villages; I will attack a peaceful and unsuspecting people—all of them living without walls and without gates and bars. I will plunder and loot and turn my hand against the resettled ruins and the people gathered from the nations, rich in livestock and goods, living in the center of the land.' ''

## Romulans and Roman gods

In Star Trek, the Romulans, a warlike people from the planets Romulus and Remus, are patterned after the ancient Romans. In Roman mythology, Romulus and Remus were twin sons of Mars and the vestal virgin Rhea Silvia or Ilia. When they were born, their uncle ordered them thrown into the Tiber. The trough in which they were placed in the river came to ground at the site of the future city of Rome. A she-wolf suckled and cared for them. Later they were found and brought up by a shepherd and his wife.

Growing up, they became the leaders of a band of adventurous youths, killed their uncle, and restored their grandfather to his rightful throne. They founded the city of Rome, and Romulus built a wall around it. Remus, in contempt, jumped over it; so Romulus killed him, saying, "Thus perish anyone who leaps over my walls." Romulus was a warrior king and founded Rome's military institutions.

In the world of Star Trek, little is known of the Romulans. It is believed that they are descended from an early Vulcan colonization expedition; because Vulcan was at that time being torn apart by violence, contact between the two planets was lost. Vulcans formed a new society based on logic, while the colonists retained their warrior philosophy. The Romulan Neutral Zone is patterned after the wall built by Romulus. It lies between the Romulans and the Federation; if either side crosses into the Neutral Zone it constitutes an act of war.

Vulcan, Spock's home planet, has a very hot climate. In Roman mythology, Vulcan was the god of fire and metalworking, with a flaming forge located under Mt. Etna.

The episode "Bread and Circuses" showed us a twentieth-century Roman Empire on a planet-wide scale. A gladiator named Achilles, the Jupiter 8 automobile, Mars Tooth Paste, and Neptune Bath Salts are all named for greco-Roman heroes or gods. In mythology, Achilles was a fighter who couldn't be wounded anywhere except his heel because that was where his mother held him when she dunked him into the River Styx to make him invulnerable. The Jupiter 8 was named after the chief of the Roman gods; obviously the buyer was intended to believe the Jpiter 8 was "chief of cars." Mars was the god of war; so Mars Tooth Paste fought cavities. And the bath salts were appropriately named after Neptune, the god of the sea.

In "Mudd's Women," the three women were taking the Venus drug, which made them more desirable. Venus was the Roman goddess of vegetable gardens, springtime, beauty, charm, and sexual desire, as well as just plain, good, ordinary lust. She was the mother of Cupid, and was equated with the Greek goddess Aphrodite, the mother of Eros. Eros was the male god of love; and *eros* means "love" as in "Let us embrace in love. For my husband is not at home, but is gone on a long journey." When Mudd's women were taking the Venus drug they were erotically attractive to men in the same sense.

The Greeks had different words for the various emotions and expressions of love, yet we have only the one word, "love." How unfortunate that Western society has lost this aspect of ancient Greek philosophy when so many other elements of it have been carried forward.

## Fertility

Here again is Star Trek's use of a very popular classic mythological theme. At no time is our race left untouched by our sexuality or the need to reproduce ourselves. Fertility involves birth, growth, courtship, marriage, death, burial, and rebirth. It ensures the survival of the next generation. Many times in our lives we practice some form of ancient fertility rites, such as dancing, dating, weddings, festivals, and funerals. Furthermore, we teach our children about Easter eggs and bunnies, to play with dolls, to play games like in-and-out-the-window, and to celebrate the first day of May with a Maypole as our parents taught us.

Fertility rites or rituals were derived from the observation of the course of nature through birth, growth, death, and rebirth, and attempted to invoke the abundant growth of vegetation, necessary for life, at the time of its development—spring. These cylic myths of recurrent fertility involve sacrifice of, or to, a savior such as Osiris (Egyptian), Tammuz (Babylonian), Orpheus (Greek), Balder (Norse), or Baal (Canaanite). Frequently the sacrifice to the savior appears in terms of sexual orgy, in the offering up of virgins, or in veneration as of the phallus, or in death, mutilation, or torture of a savior-surrogate or an effigy.

The basic story for almost all fertility myths anywhere in the world is as follows: The Earth Mother is in love with and married to a god of benevolence and vegetation. By some means he is killed and sent to the underworld. The fall harvest represents his death. The Earth Mother is in mourning. The winter months represent her mouring. The earth is barren, and all is in desolation. She then either takes a hazardous journey to the underworld to retrieve her lover (spring planting), or gives birth to an heir and marries the son. This depicts the growth of the planted fields. Upon winning the god back, the couple return to the upper world, and the earth is covered with vegetation, the growth of their love. The cycle—summer, fall, winter, spring—went on and was represented in imitative magic.

Star Trek made very good use of this basic human theme. In ''Wink of an Eye,'' the Scalosian females had to choose mates from compatible males of other races. They lured the *Enterprise* to their planet with a distress signal, and Deela, the queen, chose Kirk for her mate and accelerated him to her place in time in order to procreate with him. Unfortunately, Kirk would die if he remained in that accelerated time frame. Deela was like the Earth Mother and Kirk was like the god of vegetation.

In ''Metamorphosis,'' Zefrem Cochrane was over a century old. The cloud mass, called the Companion, came down upon him, gave him life, kept him young, and, in a sense, rejuvenated the fertility god. Ultimately, she combined with the human female and became mortal for the sake of her lover.

In "Space Seed," Khan was in deep sleep in the underworld, so to speak, of his sleeper ship. He was revived, and Marla McGivers took sides with the newly revived Khan. This episode is an excellent example of the Earth Mother's struggle. Marla went through a hazardous conflict between her duty to the Federation and the *Enterprise* and her love for Khan. At the conclusion of the episode, Marla, Khan, and his followers are exiled to a world which they can seed with new life. (In mythology, more often than not, the Earth Mother is represented in red because the waters of birth are red, and, coincidentally, Marla wears the red Starfleet uniform.)

In "The Menagerie," Captain Pike was Vina's ideal man, and she couldn't help but love him. The Talosians took him to the underworld of their barren, desolate planet, where Vina struggled to join with Pike. The Talosians wanted the two humans to breed a new race which would refertilize Talos. Pike would not and could not stay, however. Even though Vina was distraught, time was on her side, and he eventually joined her on Talos, saving himself from the suffering of his twisted body.

## Scapegoats in Space

A scapegoat is a person, group, or animal that bears the blame for the sins, mistakes, or ill luck of a people in order, symbolically, to remove these evils from the people. The scapegoat is driven away to die by sacrifice or exposure. The scapegoat may also become the symbol of frustrations and disappointments.

"The Mark of Gideon" is an interesting variation of the scapegoat theme in Star Trek. In this episode, the planet Gideon was without sickness or death and suffered from massive overpopulation. Life was sacred to the people; their morals forbade them to use contraception. Kirk's blood carried a virus which was highly communicable; through trickery, a sample of his blood was given to Odona, a beautiful young woman, who soon became seriously ill. As Kirk was trying to save her life, she explained to him the purpose of her actions

She had volunteered to die in order to set an example for other volunteers among her people. Their sickness and deaths would start the planet back toward its natural balance. Odona was to be the scapegoat for her overpopulated planet. She was a princess of a ruling family, a position of honor and responsibility. She recognized that she was supposed to be a scapegoat and accepted the situation. To sacrifice herself was a high honor.

In early Middle East mythologies, the concept of the scapegoat was first attached to kings because they were considered a link between man and the gods. Being king was a position of religious honor and had nothing to do with leadership. (Further on, we will discuss how this concept later changed.) For a year, the king was treated with honor, fattened, and pampered in every way imaginable. At the spring feast, he became the feast. Since he was the link between man and the gods, he represented all of mankind's sins and bad luck. The king would be slaughtered, his blood would be spread over hillsides and fields, and all would eat a part of him so that they might also be temporarily in association with the gods. As human sacrifice went out of fashion, this honor was transferred to animals.

During the time of the Jewish Temple, on the Day Atonement, which is observed in the fall, the high priest of the ancient Jews laid both his hands upon the head of a live goat. He confessed all the sins and wickedness of the people of Israel and transferred them to the goat. The goat was led out of Jerusalem into the desert and made to fall to its death over a cliff.

In our modern times Jesus is a classic example of the scapegoat theme. St. Peter wrote, "Christ died once for sins, a righteous man for unrighteous men, in order that he might lead us to God." Christians commemorate this sacrifice as part of their worship. The body and blood of Jesus are represented by bread and wine. The people partake of the bread and wine to remember Jesus' sacrifice.

There are other episodes in Star Trek that demonstrate the scapegoat philosophy: In "The Alternative Factor," the sane Lazarus chose to fight his insane double for all eternity in order to save both universes. Kirk had to let Edith Keeler die in "The City on the Edge of Forever" in order to restore Earth's future as he knew it. Under threat of almost certain death, Spock traveled to the nucleus of the giant amoeba to save the *Enterprise* in "The Immunity Syndrome."

## Kingship

Kingship is an idea that goes back into antiquity. It developed with the philosophy of scapegoats. The king was the scapegoat, that link between gods and man. As our ancestors moved away from human sacrifice to animal sacrifice, the kings became priests. Power rested with them, and they became political leaders as well as religious leaders.

In "The Apple," Akuta is the leader of the people of Vaal. He is the eyes, ears, and voice of Vaal. Direct contact between Vaal and Akuta was maintained through antennae located just behind Akuta's ears. To the natives of Gamma Trianguli VI, he was the king, that link between god and man.

In mythology, man's greatest sin was to compare himself to the gods, and Star Trek has a surprising number of episodes based on this theme—men who dared to think of themselves as gods or who tried to become immortal.

In "The Ultimate Computer," Dr. Daystrom invented the M-5 computer, which could perform all of the ship's functions. He had been a boy genius who could not live up to his reputation in later life. Daystrom put his brain engrams into the computer, essentially making his essence immortal. Both he and the computer were destroyed, as if the wrath of the gods had come down—as always in the mythological stories—and destroyed this mortal.

In "Plato's Stepchildren," Alexander, the dwarf, who is one of the heroes of the story, could not utilize a substance in food and thereby gain telekinetic powers as the other inhabitants did. When the *Enterprise* men discovered the means to achieve telekinetic power, Alexander refused it. He did not want to become like his evil contemporaries. Parmen, their leader, who had the strongest power, led the people to their downfall because he behaved as if he thought he was a god. Alexander left the planet and escaped their punishment.

"Lord" Garth, in "Whom Gods Destroy," declared himself to be Master of the Universe and compared himself to the gods. He practiced human sacrifice and tried to take over the *Enterprise* as the first step in his conquest of the galaxy. He was frustrated in his actions and subdued. According to the gods, man must be humble and retain his place in the universe and on earth.

In "Return to Tomorrow," Sargon and his wife Thalassa belonged to a race from the now-dead planet Arret. Sargon said that in their prime, his people were so powerful that they dared to think of themselves as gods. This led to war and their destruction; only a few survivors were able to place their minds into little orbs. Henoch failed to learn his lesson the first time; he continued to try to be all-powerful, and he decided to keep Spock's body. Sargon destroyed Henoch and the orbs; deciding to accept their punishment, he and Thalassa ended up departing into oblivion.

Gary Mitchell was contaminated by the forces in the barrier at the edge of the galaxy in "Where No Man Has Gone Before." He mutated, developing unlimited mental powers. Kirk realized the danger he posed and tried to abandon Mitchell on a barren planet. Mitchell created a garden of sorts, with Kaferian apples, called himself god, and demanded that Kirk pray to him. But he was still driven by human frailty, and eventually was killed.

Apollo in "Who Mourns for Adonais?" was another who dared to call himself a god, and even though he was once worshiped as a god in ancient Greece, still he was eventually destroyed.

The same theme occurs in the Bible: "Pride goes before destruction, and a haughty spirit before a fall."

King Herod Agrippa I put on his royal robes and sat on his throne to make a speech to an audience of people from Tyre and Sidon. He wore a garment made wholly of silver and of a truly wonderful fabric. The early-morning sunlight hit his garment, and the effect was dazzling. His flatterers were shouting, "The voice of a god and not of a man," and he did not stop them. Immediately he was stricken with a severe pain in his belly, and five days later he died.

The Bible says, "An angel of the Lord struck him."

## Khan

In "Space Seed," Khan compared himself to Milton's Lucifer and said, "I've gotten something else I wanted—a world to win, an empire to build."

When Kirk was asked about what Khan meant when referring to Milton, Kirk explained: "A statement Lucifer made when he fell into the pit: 'It is better to rule in hell than to serve in heaven.'"

The name Lucifer in the Bible does not refer to Satan. It refers only to the overly ambitious last king of Babylon, Nabonidus, who became king in 555 B.C. and terrorized the world. He made his son Belshazzar coruler. Belshazzar threw a big feast, and when he used the Jerusalem Temple vessels for drinking wine, handwriting appeared on the wall predicting the end of his kingdom. Babylon was overthrown that very night. In Isaiah 24, there is a taunt against King Nabonidus, calling him Morning Star (Lucifer, in some translations), son of the god of dawn in Canaanite mythology:

> How the oppressor has come to an end!
>     How his fury has ended!
> How you have fallen from heaven,
>     O morning star, son of dawn!
> You have been cast down to the earth,
>     you who once laid low the nations!
> You said in your heart,
>     "I will ascend to heaven;
> I will raise my throne
>     above the stairs of God;
> I will sit enthroned at the mount of assembly,
>     on the utmost heights of the sacred mountain.
> I will ascend above the tops of the clouds;
>     I will make myself like the Most High."
> But you are brought down to the grave,
>     to the depths of the pit.

Khan had failed to lay the nations low on Earth. Then his ambition was to ascend to heaven and raise his throne above the stairs of God, but how his fury has ended!

## "The Gamesters of Triskelion"

In "The Gamesters of Triskelion," the thralls were people stolen from other parts of the galaxy and forced to render service and fight each other. Each of them wore a collar of obedience. In Norse mythology, a thrall is a slave. Odin, the Norse god of war and death, had a magic ring, and whoever wore it was of the league of Odin, that is, if given a ring of Odin, service must be rendered to Odin. (The custom of giving a wedding ring also goes back to Odin because service is rendered.) The collars worn by the thralls in "Gamesters" represent the rings of Odin.

After death, Odin's top-ranked warriors would be taken to Valhalla by the Valkyries (women warriors) to do battle all day and die on the field, and then rise up at night to feast with Odin. Odin would give weapons to the kingly leaders; probably the sword of King Arthur, Excalibur, was thought to be such a weapon. The women warrior thralls, Shahna and Tamoon, were representative of the Valkyries.

Berserkers were of the league of Odin; all they did was fight. They were mercenary soldiers, and they were thought to be strange because they never wore any armor—just carried a sword, and wore bearskins. In "Gamesters," the big, ugly fighter Kloog wore a bearskin and was a true representative of a berserker of the league of Odin. It should be noted that both Kloog and Odin were blind in one eye. Spock knows of the berserkers as well—he points out that the Klingons are "not berserkers."

## Priestesses and Oracles

In "For the World Is Hollow and I Have Touched the Sky," the asteroid Yonada is a spaceship inhabited by colonists being sent to a promised new world. The builders of the ship have long since been forgotten, and the people are not aware that they are inside a ship, and they worship the computer that runs it. Natira is their high priestess. To receive instruction, she kneels on a platform in the oracle room and speaks with the computer, which she calls "Oracle of the People."

The most famous oracle of antiquity was that of Apollo at

Delphi, consulted for predictions of future events, guidance for founding new colonies, and all kinds of advice. Apollo was not the original owner; he got it by killing a dragon or enormous serpent named Python that was already in possession. Underworld powers, according to Greek mythology, very commonly manifested themselves in the form of a serpent, and the people who were supposed to predict future events were said to have a spirit of Python. To receive inspiration, the Delphic priestesses sat in the center of Apollo's temple on a sacred tripod carved with intertwined snakes. So Natira can be seen as a priestess of Apollo.

Vaal, the reptilian-shaped thing in "The Apple," spoke only to Akuta and could be considered another oracle of underworld power. Its center was deep in the planet, and the Pythonlike figure was an access point.

## "Who Mourns for Adonais?" and Greek Gods

In Star Trek there are several direct references to mythical Greek tales. In "Who Mourns for Adonais?" Apollo was the last of the self-exiled Greek gods—a near-immortal being able to direct power from a material power source. To the Greeks, Apollo was the god of the sun, youth and manly beauty, poetry, music, and the wisdom of the oracles. He was the protector of flocks, guardian of colonies and villages, and averter of evil. He was the son of Zeus and Leto, and twin brother of Artemis. He was the most loved and feared god in Greek mythology, and represented all that was sacred in Greek ideals.

In Star Trek, Apollo needed love to survive. He grabbed the *Enterprise* at Pollux IV in order to found a new colony of worshipers of himself. He and Lieutenant Carolyn Palamas became fond of each other, but she then rejected him. After a series of backslashes, Apollo spread his body upon the wind and disappeared forever.

In the episode "Elaan of Troyius," Elaan, the bride-to-be sent from Elas to Troyius to marry the Troyian leader, represents Helen of Troy. Helen (Ελένη, "torch") was the daughter of Zeus and Leda, the wife of the king of Sparta, and was thought to be the most beautiful woman in Greece ('Ελλάς,

Hellas). She had many suitors in Greece and chose one, but Aphrodite had promised the Trojan prince Paris that he could marry the most beautiful woman in the world. So he abducted Helen and took her across the sea to Troy, and she became the indirect cause of the Trojan war when the Greek chieftains tried to recover her. The Klingons and Kryton tried to cause a war over Troyius and Elaan, but the *Enterprise* prevented it. Helen was worshiped as a goddess in Sparta, and torchy-tempered Elaan expected a little worship on the *Enterprise*, and had no patience with soft, un-Spartan things.

In "All Our Yesterdays," Zarabeth lived on a planet named Sarpeidon. All of the people on the planet went back into their own history. If they went back to a place where their ancestors were, the atavachron (meaning "ancestor time") enabled them to become their own ancestors.

The Greek myth of Sarpedon helps explain how this could happen. Sarpedon was first son of Zeus and Laodamia. He was prince of Lycia and a hero in the Trojan war, killed fighting on the side of the Trojans. Apollo rescued his body and handed it over to Sleep and Death, who took it back to Lycia for burial. According to a later tradition, Sarpedon became the son of Zeus and Europa, brother of King Minos of Crete, and grandfather of the first Sarpedon; that is, his own grandfather. Minos expelled him from Crete, so he and his comrades sailed for Asia, where he finally became king of Lycia, and was allowed by the gods to live for three generations.

In "Dagger of the Mind," Dr. Simon van Gelder escaped from the penal colony on Tantalus V by hiding in a crate that was beamed up to the *Enterprise*. The penal colony was located deep under the surface of the planet. The Greek mythological theme in this episode is of Tantalus, who had committed a terrible crime, and whose punishment in the underworld was torture with eternal hunger and thirst. He was condemned to stand in water that always receded when he tried to drink and stand under branches that the wind always blew upward when he tried to reach the fruit. In the episode, the neural neutralizer was used to remove memories and to torture with loneliness. Lethe was the name of a former inmate who did not remember her crime. Her name, from Greek mythology, means "forgetfulness," and was the name of the river flowing through the underworld, whose water caused a loss of memory in those who drank it.

## Medusans and Gorgons

In the episode "Is There in Truth No Beauty?" Dr. Miranda Jones is the representative for the Federation to the Medusan race via mind link with Ambassador Kollos. The greek word καλός (*kalos*) means both "good" and "beautiful" and describes the thought of the Medusan race. In Greek mythology, Medusa was one of the three gorgons, a monster with snakes for hair, whose face would turn all who looked at it to stone; but in this episode, looking at Kollos would cause a human to go mad. Either way, one would be destroyed.

"And the Children Shall Lead" featured a Gorgon named Gorgan. He appeared to the children as a friendly angel until they saw him as he really was, evil and ugly. In mythology, the Gorgons were horribly ugly and repulsive, with dragonlike bodies, snakes for hair, golden wings, claws of bronze, and glaring eyes. They were also female, so the Gorgons were misrepresented in Star Trek.

## Bacchus Made Me Do It

In "By Any Other Name," some Kelvans from the Andromeda galaxy took on human form in order to take over the *Enterprise* and journey toward home. They were not used to human sensations, so Scotty was able to get one of the Kelvans, Tomar, drunk. One of the drinks, the green one, was from Ganymede, one of Jupiter's moons. In mythology, Ganymede had the job of filling the drinking cup of Zeus, the Greek equivalent of Jupiter.

Bacchus was the god of wine and Bacchic revelries. Originally Bacchus was not a Greek god; the Greeks threw an irrelevant goddess out of their twelve-god pantheon and put this wine god from Turkey in. The Romans picked him up without changing his name, but they polluted the myth of Bacchus, and they would have Bacchic revelries and blame their drunkenness on the god. Therefore, the Roman god of wine was a drunken brawler while the Greek god of wine was a scholar inspired by the wine. There were Bacchic revelries in mythology, where all kinds of uninhibited and inspiring things or really rude, crude, and socially unacceptable things were done and blamed on the god. In ''The Return of the Archons,'' during the Red Hour and Festival, all became totally uninhibited for twelve hours as if they were in a Bacchic revelry.

## Flint

In ''Requiem for Methuselah,'' Flint owned a Gutenberg Bible. It was not unusual that he owned a Bible, for already it has been translated into more than 1,000 languages and parts of the Bible have gone to the moon; it was more unusual in that it wasn't computerized. But this wasn't just an ordinary old-fashioned bound book; a Gutenberg Bible was the first book printed with movable, cast type. It measured eleven by fifteen and one-half inches, was set in type that resembled calligraphy, was in Latin, and had pages beautifully decorated in colors.

Flint was an immortal human. Born Akharin, a bully soldier of Mesopotamia, he later became Methuselah, Solomon, Alexander, Lazarus, Merlin, Leonardo da Vinci, Johnannes Brahms, Abranson, and a hundred others. He claimed to have known Moses, Socrates, and Galileo. In very ancient times, there were more famous people in the Bible than in the rest of ancient history, and the older Old Testament stories are older than the extant Greek and Roman mythological stories. Flint said that he was born in 3834 B.C. Methuselah was born about 3317 B.C. and died the year that his grandson Noah entered the ark to escape the flood. Methuselah was famous for his record age—969 years. Lazarus was famous for having been raised from the dead by Jesus. Solomon was famous for his unusual wisdom and insight, his almost incredible wealth, and his 1,000 wives and concubines. Solomon wrote parts of the Bible—his address and prayer at the dedication of the Temple (1 Kings 8), Ecclesiastes, the Song of Solomon, and most of Proverbs.

Flint told Kirk, ''I have married a hundred times, Captain, selected, loved, cherished, caressed a smoothness, inhaled a brief fragrance. . . . Tonight I've seen something wondrous, something I've waited for. Nothing must endanger it. At last Rayna's emotions have stirred to life. Now they will turn to me.''

An excerpt from the love poem, Song of Solomon:

All night on my bed
I looked for the one my heart loves;
   I looked for him but did not find him.
I will get up now and go about the city,
   through its streets and squares;
I will search for the one my heart loves.
   So I looked for him but did not find him.
The watchmen found me
   as they made their round in the city.
   ''Have you seen the one my heart loves?''
Scarcely had I passed them
   when I found the one my heart loves.
I held him and would not let him go
   till I had brought him to my mother's house,
   to the room of the one who conceived me.
Daughters of Jerusalem, I charge you
   by the gazelles and by the does of the field:
Do not arouse or awaken love
   until it so desires. . . .
Come out, you daughters of Zion,
   and look at King Solomon wearing the crown,
   the crown with which his mother crowned him
on the day of his wedding,
   the day his heart rejoiced.

### Adam and Eve and the Garden of Eden

The story of Adam and Eve and the Garden of Eden seems to be a favorite among Star Trek's writers. *Adam* means ''man.'' ''Adam named his wife Eve, because she would become the mother of all the living.'' *Eve* means ''living.'' *Eden* means ''delight.'' This is the story of the beginning of mankind on Earth.

In ''Mudd's Women,'' the woman named Eve was looking

for a man to whom she could be a wife and helper. She ended up with a man on a desolate planet, a planet that must have looked as bleak to her as did Earth outside Eden to the first Eve when she was driven out of the garden.

"The Way to Eden" features a space hippie named Adam looking for an Eden, a planet that was thought to be mythical. When found, somewhere inside Romulan space, it proved to be a fantastically beautiful planet of sunshine, flowers, and heavily laden fruit trees. But it had no humanoid or animal life because all the plants contained an acid which would badly burn exposed skin areas and would kill if the fruit was eaten. Adam ate the fruit and died. Dr. Sevrin, the leader of the Eden seekers, was insane—warned not to eat the fruit because it was deadly, he ate it anyway and died.

When God put Adam and Eve in the Garden of Eden, he commanded Adam, "You may freely eat of every tree of the garden; but of the tree of knowledge of good and evil you shall not eat, for in the day that you eat of it you shall die." Adam ate the fruit and tried to blame Eve, and Eve tried to blame the serpent, but God held all three responsible and punished all of them. To Adam he said:

> Because you have listened to the voice of your wife,
>     and have eaten of the tree
>     about which I commanded you,
>     "You shall not eat of it,"
>     cursed is the ground because of you;
>     in toil shall you eat of it all the days of your life.
> Thorns and thistles it shall bring forth for you,
>     and you shall eat the plants of the field.
> By the sweat of your brow
>     shall you get bread to eat
> till you return to the ground,
>     for from it you were taken;
> for you are dust,
>     and to dust shall you return.

To Eve he said:

> I will greatly multiply your pain in
> childbearing;
> in pain shall you bear children,
> yet your desire shall be for your husband,
> and he shall rule over you.

Then God banished Adam and Eve from the Garden so that they could not also eat from the tree of life, which was in the Garden, and live forever.

In "Return to Tomorrow," when Sargon explained why he called the humans and Spock "my children," he said, "Perhaps your own legends of an Adam and an Eve were two of our travelers."

In "A Private Little War," Kirk called Tyree's planet "a Garden of Eden," and explained flintlocks to Scotty as "serpents for the Garden of Eden." Tyree's wife was so beguiled by weapons that she tried to get them for her husband. The serpent in the Garden of Eden beguiled Eve, telling her, "You will not die. God knows that when you eat the fruit of the tree of the knowledge of good and evil, your eyes will be opened and you will be like God, who knows good and evil."

After Adam and Eve had both sinned by disobeying God and eating the forbidden fruit, they felt ashamed. Being naked began to bother them, so they sewed fig leaves together to make themselves aprons. In "Metamorphosis," when Zefrem Cochrane said that he and Nancy Hedford might even plant a fig tree, he was referring to everything Adam and Eve did after their experience sewing fig leaves.

In "The Menagerie," the Talosian Keepers wanted to start a race of slaves descended from Captain Pike and Vina—as in "he's Adam and she's Eve." Adam and Eve were told to be fruitful and multiply and fill the planet and subdue it and have dominion over the fish of the sea and over the birds of the air and over every living creature that moves upon the planet. The Keepers wanted Pike and Vina to do the same except that the Keepers would rule over the humans. The humans, however, believed it was wrong to start a whole race of humans just to serve the Talosians.

In "This Side of Paradise," people were under the influence of alien spores, and in return the spores would give the people perfect health and happiness. They even made Spock happy, and he said, "It's a true Eden, Jim. There's belonging and love."

Violent emotions caused the people to throw off the effect of the spores, and as they were leaving the planet, McCoy said, "That's the second time man has been thrown out of Paradise."

Kirk disagreed. "No, this time we walked away on our own."

Vaal's planet in "The Apple" seemed, at first, to have striking resemblances to the Garden of Eden, which Chekov said was "just outside of Moscow. A very nice place. It must have made Adam very sad to leave." But differences soon became obvious—dangerous plants and land mines. The people obeyed Vaal and had no vices; although they didn't age, they also didn't progress. Kirk and McCoy thought this situation to be one of stagnation and thought the Vaalians needed to be more human. The Vaalians learned to touch and kiss from Chekov, and they learned to kill from Vaal. Vaal proved to be only a machine, but Akuta revered it as if it were God and said, "Vaal is everything. He causes the rain to fall and the sun to shine. All good comes from Vaal."

God "causes his sun to rise on the bad and the good, and sends rain on the just and the unjust"; and "every good gift and every perfect gift is from above, coming down from the Father of lights." The captain had to destroy Vaal in order to free his ship; this also freed the Vaalians from stagnation, but Akuta was left without guidance and security and he and his people had to learn that Vaal was not God.

After the *Enterprise* crew members returned to the ship, Spock said, "Captain, you are aware of the biblical story of Genesis?"

Kirk answered, "Yes, of course I'm aware of that. Adam and Eve tasted the apple and as a result were driven out of Paradise."

And Spock said, "Precisely, Captain, and in a manner of

speaking, we have given the people of Vaal the apple, the knowledge of good and evil, if you will, as a result of which they too have been driven out of Paradise.''

The captain asked, ''Are you casting me in the role of Satan? . . . Are you aware of anyone on this ship who even remotely looks like Satan?'' Spock was not aware of such a person.

### Satan

It has been said that Spock's appearance is satanic, but he does not look even remotely like the Satan of biblical standards, who appeared to Eve as a talking snake or dragon, and except for size, looked a lot like Vaal. The Bible is not the point of origin of legends of pitchforks and pointed ears—Pan, the goatlike god of European mythology, is. Whenever Christianity has been newly introduced into a region, Satan has become associated with a god or some character from that region's mythology in people's minds. So in different regions, artists have depicted Satan quite differently. In France, for instance, Satan has been drawn as a pig.

Witchcraft was a part of the mythology of France, Germany, and the British Isles. It was the act of controlling natural forces and minds by the powers of magic. Their god appeared disguised in various human and animal forms, including black cats (as Sylvia appeared in ''Catspaw''). Assemblies took place four times a year, including Halloween and the eve of May Day, and included the usual fertility rites. Sylvia's method of threatening the *Enterprise* by holding a model of it above a candle flame comes from witchcraft; so did her spells over Sulu and Scott and her attempt to inspire Kirk with a desire for power.

In ''All Our Yesterdays,'' when Kirk went back in time into Sarpedon's past, he found that it was not safe to be thought a witch there.

In ''Charlie X,'' Uhura's song about Spock teasingly warns girls in space not to be beguiled by him:

Oh, on the Starship *Enterprise*
There's someone who's in Satan's guise
Whose devil ears and devil eyes
Could rip your heart from you.

The Horta, from "Devil in the Dark," was another creature unfairly compared to the devil. St. Paul wrote, "Put on the full armor of God, that you may be able to stand against the pursuits of the devil. For we are not wrestling against flesh and blood, but against the leaders, against the powers, against the world-rulers of this darkness, against spiritual things of the evil one in heavenly places." The Horta did not have the kind of flesh and blood that the men could recognize, and it was the ruling power of that dark world. The Horta had been killing the men, so it seemed evil until it was understood. Yet the men had seemed quite evil to her, too, and she called *them* devils.

In "The Omega Glory," Captain Tracy told the Yangs that Kirk was the Evil One and that Spock was his servant. The Yangs knew of God and, looking into an old Bible to see if this was true, found a picture of Satan somewhat resembling Spock. When Tracy said that Spock had no heart, Kirk, in order to keep Spock from being killed, said, "No, wait! There's a better way! Does not your sacred book promise that good is stronger than evil?" The Yangs decided that good will always destroy evil, but they forgot that if you sit back and wait for it to happen, you may be waiting until judgment day. After Sulu and security guards beamed down, the Yangs thought Kirk a great servant of God and bowed down to him.

The children in "And the Children Shall Lead" called Gorgan "friendly angel," but he seems to have had more in common with the devil's angels. The devil is the deceiver, and "even Satan transforms himself into an angel of light. So it is no great thing if his servants disguise themselves as servants of righteousness. Their end will correspond to their deeds."

Gorgan had been disguising himself and deceiving the children and crew members. He sought to maintain power by suppressing the truth, but Kirk defeated him and freed the children with truth.

In the New Testament, Jesus said, "You will know the truth, and the truth will make you free." Also, James wrote, "Resist the devil and he will flee from you."

In "Day of the Dove," Kirk said to the Klingon Kang, "Go to the devil." Kang answered, "We have no devil, Kirk, but we understand the habits of yours. I will torture you to death, one by one!"

Jesus said to the church at Smyrna, "Do not fear what you are about to suffer. Behold the devil is about to throw some of you into prison, so that you may be tested, and you will suffer persecution for ten days. Be faithful until death, and I will give you the crown of life."

## The Prime Directive

When the Prime Directive is in full force on a planet, there can be no identification of self or of mission and no references to space or to the fact that there are other worlds or more advanced civilizations. The use of phasers is expressly forbidden. There can be no interference with either the normal social development or the normal technological development of the planet in order that the people's wisdom and understanding will have a chance to keep up with their technology.

> Happy is the man who finds wisdom,
>     and the man who gets understanding,
> for the gain from it is better than gain from silver
>     and its profit better than gold.
> She is more precious than jewels,
>     and nothing you desire can compare with her.
> Long life is in her right hand;
>     in her left hand are riches and honor.

The reward of wisdom and understanding is long life and prosperity. As the Vulcans say, "Live long and prosper."

# TREK ROUNDTABLE—LETTERS FROM OUR READERS

*This volume of* The Best of Trek *unfortunately goes to deadline only a week or so after the premiere of* Star Trek III: The Search for Spock. *While we were able to squeak in a number of articles about the new movie, we hadn't as yet gotten a lot of mail. However, a few determined readers sat down and—literally—immediately wrote to the Roundtable their views on* The Search for Spock. *You'll find those letters interspersed throughout this section. Don't despair, however, for we have an unusually fine selection of letters this time around, and we think you'll enjoy each and every one of them. And why don't you write us a letter, too? It's just possible that you'll be a participant in our next Trek Roundtable!*

**Pam Watson**
**Bentleyville, Pa.**

I saw the premiere of *Star Trek III: The Search for Spock* on the evening of June 1 and I have been trying until now to figure out how I feel about it. I guess I liked it. . . .

What can I say about it? It was the second half of *Wrath of Khan*, and I don't know why they didn't just tack it onto the end of *Wrath of Khan*.

But perhaps it is the ending I found so slow. All that standing around on Vulcan waiting for the mind meld to be reversed when we knew that Spock *was* going to come out of it alive and unchanged.

Maybe that was the real problem. There was no change by the end of the movie as there had been in *Wrath of Khan*, and no growth. People were back where they always had been, and it reduced the story to just another television show episode.

"Well, they thought Spock was dead but he wasn't really."

"Oh."

And I can't help thinking that it could have been made into a much better movie if Spock's rebirth had been treated as his death was in *Wrath of Khan*—a sidebar to an otherwise interesting and enjoyable story. Why wasn't there more about David's death? There could have been the sense that his death was in accordance with the old Greek idea that nothing beautiful or worthwhile is achieved without sacrifice. There could have been just one scene between him and Kirk where we gathered that they cared about each other, or where Kirk spoke of him as his son with love to *show* why Kirk collapsed in tears at his death. We should have felt his death, he shouldn't have been knocked off casually like some unknown security guard.

And why didn't we *know* what Kirk and the others were sacrificing by stealing the *Enterprise?* A remark saying Kirk had finally reachieved command officially, being promised a new ship, would have made the action of deliberately throwing his heart's desire away more compelling.

And don't tell me we in fandom *know* how Kirk and Scotty felt ordering the *Enterprise*'s destruction. Most of the people who must pay to see this movie if it is to be a success and there is to be a *Star Trek IV* aren't in Trek fandom, and if you aren't in fandom or haven't seen *Wrath of Khan*, you wouldn't know what is going on. You certainly wouldn't know why that group of people is ready to give up their careers, and possibly their lives, for Spock.

I started by not being sure if I liked *Search for Spock*, but writing you I have decided what I feel.

This is the second Star Trek movie that misses the mark. And it is a shame.

**Deidre Simpson**
**Nashville, Tenn.**

I have purchased and thoroughly enjoyed all the *Best of Trek* books. I have been a Star Trek fan since the original series (I was fourteen when it started, so was old enough to appreciate it). No matter how many times I have seen the different episodes I still never tire of them. But in Nashville, we have been without it for a long time until recently when a new independent station started running it again.

At first they aired it at 10:30 P.M. each night; fine time if you are a kid, but terrible if you have to get up to go to work the next morning. Well, after about three weeks on the air, they announced that due to the tremendous response of fans, they were moving it to an earlier time, 6:00 P.M. This was fine except that I don't get off work until 5:30, and it's a wonder that I have not gotten any speeding tickets trying to get home in time to see it each night. In fact, one night, there was an accident on the interstate and I was late getting home and I was cursing right and left at everybody because I couldn't get home in time. Normally, I don't lose my temper, but when it comes to watching Star Trek, watch out!

One of the girls I work with is a Star Trek fan also, and we would call the station to see what episodes would be coming on and tell them how much we appreciated them airing it. This is something, in that we work at the CBS affiliate here, and we were complimenting one of our competitors on their programming. Our programming department had the chance several years ago to purchase Star Trek and passed it up. No fans there. This other station also had a month-long promotion leading up to the premiere of *The Search for Spock*, ending up with a twenty-four-hour Star Trek Marathon on Memorial Day weekend. This was fabulous.

I was able to get one ticket to the sneak premiere of the movie here simply because of my connections in the industry. I loved it. I had managed to find out definitely that Spock did come back, but not exactly why. I have now seen it twice and plan to go back again. I might try writing my impressions of it once I have seen it again. The first time, I had the unfortunate luck to sit beside a woman who had her kid with her, which meant that I didn't hear half the movie.

The strongest impression I got from the movie was how much I enjoyed seeing the crew away from the *Enterprise*. I got the impression that I was really seeing the characters as they really were away from "the battlefield," so to speak. I love the civilian clothes; this was just another touch of realism, in my opinion.

**Hilary Ryan**
**Regina, Sask., Canada**

"It is very cold in space. . . ." I couldn't get these words of Khan's out of my mind as I watched the thermometer outside our kitchen window drop below that point where the Celsius and Fahrenheit scales meet. −40 C., only 233° above Absolute Zero, where not even hydrogen atoms can move; no wonder my car wouldn't start! My shivering wasn't helped by the repeated announcements that it was warmer in Siberia and at the North Pole than in Regina. I firmly resolved to follow my car's example and not budge from the house during this holiday if I could avoid it. So saying, I curled up with my latest treasures from the bookstore, and lost myself in our beloved Star Trek universe.

The first book I plunged into was *The Best of Trek #6*. As always, I was impressed with the care with which every article was researched and written. Jeff Mason's "Star Trek Chronology" was especially good.

The Roundtable is a marvelous institution. Several things hit me when I read the letters in this and previous *Best of Treks*. First is how remarkably similar fans' feelings about themselves are when they talk about how they "came out of the closet." It strikes me that most of us felt a little embarrassed at the strong feelings we had for this show (before we realized that others felt this way, too). I know that as I was approaching my last year of high school, I tried to tell myself how silly it was to be so attached to a television program, to be sure a good one, and that it was really time I grew up and went on to more mature hobbies. Luckily, I ran into a fan who was quite open in his love for Star Trek, and ten years ago, I discovered "organized fandom." That was a terribly exciting time of my life and I've never regretted getting into, however superficially, this elite group of people.

The second thing I noticed, and have been surprised by, is that I have yet to see any comment on why Kirk was so upset by this particular birthday (in *Wrath of Khan*) and which birthday this is. It was obvious to me that he was celebrating the "Big Fifty." When we first met Kirk, way back in the first season, we are told (in the Writer's Guide and elsewhere) that he is thirty-four years old, one of the youngest captains in the Fleet. Adding fifteen years to this makes him forty-nine going on fifty. Whenever a human marks another decade it is a momentous occasion, and obviously even in the twenty-third century the half-century mark is one to reflect on even more than usual.

I am intrigued by the many ideas on how to get Spock back. As David Gerrold says, it isn't fair to play with our emotions and then say, "See, we didn't kill him after all" (especially after that beautiful and gut-wrenching death scene).

Unfortunately, I don't *want* to have Star Trek without Spock. I am quite prepared to see an "episode" which takes place before *Wrath of Khan*. I don't like the idea of a "spiritual guide" like Obi Wan, but I am also quite prepared to see him resurrected. I wondered when Spock mind-melded with McCoy if he was telling him to remember that Vulcans can slow their metabolic rate so low that instruments might not record it, and that he was in his famous healing trance and would eventually wake from it Perhaps he was telling him to remember that "our many craftsmen have the ability to place a human brain in a structurally compatible android body." If Spock has placed his consciousness in McCoy's brain, it may be that the androids on Planet Mudd can build an appropriate "receptacle" for it.

On the third hand, maybe the Genesis Wave can be a factor in his rebirth. I would think that the Genesis program would have a subroutine to handle "outside" life forms. After all, the original program was designed to make a planet "suitable for whatever life we see fit to deposit on it." This must mean that it would recognize something from outside its matrix after a certain stage in the planet's development and gear the rest of the development to an ideal environment to support that life form. Not all life forms require the same conditions, physical and organic, to sustain them. If a planet was being made for Vulcan habitation, and remembering that they were "spawned in different seas" from Terrans, the conditions would be radically different. (And if Hortas were the proposed colonizers, they wouldn't appreciate the oxygen-rich paradise we saw forming!) If Spock's torpedo casing arrived at the appropriate time in development, it may well be that the planet has prepared itself to nurture and heal him ( or that which remained of him).

I have a comment to make regarding the idea of cloning Spock. What most people don't seem to realize is the fact that cloning takes a single cell, and stimulates that cell to grow a duplicate of that organism; a few months for a carrot, a year for a frog, about sixty years for a Vulcan of Spock's age. Are Kirk and company going to be hanging around that long waiting? Are we? Even if the growth period is sped up, there still remains basic learning and training, which surely cannot duplicate the original's. We would have a totally different Spock who just looked like our friend; that could be more painful and harder to accept than his death.

The other book I read was *The Wounded Sky* by Diane Duane. This has to be the most stunning and thought-provoking Star Trek book yet. I heartily recommend that all fans read it (at least a couple times!).

**Monica Spencer**
**Summerland, B.C., Canada**

I have loved Star Trek ever since I first saw it several years ago. At first I was attracted to its creative storylines and its thought-provoking ideas. It wasn't long before I was "hooked," and I began to realize that there is much more to Star Trek than meets the eye. (I still haven't figured out just *what*, exactly.) I have *The Best of Trek #1–6*, and I love them; the articles are interesting, stimulating, and reflect deep insight. It means a lot to me to know that there are other people just as "crazy" as me—intelligent, normal people who have a lot to offer. Thank you, *Trek!*

A little about myself. I am twenty years old, and majoring in Biology at the University of Victoria. Besides Star Trek, I enjoy riding and showing horses, reading, writing, and turtles (I have a box turtle named Tobias).

Now that I have seen *Star Trek III: The Search for Spock*, I feel the need to share some of my thoughts with people who will not think I am being soft in the head. I loved the movie! It was real Star Trek; even better, I think, than *Wrath of Khan*. I had not expected to like Robin Curtis's Saavik (how dare they change actresses like that!), but in many ways I liked her better than Kirstie Alley. She seemed more Vulcan and less glamorous. The unshakable loyalty of the command crew was touching (though not, of course, unexpected). Sulu and Uhura *finally* got to show their stuff. It was wonderful! It's about time they had more to do than fill up space in the background. I only wish that Uhura had gone to the Genesis Planet with the rest of them. (It also would have been nice if *she* had thrown someone on the floor!) Kirk, Spock, and McCoy were, as usual, superb. Sarek was also very good. He projected an aura of quiet power and arrogant Vulcan assurance. The Klingons were fantastic! Kruge was everything a good Klingon should be—fearless, unpredictable, and completely ruthless.

During the battle with the Klingons, I could feel everyone in the theater looking to Kirk, trusting him to find a way out of an impossible situation. It was a no-win scenario all over again, but Kirk got them out. Out of the frying pan, into the fire . . . into molten lava! But he won in the end. No wonder his crew will follow him anywhere!

When Kirk gave the order for the *Enterprise* to self-destruct, I felt as though he were ordering the death of an old friend. I was horrified, but I knew how much it cost him to give that order. Still, he had no choice, as McCoy said, and I would rather see her go out in a blaze of glory than see her end up in a scrap heap.

About Spock's resurrection: I was pleased to see that it made sense. So *that's* what the mind meld with McCoy was for! And the regeneration and aging of his cells is plausible, given the Genesis Wave and the use of protomatter. (A nice touch, that; it explains any anomalies.)

There is one thing that bothers me . . . Spock's *pon farr*. When the Spock on the Genesis Planet went through it, he appeared to be much younger than Spock in "Amok Time." In that episode, all indications were that it was his first *pon farr*. (I can't help but wonder now whether Saavik will end up pregnant. It certainly looked suspicious, but then you can never tell with Vulcans.)

I am curious to see what direction the next movie will take. The *Enterprise* is lost, and it looks as though the entire command crew is out of a job. I imagine that the Vulcan elders will come to their rescue as T'Pau did in "Amok Time," but I wonder if even they have enough weight to be effective in this case. Whatever happens, the command crew is still together, and it is this group of people—their courage, loyalty, and love for each other—that keeps Star Trek on the screen.

**Ellis Cambre**
**Gretna, La.**

I can't believe it! She's gone! NCC 1701 scuttled by her crew's own hand! Not destroyed in glorious battle with all flags flying and all phasers blazing, but burned up in the atmosphere of a dying planet. She was a good ship and deserved better than this!

Oh, I am quite sure that somewhere down the line there is an X2001 or an *Enterprise II* or some such successor. But it won't be the same corridors around which the crew gets tossed. The ship of the Tribbles that did battle with the Klingons and Romulans many times and sometimes returned bloodied, but always undefeated and unbowed. How can we have "continuing voyages of the Starship *Enterprise*" when it is not *the* Starship *Enterprise?* Every sailor can tell you each ship has a personality, a magic all its own. They killed NCC 1701, and we all lost something special.

**David E. Novak**
**Operation Deep Freeze, Antarctica**

As you can tell from the letterhead on this stationery, I am writing to you from about as far south as one can get.

Presently, I am a member of Antarctic Development Squadron 6's Parachute Rescue Team, currently deployed on the continent of Antarctica.

Being more or less isolated as I am, my only contacts with the world of Star Trek are my well-worn copies of Bjo Trimble's *Star Trek Concordance*, an almost complete set of Star Trek Fotonovels (Fotonovel #2 having been stolen while on deployment aboard USS *Midway* in 1978), and a video cassette of *Star Trek: The Motion Picture*, together with several TV episodes.

Recently I purchased *The Best of Trek #6*. I had never seen *BOT* before and I feel I have really missed out on something. *BOT* #6 was great, but I must make comments on two of the articles presented in this volume.

In Diane Rosenfeldt's "The Wrath of Khan: In Print/On Screen," she states, "Saavik's existence also allows us our first exposure to spoken Vulcan." This is most incorrect. In *Star Trek: The Motion Picture*, there were at least six or eight lines spoken to Spock by the Vulcan woman whom I assume to be the successor to T'Pau. (Celia Lovsky, who played T'Pau in "Amok Time," was, in my opinion, marvelous in the role. I can't imagine anyone else playing T'Pau.)

In the article "Star Trek Mysteries Solved—One More Time," one question concerned who was Captain Spock's first officer/who will be Kirk's new first officer. I must wholeheartedly agree with the choice of Commander Uhura to fill the position. But I don't think that we should assume that Kirk will remain in command of the *Enterprise*. Let me try explaining that by drawing on my experience during the last thirteen years in the Navy, and relating it to the nautical theme and background upon which Star Trek seems to be based.

First: Kirk is now an admiral. He is now of "flag rank," and would not command a ship. A present-day example (taken from my world of naval aviation) would be the admiral onboard an aircraft carrier. (Many Federation starships seem to be named after carriers: *Constellation*, *Enterprise*, *Lexington*, *Yorktown*, etc.) In my experience, the admiral would be on board as commander of a certain task force during a specific evolution, such as one of our various war-game scenarios so often played out while at sea. But he was definitely not in direct command of that ship, the captain was. And if we recall in *Star Trek: The Motion Picture*, Kirk had to be temporarily reduced in rank in order to captain the *Enterprise*.

In *Wrath of Khan*, Admiral Kirk was more or less forced to take command of the vessel in this emergency, at the insistence of the less-experienced "new" captain. And again it was understood that this was a temporary command.

So, seemingly, we are not faced with finding a new first officer, a billet probably being quite capably filled by Commander Uhura, but instead faced with finding a new captain!

Let me get off the track for a moment to bring up a question:

On page 31 of *BOT #6*, after it was revealed that Uhura was Spock's second in command, Leslie Thompson states that "she returned to her old post at communications for the purpose of the training voyage." *Returned* to her old post? That doesn't make sense. Are we to assume that someone of Uhura's obvious experience couldn't handle *both* duties? Spock's being first officer didn't interfere with his duties as science officer, or vice versa. He was science officer when he was promoted to first officer after the death of Lieutenant Commander Gary Mitchell, Kirk's original exec, and, if I'm not mistaken, chief navigator. What I'm getting at is that other *Enterprise* officers were not divorced from their job specialties as they rose in rank; shouldn't it also be so with Commander Uhura?

Anyway, let's get back to the problem at hand: Who will be the new captain of the *Enterprise?* The one logical choice to fill the command chair was the one most quickly "passed over" in the search for a new first officer, Commander Montgomery Scott! Above anyone else, he should be due for a promotion. He was already a lieutenant commander when Sulu and Uhura were both lieutenants, and although it's easy to picture Sulu in command of his own ship, I cannot see Scotty just stagnating at the rank of commander, not someone of his talent and caliber.

In character profiles put out during the early years of Star Trek, I believe that Scotty's read that he rose to lieutenant commander from the ranks. That must mean that he began somewhere along the line as just an ordinary crewman, Star Trek's version of our enlisted ranks. I don't think that anything can prepare you better in the leadership/management skills needed for command than to experience the service from both sides of the fence.

I think that one question that might be asked at this point is how Scott himself would feel about being taken from his engine room and away from his "precious bairns." Here's another example from our present-day fleet: One of the busiest men I can think of is an aircraft carrier CO. Almost invariably a naval aviator, he still can find the time to fly occasionally. I'm sure Scotty, as captain of the *Enterprise*, would make the time to occasionally visit his old engine room.

Now, let's put Leslie Thompson's theories and my own ideas together and see what kind of a bridge crew we come up with. As she said, "For all we know, the *Enterprise* could have been more or less permanently assigned as a command/ cadet training vessel." Okay, let's go with that premise. As things would now stand, Admiral Kirk is in command of a certain specific training task force, berthed aboard the largest of the training ships, USS *Enterprise:* Captain Montgomery Scott, captain; Commander Uhura, exec and communications officer; Dr. David Marcus, science officer; Lieutenant Saavik, navigator. That leaves only one empty major billet, helmsman. A position that could very well be filled by Lieutenant Commander (formerly Yeoman) Janice Rand. To me, that really doesn't sound too bad.

And what better way for a fairly seasoned bridge crew to train cadets than on an actual deep-space mission of the routine, nonviolent sort? A mission similar to our present-day Naval Academy's Summer Cruise, wherein the midshipmen get a chance to go to sea and actually experience what shipboard life is all about.

A deep-space mission somewhere in the vicinity, say, of the Genesis Planet?!?

Food for thought, if you ask me. . . .

**Arden J. Lowe**
**South Hadley, Mass.**

I want to thank you for your help. Last week I brought and read *Best of Trek #2–5*. (Yes, one after the other.) It was quite therapeutic. Not only was I given reassurance that I was not crazy—that there were other people as obsessed with Star Trek as I was and for the same reasons—but I was also able to enjoy my beloved Star Trek universe again. You see, I live in a cultural void—plenty of art, dance, drama, and music, but no Star Trek. The only TV station that carried Star Trek took it off the air in lieu of *Buck Rogers*. (Well, that's not what my husband and I call it, but this is a family publication.) None of the fanzines, including *Trek*, are available around here. If it weren't for the Star Trek novels and your essay collections, things would be really bleak.

I have a few comments to make on some of the articles in *Best of Trek #5*, beginning with Joyce Tullock's article, "The Myth and the Journey of Dr. Leonard McCoy." While I enjoyed reading the article and appreciated Ms. Tullock's insight into McCoy's character, I disagree with the point she made about "Bread and Circuses." In discussing the prison scene, she stated that "when McCoy loses his temper, his cutting remarks bounce back at him. He discovers that he is punishing others as a means of dealing with his own pain." She goes on to say that after McCoy lashes out at Spock, he realized that he is saying those things about himself and is sorry. However, Ms. Tullock had stated earlier in the article that McCoy is "unmerciful with the truth" and that his most valuable contribution is "his unrelenting realism." I believe that is what has happened in this scene. McCoy, being "unmerciful with the truth," has stated that Spock is not afraid to die because it would release him from his daily fear of slipping and showing his emotions. McCoy has, in fact, hit the proverbial nail on the head, as can be seen by the look on Spock's face. While he is too Vulcan to admit that McCoy is correct, the expression on Spock's face is that of one who has been "found out" and exposed. Well, that's my opinion, anyway, and I'm sure there are many more who would agree with me as well.

Secondly, I have a couple of questions on Jennifer Weston's article, "Of Spock, Genes, and DNA Recombination," keeping in mind that I am a musician, not a biologist. The first thing I wonder about is the necessity of the placental environment for Spock's prenatal development. After all, we are talking about the twenty-third century on a technologically advanced planet. Wouldn't Vulcans have developed *in utero* obstetrical techniques to compensate for any problems? We have some techniques now for Rh factor and other prenatal complications. I wonder. Of course, by the twenty-third century, the placental environment might be the preferred method of childbearing for both humans and Vulcans. Who knows?

The other question I have is about Spock's sterility, due to hybridization. If he were, in fact, sterile, why would he feel the effects of *pon farr?* Sterilized animals don't go into heat; why would a sterile Vulcan feel the mating urge? And, as has been demonstrated in "Amok Time," Spock does indeed have a *pon farr* cycle. Anyway, I was just wondering.

Finally, I disagree with one of the points in Rowena Warner's letter, which was in Trek Roundtable. In her letter, Ms. Warner discusses how Kirk hides his affection for Spock, and she states that she was "almost shocked by Kirk's rather harsh 'Spock, are you all right?' " Fortunately for Ms. Warner, she is not as accident-prone as I am, because if she were, she would have heard that tone of voice very often. My father, my husband, and our gentlemen friends use that tone of voice every time I injure myself. (Usually with a sharp implement of some kind.) Our twentieth-century American society encourages men to be near-Vulcan when it comes to emotional reactions. Such emotions as terror or concern for a loved one have to be checked very carefully. The tone of voice that Shatner chose to use for that particular scene is that of a man who is trying to keep both terror *and* concern in check, trying to keep calm. Unfortunately, the result *is* a rather harsh tone.

Kirk is a captain, and as such must remain calm and stay in control, at least on duty. After all, he is responsible for 430 lives. In the events that occur before Spock is attacked, Kirk has found his brother dead, seen his sister-in-law die, and discovered that the inhabitants of "one of the most beautiful colonies in the galaxy" have gone mad. Then one of the

creatures responsible for this mayhem attacks his friend, one
of the few friends he has allowed himself after Gary Mitchell,
Matt Decker, et al. Naturally, Kirk would be terrified to see
Spock suffering the same agonizing fate as the Denevans,
and, of course, would be very worried for his friend. However,
he is still the captain and still in control of both the ship and
the landing party. Not only that, but if he were too emotional,
Spock might react to Kirk's responses, and possibly make
matters worse. Hence the command-like tone of voice. Kirk
isn't entirely undemonstrative, however. After all, when Spock
doesn't respond to his questions, Kirk turns him over and
supports him in his arms. He could just as easily have rolled
Spock the other way, onto the floor.

Well, I'll shut up now. I appreciate the opportunity to
"spout off" about a pet subject—especially to people who
understand. I'm looking forward to *Trek*, and I'm thinking of
writing an article myself. Thanks again for making the last
week so enjoyable.

**Melanie Thorne**
**Anderson, S.C.**

I have been a fan of Star Trek for many years. In fact, I
have been a fan since the second season of the television
show. I have always been interested in the stories as well as
the characters, especially the triumvirate (Kirk, Spock, McCoy).
The last few years, my enthusiasm for the show diminished
because it was not on in my area, and the movies weren't out
as yet. Since I have been watching the reruns, my love for
Star Trek has been revived, and the new movie has added
fuel to the flames of that love. My personal opinion is that the
new film, *The Search for Spock*, is the best of all the movies.

I have just completed reading your books *Best of Trek #1,
3*, and *6*. I have never read more comprehensive analyses of
any subject than those of Star Trek in your magazine. I feel
as though I have met some new friends through your books. I
am now trying to get my hands on everything connected with
Star Trek since you helped rekindle my appreciation of the
series.

My favorite writer in your magazine is Leslie Thompson.

She seems to be a very smart lady. I have specially enjoyed her projected histories of Klingons and Romulans, as well as "Star Trek Mysteries Solved." I might not always agree with her, but I do agree with her most of the time. I, too, am a fan of the Klingons, and I also do not like the changes made in the movies from the way they are in the TV show.

One thing that really impressed me about the articles in *Best of Trek #6* was the uncanny predictions about what *The Search for Spock* would be about. To steal a word from Mr. Spock, it was quite "interesting."

**Portia Olson**
**North East, Pa.**

I have just finished reading *The Best of Trek #6*, and would like to tell you how highly impressed I was with it—later I went out and bought *#4 and #5* (they were all I could find). I think this would be a good time to give an "explanation" (for lack of a better word) of myself.

This letter is an attempt to relate how, in the past year, I am finding that I am apparently a "coming-out-of-the-closet Trekkie." I'm sure that when the closet door finally shuts, I will look around and see a sign posted on that door stating "Caution—Do Not Open—Trekkies Inside." Not only have I become/am I becoming a Trekkie, but also a "Sci-Fikkie" (if there wasn't such a word before, there is now!). Let me tell you how this came about. Even though I have had an active interest in SF since seeing *Lost World* in the theater when I was about five years old or so, never did I realize how starved I had become for it until the end of my year's stay in Sweden during 1981–82. Later, I found a line in an intro to one of the *Analog* books that said people who are avid readers of science fiction actually go through withdrawal symptoms after stopping for a while! I believe it!

Just before I was to come home, I decided to go all out and read in English instead of Swedish—naturally I chose SF. (I hadn't read any for at least a year.) Well, in less than two months I went through the whole collection of English-language SF books the library had, which, incidentally, didn't number over two dozen. After I got home I started in on the SF section at the library and worked my way in from both ends. In one year's time, I've gotten to the B's and W's.

I'll never forget taking the taxi from Kennedy Airport after I returned from Sweden in July of 1982. I had no idea what/who an E.T. was and had heard through the grapevine (i.e., the taxi driver) that in *Wrath of Khan* one of the characters dies. Of course, first of all I thought, "Could it be Spock? No, how could they? But, then, who else *could* it be?" Stupid though I may sound, Spock seemed to be the only logical choice.

I did, of course, see the movie and thoroughly reveled in every second of it. I stayed until the screen went blank. (I have to pay my respects to the artists, as I am one myself and must see who contributes all of the special effects and artwork.)

Even though I was only ten years old in 1966 when Star Trek debuted, I have always been a fan—it's just that now I'm a more avid fan! This past year has found me keeping track of all the Star Trek episodes on TV; I can tell you when I last saw such-and-such an episode, or how many times I've seen it. Not only do we pull in Star Trek from the local Erie station five days a week, but also twice a week from two stations in Canada, and, when the weather's right, we can get it at 6:00 P.M. on channel 50 on Saturday and Sunday from Detroit, five hundred miles away. It may be snowy almost to the point of oblivion sometimes, but I'll watch it all. I also have memorized all the titles, have read *The Making of Star Trek,* and have bought and read eleven Trek books. From the book *Star Trek Compendium* I have listed alphabetically all of the film and TV appearances of each of the Star Trek regulars and watch for them on TV. I have an '84 Star Trek calendar on the wall and the cassette soundtrack to *Wrath of Khan.*

I live at home. Dad is a *Doctor Who* fan, and my mother and brother just shake their heads sadly when I even mention anything pertinent to ST. Let me hasten to say they aren't averse to it—my brother watches sometimes, and has certain lines from various episodes memorized, and Mom watches somewhat while she's fixing dinner (ST is on at 5:00 P.M. and the TV is in the kitchen). She knows who Mr. Spock is now and is beginning to distinguish which is Captain Kirk and which is McCoy. (She knows that Kirk always seems to get the beautiful girls.) But they as yet don't seem to understand why I would rather miss something else and instead watch Star Trek, and "waste all my money," of what little I keep scraping up, on Star Trek books and so on.

I have even written a fan letter to the Star Trek crew at Paramount (my first fan letter ever), and now I am writing to you people. After reading from "A Sampling of Trek Roundtable," I decided to contribute, particularly after reading the letter from Linda Knight of Walla Walla, Washington. Dear Linda, yes, there are people "out there" like you—and I'm one of them! This past year when I found out there were such things as Star Trek conventions . . . ! Boy, did I ever feel cheated—it was like "Why didn't anyone tell *me* about it?"

I have been "fascinated" by all the imput and ideas about Star Trek in fan fiction and philosophical speculations and opinions such as are found in *The Best of Trek* books. I eagerly await #7.

Now that I'm beginning to write myself dry, I would like to make a few comments on *Wrath of Khan*. I was disappointed with the music on the cassette. Why? Because there wasn't enough of it! Come on, guys—you want me to wear my tape out or something? I *know* there are bits of music from the movie that aren't on the tape, even though I haven't seen the movie since it came out. (I'm not a recipient of cable TV, nor do we have a video system.) I do hope that *Wrath of Khan* will be rereleased or put on network, independent or Canadian TV, so we can "refresh our memory banks" once more before seeing *The Search for Spock*—which, needless to say, I await with bated breath.

My only other comment, I guess, is about Spock's demise and revival. I have read other opinions and postulations, all of which are very intriguing, but I say, how can you be certain that Spock is going to be found and revived in *Star Trek III*? After all, isn't it titled *The* Search *for Spock*? Maybe it will end with Kirk and McCoy twenty feet from the coffin with their backs turned to it and no one knowing it's there except for us fans in the audience. How would that be for a cliffhanger to make you go and see *Star Trek IV?*

**Betty Ragan**
**Pennsauken, N.J.**

I am twelve years old and I have been a Star Trek fan since I was ten. Let me tell you something about myself.

When I was very young, not even school age, Star Trek reruns were on right before dinner. I always watched them with my mother. I suppose most of Star Trek's meaning was lost on my four-or-five year old self. I don't remember much from those days, but certain episodes must have made a great impression on me, for I remember most of "The Empath" and "The Naked Time" clearly. Much dimmer is "Spectre of the Gun."

At seven, I saw my first and, unfortunately (or maybe not so unfortunately, from what I've heard), my last animated episode "Yesteryear." My sister had been watching cartoons and Star Trek came on. I can remember her saying, "Look! A Star Trek cartoon!" I had been reading, and merely spared her an "Uh-huh." But I found I was watching interestedly in spite of myself. I think I found it "fascinating." Unfortunately, I never bothered to watch another, although sometimes I wanted to.

Then, one summer, I discovered the Blish books on my library shelf. Remembering the bygone Star Trek days, I thought they might make interesting reading during an otherwise boring summer. Little did I know! I definitely loved them. When reading them, especially when just holding them, anticipating the delightful plots inside, I felt a wonderful, unexplainable feeling. At first I thought it was merely a renewed joy in books. I do not know when I realized I was a Trekkie (or Trekker; I'll get back to that), but now I know I am. Just walk into my room and look at my posters, books and paper models!

I have found a joy in Trekdom that I desperately want to share; that's why I'm writing to Trek Roundtable.

I promised to discuss earlier the difference between "Trekkers" and "Trekkies"—I think it's so much nonsense. I'll be a Trekkie and *proud* to have a title that shows my love for Star Trek! However, some do not see it that way; if they consider a "Trekker" as a mature fan, and "Trekkie" as an immature fan, then I respect that. And if anyone ever calls me a "Trekkie" in that sense, he or she had better run!

**Rowena G. Warner**
**Louisville, Ky.**

I read *Trek Movie Special #3* with a great deal of interest and feel as if I could write a hundred-page thesis agreeing and disagreeing with several points raised in the letters.

Every single letter was fascinating, but there are a couple I would like to zero in on. Lynette Wood's letter was quite stimulating because it raised a number of issues on which I would like to respond.

I have little difficulty accepting the fact that Khan and his people survived on Ceti Alpha V. Kirk obviously left them with more than just perishable supplies. Since they were to build a world on that planet, seed and the like would have been furnished in order for them to grow their own crops. No doubt, Khan and his followers had a thriving community in operation when the explosion occurred. Since this catastrophe was probably forecast by earthquakes and a sudden erratic climate, Khan had sufficient time to switch his farming to caves. The man was a genius; I'm certain he would have worked out something. Also, just because a planetary orbital switch occurred, it does not necessarily follow that water and a breathable atmosphere would have been stripped away.

Lynette Wood also raised the subject of the pulsar in the Mutara Nebula and felt the *Enterprise* would not have been able to escape the gravitational effects of this neutron star. She stated the star would have to be at least thirty-two times as massive as our sun to create this nebula and pulsar. Actually, the star could have contained *no more* than two and one-half solar masses in order for the pulsar to have been formed—any more and it would have become a black hole. With regard to the *Enterprise* escaping the gravitational field of this pulsar, we have to keep in mind that the *Enterprise* has warp drive. Theoretically, the ship could even escape the event horizon of a black hole since its speed is *greater* than that of light.

In the formation of the second generation star and its attendant planet, Genesis, we have to remember this was not a planned, controlled experiment. When Dr. Marcus and her people reached a point at which they wanted to test the Genesis process on a planetary scale, no doubt they would have worked up a list of criteria for searching out a suitable location, i.e., age, size, and mass of a nebula.

No controlling factors existed when Khan activated the Genesis Device; as a result, the consequences would be totally unpredictable. The Genesis Process itself could also be defective on a planetary scale. Herein, I believe, lies the key to Spock's subsequent return to life.

I have decided to accept the challenge and attempt to set forth a possible *theory* (remember that word) as to what might transpire in *Star Trek III*.

According to the explanation of the Genesis Process, it breaks down matter into subelementary particles-waves, then by manipulation of nuclear forces, such mass would be formed into a new matrix.

This manipulation could involve the introduction of an additional electron in an entirely new orbit around the nucleus of an atom. A hydrogen atom (the most common element in the universe) has one electron. If another is added, one would think it would become a helium atom, since that element has two electrons. However, the two electrons in a helium atom follow the same orbit, so if this new introductory atom is in a different orbit, it would create an entirely new atom with an increased gravitational pull. These new atoms would collide faster, and matter would form more rapidly. After the planetary system had been formed, the introductory electrons would fall into and become part of the atoms' nuclei, thereby reverting the "aging process" to the evolutionary norm.

But what if something was defective about the Genesis Processes and the "aging process" did not halt? The star created could be born and die in a matter of months, weeks, or even days. I can see a whole story evolving here, for we have Spock's coffin lying in repose on a planet whose sun could go nova at any time.

But what about our favorite Vulcan? What does all this have to do with his return to life? Contrary to Vonda McIntyre's description of a wolf and a winged creature in the Genesis Cave, I am strongly against the supposition that Genesis can create animal life so advanced. I am not taking a moral stand on this issue, but rather a practical point of view. Man is supposed to have evolved from lower forms of life, and if the Genesis Process creates animals at a greatly accelerated evolutionary pace, I am going to find it quite difficult to believe Man will not also evolve. If so, this would defeat the whole purpose of Genesis—to create a planet suitable for human habitation.

But if the Genesis Process has "gone haywire," the results could be mind-boggling, including Spock's return to life. Here again we could get involved in a sticky situation. It has to be explained in such a manner that we would not be led to believe that *every* individual could be rejuvenated by the Genesis Process. If that were the case, no one in the universe would ever again remain dead, and that is a definite no-no.

I believe Spock's physiological makeup is an important factor. Perhaps his body received just enough introductory electrons to begin a regenerative process. At a certain point, his Vulcan healing powers could intercede and complete regeneration. From an ancient ritual he learned on Gol, Spock could now bring himself out of the healing trance. The antibodies in his human blood could then oust these extra electrons. *Voilà!* We have a living and breathing Vulcan!

I can see it now. The camera pans across the Genesis Planet, soft music playing as we are shown the beauty of creation. Music builds, and the camera rests on the ebony torpedo. We are all on the edge of our chairs as the music reaches a crescendo, threatening to deafen us. Quite suddenly— all is silent. We wait, holding our breath, five seconds, ten seconds . . . it happens! A hand crashes through the torpedo, then another. Fragments fly in all directions. The lid is violently torn apart and he stands. Spock has returned to life!

But should this happen? Should Spock return in *Star Trek III?* There seems to exist a major controversy in this area. I agree with Judith Wolper in *Trek Movie Special #3* that we Trekkers have never had to face the death of our favorite people. In the episodes "The Tholian Web" and "Immunity Syndrome," for instance, we never once suspected that Kirk

or Spock might really be dead. In the movie, particularly after
the controversy which surrounded it, we weren't quite sure.
Doubt hung heavily until we heard that magnificent voice—
"Space . . . the final frontier. . . ."

Paramount engineered the Vulcan's death before the controversy began, and, of course, they did it for the Almighty
Dollar, but what studio does not? I am willing to give them
that dollar and more, when they give me such a beautiful,
subtle, and totally heart-rending death scene which was really
the beginning of life.

My only regret is that Leonard Nimoy, a man for whom I
have the highest degree of respect, was shabbily treated
during the controversy. Whatever his thoughts were at the
time, and whatever his decision may be on movies subsequent to *Star Trek III*, we fans have no right passing judgment on him. William Shatner said it best—"You have to
love him." Not for what he *may* give us in the future, but for
what he has already given us in the past.

**Stan Rozenfeld**
**Brooklyn, N.Y.**

I have read *The Best of Trek #3–6*, and I enjoyed these
books very much, but there are a few questions that I want to
ask and a few matters that I want to discuss.

In the article "Love in Star Trek," it is said that Organians
in "Errand of Mercy" show brotherly love by intervening in
the Federation-Klingon War. I disagree, and think that they
stop the war because they despise violence and unnecessary
death. At the end of the episode, Ayelborne says, "In fact
you will have to leave. The mere presence of beings like
yourselves is acutely painful to us." I don't think that this is
brotherly love talking.

Also, a lot of things in that article really stretch the concept
of love. We can't throw romantic love and love of wisdom
into the same category and label that category "love." The
article offers no definition of love. And without even a
general definition, how can we judge what is done out of
love, as opposed to what is done out of duty, or reason, or
even out of a simple desire to avoid pain and experience

pleasure? What is love? What is friendship? What is compassion? What is duty? What is reason? These are the questions we must answer before we jump into a discussion about love.

The article that I liked most was "The Alien Question." It was a very interesting article because it pointed out Star Trek's main flaw. Despite Star Trek's obvious tolerance and appreciation of the diversity of life and alien ways, everything seems to be centered around Earth and humanity. Why is the *Enterprise* or any other Federation ship always referred to as an Earth ship? Why does Kirk, in "Friday's Child," refer to the Federation as "Earth-Federation"? In "The Immunity Syndrome," it is implied that there is only one starship with an all-Vulcan crew, when Kirk says that *Intrepid* was built in honor of Vulcan's contribution to the Federation. And how many starships are there with an all-human crew on board? *Defiant, Constellation,* and four ships seen in "The Ultimate Computer." In short, why are humans running the Federation, although Vulcans, Andorians, and Tellerites were also the founding members?

Why, in many episodes, do aliens have to acknowledge the human way as the best way? Though Kirk's actions were necessary in "By Any Other Name," his attitude toward the Kelvans was disgusting. In "The Tholian Web," McCoy accuses Spock of trying to take Kirk's command, not realizing that Vulcans act out of different motives than humans do. Because of his ignorance, he judges Spock by human standards. In "The Galileo Seven," everyone seems to hate Spock, and the whole group is on the verge of rebelling against him, because he is more concerned with the survival of the living than with respect for the dead. (The only exception is Mr. Scott.) And in the end, instead of acknowledging that they were wrong, they start picking on Spock about his "emotional" decision, and basically try to make the whole thing look like a joke.

In "Requiem for Methuselah," McCoy gives Spock a big speech about how Spock does not know love and how McCoy pities him for it. He does not realize that it is the calm and rational Spock who saw that Reena was free and urged Kirk to control his "primitive impulses." It was Spock who saw the danger to Reena and urged Kirk and Flint to stop, but like stubborn jackasses, they kept going through their "come with me, stay with me" routine. Spock's human half might have been instrumental in helping him understand, but it was also his calmness and objectivity which enabled him to see what humans did not. The word "love" might not be written in Spock's book, but the word "wisdom" is.

I am glad, however, that in "The Immunity Syndrome," Spock finally gives McCoy a piece of his mind. "You have always wondered at the objective hardness of the Vulcan heart, yet have so little room in yours." Here is something for us to ponder.

Spock represents many things to us. Not only is he an outsider and an alien, looking at our society and humanity and criticizing, but he is also an individual trying to come to terms with his dual nature. In *Wrath of Khan,* we see a new Spock who has come to terms with his duality . . . he admits that he has emotions, potential for unpredictability, and intuitive insight, and that they can be a great asset, provided that they are controlled and coordinated by his Vulcan logic and discipline.

Unfortunately, the price for that is his status as an alien. It would be great indeed if, when (and if) Spock returns in *Star Trek III*, the writers would find a way to preserve his outsider status, while keeping him as the new Spock we saw in *Wrath of Khan.* In that way, he will be able to serve his dual purpose in Star Trek, while continuing to evolve as a character.

In *Star Trek: The Motion Picture,* Spock states that logic without need is barren, implying that emotions provide the needs. However, if you think about it, reason can determine the needs of the individual as well as emotions.

I have also noticed that fans tend to criticize Vulcans for their lack of emotion and flexibility. And I agree that Vulcans have taken their measures to extremes. But it's not like Vulcans were created so they will learn from us, but rather that we compare ourselves to them and learn from them. We try to protect humanity by criticizing others, but we often forget that for all the optimism in Star Trek, its function is to criticize human nature. Its optimism is not about what we are, but what we can—and must—become. I think that we shouldn't judge Vulcans too harshly; in many ways they are a race much wiser than we. We must direct that criticism at ourselves, as Kirk does in "A Taste of Armageddon." After all, shouldn't we control our passions with reason?

Everywhere in the series it is stated over and over again that passions and intuition are good for you. Nowhere in the series is it stated explicitly that logic and intellect, although not everything, are still the best faculties we have, and that passion, uncontrolled and uncoordinated by reason, is a very dangerous thing.

Although Star Trek makes many mistakes with aliens, there a number of episodes that more than make up for those mistakes. In "The Savage Curtain," Kirk seems unwilling to judge the rock creature by human standards, despite the fact that he and his crew were guinea pigs in its deadly experiment. These creatures, it must be noted, were definitely not sadistic; they thought that they were doing great honor to Kirk and Spock. We, too, ofttimes value knowledge more than we value the lives of lower, "insignificant" creatures. Perhaps now that we've seen how experimental animals feel, we may change our minds about animal rights. Other episodes, such as "Arena," "The Devil in the Dark," and "Errand of Mercy," show aliens in a better perspective and with less bias.

I also disagree with a short article called "Emotion Vs. Logic—No Contest." In this article, it is stated that intuition is a form of extremely fast unconscious reasoning. It is also stated that intuition is powered by emotion. Therefore, emotion is superior to logic. However, we don't know exactly what intuition is. While one possibility is stated above, another plausible explanation is that intuition is a direct insight into nature without the benefit of reason or the senses. Taoist and Buddhist philosophies are based on such intuitive insight, and their world view amazingly parallels the developments of modern physics. (Read *Tao of Physics* by Fritjof Capra.) Yet both religion-philosophies preach control of emotions and repression of desires. Intuitive insight comes as a result of training in meditation. Meditation is a state of calm awareness and concentration. One must avoid reasoning and emotions to achieve a meditative state.

In his book *The Dragons of Eden*, Carl Sagan draws upon

the idea of the right and left brain functions to explain intuition. Our left brain is the dominant one and contains the rational and analytical part of ourselves. Our right brain has little capacity for language and rational thought, but it contains high-data-rate cognitive abilities that bypass our analytic consciousness. This intuitive brain is responsible for creativity and pattern recognition.

**Linda Houck**
**Fort Smith, Ariz.**

I am a devoted Star Trek fan. I have watched Star Trek on television since it was released in 1966; I was then six years old. My father worked on government contract work, and many of the contracts he worked on were for the space program. This made me very curious about space, and then came Star Trek, a very realistic look at people and space. I am now twenty-four and have seen the reruns probably a million times; each time I see something new, an expression or detail I missed before.

I have just been to see *Star Trek III: The Search for Spock*. We arrived an hour and a half early for the 2:00 showing. The local Walden bookstore in the mall was being besieged by Trekkers and was immediately sold out of its entire stock of the different selections of Star Trek books. Naturally, these Trekkers were in the movie line reading about their favorite characters. What devotion we have! *The Search for Spock* was sold out before the ticket office even opened, and many had to wait for the 7:00 showing.

The characters reacted as we knew they should. Was it really necessary to destroy the *Enterprise?* She was as important as any character. It was a fitting end for her years of service, however, much better than the end planned by Starfleet.

# STAR TREK III: A RETURN TO THE BIG STORY

## by Joyce Tullock

*Joyce Tullock, one of our most popular and prolific authors, did just what many of us did this summer: She went to see* Star Trek III: The Search for Spock *several times, thought about it, and, finally, wrote about it. But unlike many of us, Joyce has the talent and insight to see just a little bit deeper into the story, to glean a little bit more from those pictures flashing up there on the screen. In the following article, Joyce tells us why she feels that* The Search for Spock *is the best Star Trek movie so far . . . maybe the best there will ever be.*

The original concept of Star Trek has suffered much in the last few years, partly due to its massive popularity, partly due to the demands of its fans. But like some grand idea whose time has finally come, it has endured . . . endured almost in spite of those who love it, endured to become something very fine indeed. I am speaking, of course, of that unexpected hero *Star Trek III: The Search for Spock.*

What a surprise to the fans, what a *revelation* to Paramount, to discover that it is, indeed, greener in their own backyard. In *The Search for Spock,* through the skilled—perhaps even inspired—direction of Leonard Nimoy, Star Trek has come home. Not to roost, but to crow. It may be the closest we ever get to the spirit of Star Trek that every fan feels in the heart. It is real. It is fantasy. It is more than it appears to be.

And it's time to talk about it. Fandom has gone through something of a roller-coaster ride of emotion about the Star Trek movies, bickering, loving, hating, admiring, sometimes quite simply numbed into apathy about the direction of the series. Will it continue? Should it? Will its need to please the masses finally lead to the worst kind of death—that of a mindless, meaningless action-adventure sci-fi series? One of many. It could happen, of course. It may very well happen. But most fans will now at least be able to say, "Ah . . . but we had *The Search for Spock*. We had Kirk. We had McCoy. We had Spock." They will stop a minute and smile to themselves and add, "Now *that* was Star Trek. The friendship, the love which showed that man will not grow out of his humanity."

No kidding. In *The Search for Spock* we have—after some nervous wavering—a return to the "big story" as only Star Trek can tell it. In *The Search for Spock*, a man grows *into* his humanity.

Not that there weren't other times when mankind was presented well in Star Trek. In both *Star Trek: The Motion Picture* and *Wrath of Khan*, we get glimpses of mankind at its best. In the first movie, we see the positiveness of man's complicated spirit and the direction of his evolution. In *Wrath of Khan*, something of a lesser picture, we see human courage and sacrifice. But *Wrath of Khan*, as Star Trek, is clouded with a certain prejudiced "Hollywood" look. A kind of fear of anything "imperfect" pervades the picture—whether it be a matter of cosmetics (no real aliens) or philosophy ( a story in black and white). Khan is evil and must be destroyed. The End.

But in *Star Trek III: The Search for Spock*, we find something different happening with Star Trek—something as old as "City on the Edge of Forever," as new as V'Ger. With a kind of controlled scream of elation, *The Search for Spock* stretches its gangly limbs and steps onto the big screen. And this time, it fits. It is, indeed, a new being, self-confident, warm, mature, but always with that childlike sparkle of fun in its eyes.

Almost like a living being, it has grown and it has learned. The characters fit together, very much acting as a whole unit.

No more is it simply "The William Shatner Hour." (With all due respect to that fine actor's talents, Star Trek was intended to be more than that.) And for the first time since the movies began, we are reminded of the Kirk/Spock/McCoy triad as it was known in the series. We see Kirk, shattered by the death of Spock, standing in the dimness of the Vulcan's "forbidden" quarters, McCoy crumpled in his arms. He is a man on the verge of losing the last of a very special friendship. Never before on the motion picture screen has the Friendship been given such direct, unembarrassed attention. And we see, as we saw to a less obvious extent in *Star Trek: The Motion Picture*, that the friendship of these three men is a beautiful thing indeed. Almost a living entity.

But more than that, *The Search for Spock* is a story about the *entire* crew and what they are willing to do to save Spock and McCoy (and thus Kirk).

There is Mr. Sulu, the dashing, sexy swashbuckler—*and we want to see more!* There is Uhura, with her warmth, beauty, and elegant presence of mind. Here is a dignity which rivals even that of Mr. Spock. Engineer Scott becomes the eager rebel, a little tired of business-as-usual. He is a quick-witted conniver, and without his know-how and courage, *The Search for Spock* and its glorious adventure would never have made it outside the barn door. He is Kirk's right hand.

Mr. Chekov, already a hero for his conduct in *Wrath of Khan*, works with his own uncomplicated Russian fervor to help his friend McCoy reach "the promised land" of emotional peace and reunion with Spock. He seems to be the most clearheaded of the crew, in fact, lacking both Scott's rebel cynicism and Sulu's passion for adventure. He is out to do what is noble and right—for those reasons alone. Of all the crew, he probably has the best reason for staying behind. His experience with Khan was traumatic. But he is a man whose dignity, loyalty, and love run passionately deep, whose perspective is clear and unaffected. He will help McCoy and Spock and Kirk because he loves them. There is no better, no more practical reason than that.

But the loyalty of all the crew is equal, no one can dispute that. The varied and complex reasons for all the courageous behavior of Sulu, Uhura, Chekov, and Scott are worthy of articles themselves, but we still know that it all boils down to one simple theme. *The* theme of Star Trek at its best: friendship. Jesus of Nazareth told us, "Greater love hath no man than this, that a man lay down his life for his friend."

And as the Teacher would no doubt remind us, life itself involves a whole lot more than flesh and blood. It involves the happiness of being, of enjoying living in the world. And it involves caring. In *The Search for Spock*, Sulu, Chekov, Uhura, and Scott elected to risk losing all that they have lived for up to this time—their careers, their families, their homes—for the sake of friendship. It is a grander kind of love than we have seen before in Star Trek because of the sheer scale of personalities and potential loss. Because of this, *The Search for Spock* becomes a very large story, complex in its ramifications, simple in its direction.

Hopefully, the days of the "black-and-white" good-vs.-evil Star Trek are done. It's as though our friends have passed through an awkward period of oversimplification (in *Wrath of Khan*) to finally come of age. Even David Marcus, the preppie, insipid son-of-Kirk in *Wrath of Khan*, matures in *The Search for Spock* to be a more realistic individual. Gone is the self-righteous pseudo-idealist who berated Kirk for "cheating" on the *Kobayashi Maru* test. Now we see David in a new light, flawed himself. He realizes that his ambitions got in the way of good science, and that in employing a controversial form of "protomatter" in his Genesis experiments, he has loosed terrible demons on the world. He is shown up for his hypocrisy, and is the better man for it. More believable, more likable. And when he "lays down his life" for Saavik and young Spock, we are sorry to see him go. But at least we do not think of him as son-of-Kirk anymore. Now he is David Marcus, Jim Kirk's son.

Lieutenant Saavik, played now by Robin Curtis, is a more complex character as well. Her prissiness is gone, and with it, her premature air of Vulcan superiority. This Saavik is not so sure of herself as she was in the previous movie, which, ironically, makes her seem somehow more trustworthy. Like the Spock of Star Trek's early days, she moves with knowledge and determination to do the right thing, but not necessarily with complete self-confidence. And while she knows nothing of the *Enterprise*'s mission to save McCoy and Spock, she certainly does help Spock in a very special way. Needless to say, she guides the maturing Spock through the torrid experience of his first *pon farr*.

Saavik did what she had to do to help Spock. She did what was logical. Yet, at the movie's end, she finds it difficult to look into Spock's eyes. What does it mean? Either she is being somewhat illogical, or she has a very Vulcan kind of shame to deal with. One wonders how she will come to terms with it, and who she might turn to to help her deal with any problems that have developed.

It is themes like this, complex, sometimes controversial, carefully underplayed, that make *Star Trek III: The Search for Spock* a larger film than the one that came before it. Even Commander Kruge, the brutish Klingon warrior, is not as easy a character to pigeonhole as we might like. When he first discovers the Genesis project, we are allowed to see the way he thinks. He speaks with wry contempt of the possibility of a spreading Federation which would colonize newly formed planets, strengthening its power and broadening its boundaries in galactic space. And in that glimpse of his thought processes we are able to understand just a little bit more about the violent, aggressive mind of the Klingon warrior. He thinks as he was trained to think, that much is clear. His remarks about the humans, with their wives by their side, could just as easily have been read from a Klingon textbook on the evil of the weaker races. The evil which Kruge here represents is *not* the black-and-white evil we'd like to think it is. It is an evil to be respected as one would respect and fear a talented opponent.

Clearly, Kruge's mind was developed through the process of totalitarian indoctrination. He sees the world as he does because he has the mind, the education, and the blood of a Klingon. And it is more than apparent, despite his ruthlessness, that he has a kind of moral or ethical standard. He appreciates things like loyalty and honor—even love. And as we see in the scene between Kruge and Valkris, the Klingon spy (his lover), he is capable of "feeling." (Not to mention his affection for his ghastly pet!) It is not a sense of love that we can understand or define by our terms, but it *is* a Klingon version of affection for another. So as much as we might like to, we cannot judge Kruge as being simply evil. Nor can we clearly understand him or judge him by our own standards. We need very much to look at him as an alien, brought up in a brutal society, indoctrinated in hatred and distrust of the so-called "weaker" races. So the evil represented in Kruge is the most dangerous kind of all; it is the "real" kind. No fantasy here.

"I . . . have . . . had . . . enough . . . of *you!*" Kirk yells. Exit, Lord Kruge.

Kirk is no fool in *The Search for Spock*. He *tries* to do things by the book first, and when that doesn't work . . . well, it's a boot in the face or a stolen ship. But the point is, he tries. In this movie, as in the series, Kirk's ego is in perfect balance. In this movie, he isn't trying to "beat" anyone. He isn't vying for power or the center seat. On the contrary, in *The Search for Spock*, more than ever before, we have a Kirk who has found himself. He will give up his career—the thing that once seemed to be his dearest possession. What Kirk sees most clearly now is that nothing means more to him than his friendship for Spock *and* McCoy. All he knows for sure is that he must salvage what is left of the friendship by saving McCoy and helping Spock to his rest.

The three friends have so long been united in a bond of love and trust that Kirk, always the mediator in the triad personality of Kirk/Spock/McCoy, must act now out of a deep-rooted instinct for the survival of the three of them. He tells Sarek at the end of the film that to do less would mean the loss of his soul. For the Kirk of the Friendship, that statement refers to more than a sense of honor or love or even the eternal spirit. It refers, quite literally, to who and what Kirk is. To the part he plays in the Kirk/Spock/McCoy personality. Perhaps it is fair to say here that they are, and always have been, one mind. So many times in the series we've seen McCoy and Spock at odds and we've seen how Kirk works to keep them balanced around him. It is no different here. As the willful part of the triad mind, he works tirelessly to see to it that balance is regained—or at least as much balance as may be salvaged.

So at long, long last, the *real* story of Star Trek is brought to the big screen: the Friendship. And through the Friendship, the journey of the human mind and heart. Kirk's love for Spock is clear, but it is no clearer than his love for the three of them. The power of their friendship is, after all, the very heart of the Star Trek phenomenon. It is also the kind of surrealistic theme which separates Trek from the "whip-dash-flash" screen sci-fi of our time.

We've determined several things which have made *Star Trek III: The Search for Spock* exceptional Star Trek: it employs the *entire* Star Trek family (with the exception of Chapel), it deals with somewhat controversial matters such as the Saavik/Spock liaison, the horrid and devilishly complex Klingon mind, rebellion against respected authority for the sake of individual good (the needs of the one outweigh the needs of the many); it finally admits to the existence of the surrealistic threefold relationship of Kirk/Spock/McCoy and uses them as they should be used. But wouldn't you know, there's still just a little bit more. It appears in the movie as a whisper, and is treated with a cautious, almost matter-of-fact approach. In *The Search for Spock*, our heroes establish, as fact (in their future twenty-third-century time), the existence of the immortal soul.

Leave it to Kirk, Spock, and McCoy.

And while their rather astonishing discovery really comes as a surprise to no one (the film virtually takes it for granted), we find a certain pleasing twist to the plot's direction. It is McCoy, of *all people*, who becomes the custodian of Spock's spiritual essence!

Nice touch. Not to mention the fact that McCoy's participation in the Star Trek movie plots has been *long* overdue. But what is so significant about the McCoy/Spock meld is that it has brought the two opposites, both cynics in their own ways, to be as one. Spock and McCoy together at last! The very humor and irony of the situation intensifies the drama. DeForest Kelley handles this difficult role beautifully, never overplaying it, coaxing his audience along, teasing them, as McCoy seeks to understand his problem and get it under control.

If the fans seem disappointed in anything about *The Search for Spock*, in fact, it is about McCoy's part in the film: They wanted to see more. After all, there is a struggle of phenomenal proportions going on inside the very human Dr. McCoy. We can see it in his face as much as hear it in the sometimes Spockian voice. But there is no doubt that McCoy is willing to accept his own very personal duty to Spock . . . once again, the Friendship is at work. Though we aren't at all certain *who* is in charge when the good doctor tries to commission a private ship in the barroom scene. Ironically, it could be either. Both Spock and McCoy are men who take burdens on themselves, not seeking outside help. One thing is clear—McCoy had every intention of going to the Genesis Planet without Kirk's help. He is a man driven.

But, of course, that isn't the way of the Friendship. It's a three-part deal, and Kirk is very much the man in charge. With the help of his longtime friends Sulu, Uhura, Scott, and Chekov, he steals his old friend McCoy from Starfleet's lockup, and they're off to Genesis, disregarding every rule Starfleet can throw at them in order to see to it that McCoy and Spock are put right.

So the hugeness of the story comes to light. Our friends have, indeed, shown that spiritual essence exists within the individual. Perhaps not so immortal as we had once thought (the essence *can* be lost), and definitely bound somehow to the physical (McCoy, the storage house). Nevertheless, for the people of the twenty-third century, the return of Spock's essence must be received as a kind of proof of the existence of a very real spiritual essence—at least in Vulcans! And so we wonder, what will become of them all now? Have they perhaps gone too far? Is there a god, or is one's spiritual essence actually part of All That Is? Are we all a tiny part of the essence which forms to make godhood?

The religious implications are far-reaching, for in the Star Trek universe, we must accept that Mr. Spock is neither Christian nor Jew nor a follower of Islam—nor is he bound by any other Earth-grown faith. He is Vulcan, trained in logic, not influenced by the "emotionally based" religions of our world and time. And yet, he has a soul. And why, instead of allowing his spirit to vanish into the cosmos, does he chose to embrace McCoy—of all people? The doctor is, after all, the opposite of all that is Vulcan, and yet Spock judges him worthy and capable of keeping a most precious trust, his own logical essence. There were others in the engineering section (where the mind meld took place)—some surely with more logical natures than McCoy.

Was Spock's final choice founded in love?

*Star Trek III: The Search for Spock,* for all its very fanzine-type storyline, is a renegade movie. It rebels against the simplistic action/adventure sci-fi movies of the day (very much as the *Enterprise* crew rebelled against an unimaginative Starfleet). It does it carefully, even shyly, knowing that it will be compared ruthlessly to the works of Lucas and Spielberg (apples and oranges)—and who can blame it? If the makers of Star Trek—from Gene Roddenberry to Harve Bennett to Leonard Nimoy—have learned anything over the years, they've learned to be careful when they have something dangerous, or even worse, intelligent, to say.

And for some, even the simple friendship of our ship's crew is a dangerous thing, for it is a sign that there may be more to life than values rooted in prestige and self. In *The Search for Spock* those things were given up for something greater, and yet frighteningly realistic—concern for a friend. The needs of the one outweigh the needs of the many.

Even the *Enterprise,* so representative of man's hope and courage, gets into the act. And when she blazes to earth, Kirk's greatest sacrifice, we know it is a new beginning.

## ABOUT THE EDITORS

Although largely unknown to readers not involved in Star Trek fandom before the publication of *The Best of Trek #1*, WALTER IRWIN and G. B. LOVE have been actively editing and publishing magazines for many years. Before they teamed up to create TREK® in 1975, Irwin worked in newspapers, advertising, and free-lance writing, while Love published *The Rocket's Blast—Comiccollector* from 1960 to 1974, as well as hundreds of other magazines, books, and collectables. Both together and separately, they are currently planning several new books and magazines, as well as continuing to publish TREK.

## Great Science Fiction from SIGNET

# *TREK*®

## The Magazine For Star Trek Fans